The Plague Legacy:

ACQUISITIONS

This is a work of fiction. Any similarities between actual people or events is purely coincidental. All characters, organizations, and events portrayed in this work are a figment of the authors imagination or are used fictitiously.

The Plague Legacy: Acquisitions

Edited by Danielle Kent
Cover art by Joshua Weekes and Scott Taylor

Published by:
Fox Hollow Publications, LLC.
P.O. Box 1113
Midway, Utah 84049

www.foxhollowpublications.com

ISBN13: 978-0-9912551-1-5
ISBN10: 0-9912551-1-9

First Edition: January 2014

Dedication:

To Liam, Conor, and Dylan for surviving as my orphans, and to Sean, for believing absolutely.

TABLE OF CONTENTS

CHAPTER I

The Stalls

"Put him down, Devon!" Cam spit out dirt.

"Or what, Pig Boy?" Devon sneered and shook Cam's new stallmate like a rag doll. A small boy, Peter hung by his coat, his collar riding up against his throat as he kicked his legs in the air. With his eyes pinched shut and his hands balled into fists, Peter twisted and swung his arms, trying to reach the blond mutant who held him at least three feet off the ground.

Cam's stomach clenched as Peter's face turned colors. *Why didn't he just run? I told him to run. He's small. He could've hid with the pigs and this idiot would've walked on by.* "He's just a little kid, Devon," Cam tried reasoning with the mutant. "You're choking him."

Devon grinned wickedly and shook Peter again, "Whatcha gonna do about it?"

Grinding his teeth, Cam reached behind him, searching for a rock or stick. The ground was cold, not fully thawed, and Cam's fingertips found only a few small rocks through the thin layer of topsoil. *I'm gonna smash in your empty mutant head.* But Cam didn't dare say it out loud. Devon had a mutant-strength temper to match his mutant-strength arms.

Peter squeaked and clutched at his throat, freckles speckling the tops of his cheeks like pepper flakes as his face turned white and then red.

A few feet away, a blond girl shifted her weight and rubbed her arm nervously, "Devon, I think you're actually hurting him."

"Good, then maybe the Pig Boy will do something about it," he shook Peter again and looked at Cam. "You gonna tell the Regulators? You gonna tell them to bring their tasers and stop the big mean mutant so he don't hurt the little boy?"

Cam's fingers curled around a rock half the size of his fist and he glared at Devon.

Devon laughed, "No, you aren't gonna tell the Regulators. You're gonna tell Mama Lucy, aren't you? You're gonna run and tell her poor little Peter's in trouble." He smirked, "I bet she don't even know his name. I bet she tells me to chop him up and throw him in the soup. She hates the little ones cuz they ain't worth feeding. Not when she's got mutants like me."

"Devon, just let him go," the blond girl pleaded.

"Shut up, Tara," Devon growled at her, keeping his eyes on Cam. The muscles in Devon's bare arm bunched and flexed with the weight of the boy in his hand, but Cam had too much experience to hope that Devon was getting tired. He also had too much experience to think that he could make Devon let go by getting up and fighting him. "So what's it gonna be, Cam? You gonna save your little friend?"

"Let him go," Cam warned again.

"Piggy boy, piggy boy, piggy boy," Devon danced while Peter's face went dark purple and his eyes rolled up in his head.

"Let him go!" Jumping to his feet, Cam stepped to charge Devon, but Tara pushed between them. She pulled Peter's coat out of Devon's grip and the small boy flopped onto the ground next to Cam, his breath coming in a rush as he rolled onto his back and coughed.

A look of pure hatred twisted through Devon's face as he wrapped his fingers around Tara's slender neck and pushed her up against the weathered wall of the horse stalls. "Why are you interfering?"

She clutched at his fingers and met his eyes in silence.

Cam's breath rushed in and pressed against his ribs as he watched Devon squeeze the girl's throat. The strawberry colored mark that identified her as a mutant was mirrored in the face of her brother, along with her hazel eyes and blond hair.

Twins.

Lifting her up, Devon stretched Tara's chin so far it looked like her neck would snap, then let out a growl and snatched his hand back. "Stay out of my way."

She rubbed her throat and watched Devon stalk off to the pavilion where Mama Lucy was calling the orphans in for dinner.

"Tara," Cam reached for her to ask if she was okay, but she just glanced at him with pain and sadness and followed her brother to the tables.

On the ground next to Cam's feet, Peter wheezed on all fours. Cam pulled the boy back to a sitting position and unzipped his coat. A dark purple line had formed where the blood rushed to the surface of his throat, but he was breathing.

"I told you to hide!" Cam grabbed Peter's shoulders and made the boy look him in the eyes. "Why didn't you run? You can't win if he catches you, but if you hide with the pigs, he'll never go in there for you. Devon hates the pigs."

"Sorry," Peter croaked out in a small voice. "Sorry, I wanted to warn you." He curled up and coughed into his knees, a faint scar on the back of his neck peeking above his shirt collar. "I heard Devon saying that he was going to find you with the horses," he looked up with tears in his eyes. "I didn't want him to hurt you again."

Relieved to see Peter's freckles return to their normal shade of brown, Cam pulled him up by the arm. "C'mon, let's go get you some dinner before it's all gone," he tucked a pair of silver tags inside the boy's shirt, "and next time, at least unzip your coat so that he has to pick you up by your overall straps. That will keep him from choking you with your own clothes."

Peter nodded and sniffed, wiping a tear from his cheek as he jogged to keep up. They walked around the south run of horse stalls and passed by the pig yard that sat on the east end.

The pigs were out sniffing at the sun, three big ones and five sucklings, shuffling around their pit of half-frozen mud. It had been a litter of twelve; the squealing mess born only a month ago, but the orphanage was so desperate for food this time of year that seven of the piglets had already been chopped up for stew.

A mixture of girls and boys swarmed under the pavilion, half of them slopping sludge into their mouths and the other half jostling for a place in line. Devon already sat at a table near the orchard with his bowl and a withered apple, his feet bare on the cold, packed dirt.

While he's loading up on sludge, maybe he could also load up on some brains. Cam glared at the mutant for a moment as he and Peter tacked themselves on to the end of the line. Peter zipped up his coat and winced.

"Hey, little man, don't do that if it hurts." Cam tugged down the zipper to ease the pressure on the bruised flesh and crouched down to meet Peter's big, brown eyes. "Mama Lucy won't care if you have a few bruises, won't even wonder why, so don't suffer for her sake."

Peter frowned, "I don't care about Mama Lucy." He nodded up at the ragged orphans bent over their bowls. "But they call me names when they see what Devon does."

"What kind of names?" Cam swallowed. *Devon only picks on Peter because he shares a stall with me.*

Peter tugged on his ear and looked down at his sloppy boots, "'Stew Meat,' 'Sty Fly,' 'Sludge Face,' stuff like that."

Cam shot a warning look at the grungy smattering of kids even though all of them hovered over their bowls, eating as quickly as they could. They reminded him of the wild dogs who sniffed around the pavilion at night, looking for scraps of food.

He patted Peter on the back, "Stick by me, little man, and they'll leave you alone."

"I know," Peter shrugged, "but then I never get to play with anybody."

"I'll fix it," Cam promised. "I have a plan."

Peter smiled at him, "You do?"

"You bet," Cam's stomach tightened, "but you can't say anything to anybody, okay?"

Peter nodded, serious.

The Stalls had just fewer than thirty orphans, ages spanning from seven, like Peter, to sixteen, like Cam and the mutant twins. Peter's group had arrived from a daycare somewhere on the other side of the mountains three days ago. Many of them were undersized and underfed, soulless children who cried for their dead parents as they dug themselves into the straw at night.

He reached the pot, last in line with Peter behind him. The girl serving looked at him with hollow brown eyes, her hair a rat's nest with straw sticking out of it. Cam watched her hands, which were at least cleaner than her face, as she handed him a bowl and scooped the bottom of the pot with a bent ladle.

"Almost gone," she wheezed out as she turned the ladle over. His dinner oozed into the bowl in clumps of oat sludge, making a sucking sound as it separated from the spoon. "That's all you get. Next!"

Cam shuffled forward and waited for Peter, whose bowl was only half full when the girl handed it to him. The small boy pouted and followed Cam to a table on the far side of the pavilion from Devon. A skinny boy with spiky black hair and narrow eyes looked up when they sat down by him.

"Hey, Cam," Jake smiled and scraped up the last of his mush. "Wondered where you were, then I saw Devon come across the field. What's he been up to this morning? Tormenting your horses?"

"What he's always up to," Cam sat down and winced, his butt tender from landing on the packed dirt behind the old horse stalls where Devon had shoved him.

"You mean skinning live rodents, wringing chickens' necks, threatening small children? Or just generally making our lives the hell it is today?"

Cam didn't answer as he helped Peter climb onto the tall bench that ran the length of the table.

Jake's eyebrows shot up. "None of those?" his eyes narrowed, "Has he expanded his repertoire?"

Shaking his head, Cam glanced over at Devon, hoping the blond boy would leave before Jake said something stupid and loud enough for the mutant to hear, which happened often enough. Jake had the bruises to prove it. "Shut up!" Cam elbowed Jake's arm. "When will you learn to control the things that come out of your mouth? Do you have any sense of self-preservation?"

Twirling his spoon, Jake answered in a low voice. "He's a mutant, Cam, he can hear everything. He's like the official Emperor of Evil. There's no getting away."

Unless you run away. Cam dropped his eyes to his bowl and scooped a bite of tasteless oats as Devon looked over at them. Peter's dinner was already nearly gone, the small boy swinging his feet as he chewed.

Jake pushed his bowl away and leaned his elbows on the table, his hands squishing his cheeks up into narrow black eyes as he rested his chin on his palms. "I swear sometimes he can hear what I'm *thinking*. He's even worse than Mama Lucy."

Once a mutant slave across the ocean in Salvation, Mama Lucy was now the domineering matron of the Stalls. She watched her orphans from a rocking chair only a few yards away from the pavilion, swinging herself back and forth as her boots dangled in the air. She was a round woman who looked like she was made of dough, with a House mark branded on the right half of her face. The two concentric circles puckered in the fat of her cheek, like someone had punched a permanent dent in her face.

Both short and short tempered, her beady eyes stared straight ahead. Cam couldn't tell if she was looking at them because her eyes never seemed to move, but he figured she knew what they were saying. He had the feeling she could see and hear everything as she sat tearing the meat off a greasy chicken leg with her teeth and smacking a broken porch spindle against the leg of the rocking chair.

She had a mean swing with that spindle, and she never missed.

Devon dropped his empty bowl on one of the tables

and snatched a spoon out of another kid's hand. The boy, probably about ten or eleven, wrapped his body around his bowl of sludge and tried to escape under the table. Devon caught the boy's coat and hung him on an old iron hook that bent up out of a pavilion post.

"I'm still hungry," Devon grabbed the sludge, leaving the boy to hang, and snatched another bowl from a girl at the same table.

We're all still hungry you mutant bastard, a mouthful of food caught in Cam's throat and he fought it down. Beside him, Peter circled his arms around his own bowl.

The boy hanging from the post whimpered and squirmed out of his coat, and the girl cried quietly at the table, her long hair caught under the chain of her tags.

"Shut up!" Mama Lucy waddled between the tables and smacked the girl on the knuckles. "Quit your whining!"

The boy scooted back and hid behind the post as the girl sniffled in an effort to smother her sobs.

The grease on Mama Lucy's chin caught the light as she shook her spindle at the orphans' haggard faces. "All of you, quit your complaining! I hear you cry for your mamas at night, you bunch of babies. Don't you know that the dead can't hear you?"

Nobody dared meet her beady eyes except Cam. She was the authority, the gateway to their meager food and supplies, and her temper left many of them out in the cold or without meals as punishment for no more reason than that she hated them.

Her smile hung crooked in her sagging cheeks. "You look like you got something to say, Mr. Landry," she stretched the spindle across the table and dug the broken end into Cam's shoulder. "Well, spit it out, boy, or would you rather I beat it out of you?"

Why does someone as stupid as you get to be in charge? Cam glanced behind Mama Lucy to where Devon grinned through a mouthful of stolen sludge and answered her. "I don't think Devon should take food from the little ones. It's not fair."

Mama Lucy licked the grease from her lips, then shoved him back with her spindle and laughed. "You want things to be fair, huh? Stupid boy, nothing's fair, nothing's equal. Devon's a mutant. When the Scouts come, I'm gonna trade the boy and his sister for something good, something fat. They'll be here soon, in their fancy uniforms, and I might even get enough for the blondies to get me out of this pig pit. You immunes," she spun and waved the stick at the kids cowering at the tables, "you ain't worth the slop in them bowls. Worthless, squealing rats. Salvation only wants the strong ones for the arena, the fighters, the mutants. Their *entertainment*." She emphasized the last word, a drop of spittle clinging to the corner of her mouth.

"We deserve just as much as the mutants," Cam ignored Jake, who was pulling on his sleeve, and instead gave Mama Lucy a stern glare. "We're worth something, too."

The black eyes twitched and Mama Lucy dug the end of the spindle deeper into the center of Cam's chest with each word, "No. You. Ain't," she leaned over the table. "You're a worthless stray, and I know you've been stealing out of my cellar, boy. I could kill you for it, and nobody would come looking."

Cam held her eyes, determined not to even flinch, but Peter climbed off the bench and hugged Cam's knees, hiding,

Mama Lucy grinned, showing gaps in her yellow teeth as her eyes shot a glance down at Peter. "Got yourself a little rat to protect now, huh? Knew I was smart when I stuck him with you and those pigs." She backed away slowly, the grin like a scarecrow's in the early spring twilight. "Didn't learn your lesson when your brother burned, did you? Still stupid enough to go on and *care*."

The pavilion was silent as Mama Lucy waddled up the porch steps and into the house, chuckling to herself. When the door banged shut behind her, the orphans quietly left the tables and dropped their bowls in a tub next to the sludge pot. The girl with the hollow eyes watched the dishes pile up.

"Hey little man," Cam untangled Peter's arms from his legs. "You alright?"

Peter nodded. "She scares me."

Jake huffed at Cam, "And you scold me for saying stupid things? It's one thing to piss Devon off, but Mama Lucy's on a whole other level. What were you thinking?"

"I'm not scared of her. Besides," Cam shrugged as he watched Devon throw his bowl in the dish tub and walk off toward the horse stalls where the orphans slept, "it's our job to stand up for the smaller ones."

"Says who?" Jake asked.

"I don't know," Cam handed his bowl of sludge to Peter. "We're all they got. They're so small they don't have a chance, Jake."

Jake pressed his fingers to the sides of his head, "There is so much wrong with what you're saying right now, I don't even know where to begin. First, you *should* be afraid of Mama Lucy. That one should be self-explanatory. Second, protecting the little ones is pretty much suicide since it just gets you the attention of the aforementioned Mama Lucy, and even worse, Devon. Third—"

"I get it, Jake," Cam put his hands on Jake's shoulders and held the boy still, "I get that mutants are stronger and faster. I get that we aren't worth as much to Salvation because we can still get hurt and die while the mutants can nearly get cut in half and still swing a sword. I get all that. What I don't get is who decides that it has to be that way? Who's making the rules?"

"Right here, right now, it's Mama Lucy who gets to make the rules. And mutants like Devon. And the Regulators who've hauled you back here every time you've run away. That's who gets to make the rules." Jake pushed Cam's hands off of his shoulders.

"Yeah, well, I'm getting smarter. I'm making plans this time," Cam looked around at the empty pavilion, then sat down next to Peter while the small boy scraped the last of the sludge from the bowl Cam had given him.

Jake huffed, "If you were smart, you'd stay out of their way, be invisible like you say your brother always told you. What was it Devon did to you yesterday after you called him a cow's butt? Um, let me see if I can remember..." Jake rolled his eyes up at the pavilion rafters, then pinned Cam with a hard look. "Oh, yeah, he tried to drown you in the river."

"Mama Lucy wouldn't have let him go that far," Cam said, but he wasn't sure. "Besides," he shrugged, "I got away."

"No, Tara saved your freezing ass. You couldn't hear what she said because your head was under water, but she's the only reason her psycho brother pulled you out." Jake nodded toward the far corner of the main house, where Tara sat alone on the cold ground.

"Maybe I should go and thank her," Cam watched the blond girl dig a toe into a patch of dead grass.

"You're going to just walk up and talk to her? Do you want her brother to have more reason to hurt you? If he saw you talking to her, he'd do more than just try to drown you."

Jake pushed past Cam and Peter, then paused a few steps away. He turned around and pointed at Cam, "You're the one who seriously lacks a sense of self-preservation."

Now you've gone and started to care, Cam thought of Mama Lucy's taunt as he let Jake go and looked at Tara. She hugged her knees, her arms long and golden out of the short sleeves of her thin, white tee shirt. The deepening twilight made her blond braid turn copper over her shoulder, long lashes touching her mismatched cheeks.

Beautiful. Cam remembered what he had thought the first time he saw her seven months ago when the Regulators first dragged him to the Stalls. Beautiful and unpredictable. Cam wondered what she would do if he did talk to her. *Probably tell me I'm just an immune, tell me to go away, punch me like her brother. Or worse,* a thin shudder snaked along his spine, *tell her brother.*

Peter tugged on Cam's sleeve. "I'm tired."

"Full?" Cam picked up the bowls, both of them licked clean.

Shrugging, Peter picked at the tabletop, "Sort of."

"Enough to sleep?"

Peter nodded, the bruise like a dark red noose on his throat.

"Alright then, little man, let's get you to bed. It's getting dark. Stay by me." Cam wound his way to the dirty dish tub. Bowls leaned in a haphazard tower, spoon handles sticking out of the apocalyptic sculpture like branches of a dead tree. The girl who had served the sludge was gone, along with the cooking pot. He dumped the bowls in the corner of the tub and reached down to steer Peter toward the pigsty.

He was gone.

Dammit. Heart pounding, Cam scanned the garden and

the yard, then caught a glimpse of Peter's head peeking out from behind the house, his reddish hair sticking up in chunks.

Peter, Cam headed toward him, then stopped.

Tara walked out from behind the house, watching her bare feet trace a path on the frozen ground until she reached the dish tub. Looking up, she caught Cam's eyes and scowled. "What did you see?" She closed the distance and grabbed his arm.

"Nothing," Cam said, pulling away.

Her grip tightened. "What did you see?"

"Nothing!" Cam wrenched his arm away. Tara couldn't get a good grip on him through the sliding fabric of his sleeve, so she let go and curled her fingers around his wrist and pulled him toward her.

"I was looking for Peter," Cam stammered, his breathing shallow. "Did you do anything to him?"

"Let's stick with the 'nothing,' shall we? You saw *nothing*, I did *nothing*. Got it?" Her breath was hot on his neck, and she smelled like frost and sweat and girl.

Cam met her eyes. "Got it."

Tara nodded and dropped his wrist, pushing past him toward the stalls. Cam watched her go, then caught up to Peter coming around the corner of the house.

"Are you okay?" Cam asked.

Peter nodded but hung his head.

Taking the small boy's thin wrist, Cam tugged him toward the lean-to where they slept with the pigs. He was mad, mad that Peter had gotten hurt, mad that Tara had acted even a little bit like Devon, mad that his brother had died and left him alone.

Mad that he had let Peter out of his sight again. Mad that he *cared*.

The sty smelled like moldy straw and frost, the cold seeping up through the frozen ground now that the sun was gone. The pigs curled up in one big heap, the bigger ones snoring over the soft squeals of the nursing piglets. Cam lay with his hands behind his head, watching what stars he could through the open front of the makeshift shelter. One bright spot peeked out and then disappeared behind a cloud.

Peter squirmed restlessly, trying to wrap himself up in the wool blanket that Cam let him use, but he couldn't seem to get both elbows inside it at the same time.

"Here," Cam tightened the blanket around the small boy like a cocoon, then pulled him up farther on the straw and built a nest around him. "That should be better. Can you go to sleep now?"

He heard the straw rustle, then Peter murmured, "Uh-huh."

Lying on his back again, Cam shifted around until he caught a glimpse of the star as the cloud passed.

"Hey, Peter?"

"Yeah?" The boy yawned.

"What was Tara doing to you behind the house?"

"Oh," more rustling, "I'm not supposed to tell."

Cam swallowed. "Did she hurt you?"

"No."

"Peter," Cam bit his lip, not sure how to convince the boy that he had to tell or whatever it was could get worse. "You can tell me. Tara already knows I saw something."

"She does?"

"Yeah. But I couldn't see you very well, and she wouldn't tell me." Cam swore he heard Peter thinking, the boy's breath speeding up in the darkness. "Did she hurt you?"

"Well," Peter stalled, "Do you promise not to tell her I

said anything? Promise?"

"I promise."

"Pinky promise?"

Cam rolled his eyes. *Little kids.* "Pinky promise."

"You know if you break a pinky promise you'll die, right?"

"Peter, I pinky promise. What did she do?"

The cloud passed over the star again.

"She gave me her apple."

Swallowing, Cam stared as the star winked on. *She wasn't angry,* he realized as he recalled her scowl, the darkness in her eyes, *she was afraid.*

CHAPTER 2

Apples

Cam sat up in the straw, panting. Moonlight streaked in through the open front of the pig shelter, painting the back wall silver. He smelled rain, damp and clean, and looked over at Peter curled up in the wool blanket a few feet away, sleeping.

At least I didn't scream. Cam steadied his breath, hugging his knees until the visions in his head settled.

Not all of his nightmares woke him. Some of them swam in his head and made him turn restlessly through the night, others he forgot as soon as he woke.

But this one never left him, waking him every few weeks since he'd arrived at the Stalls seven months ago. A few days earlier, when Peter first arrived, Cam had woken the small boy in the middle of the night, turning and screaming his brother's name.

Dom.

He rubbed his eyes and his face, then stood and stretched, kicking the straw off his boots. Since he was awake, he might as well take care of the animals. At least Devon wouldn't be around to harass him, and he could brush the horses until breakfast.

He glanced over at Peter to make sure the boy was still sleeping, then headed out into the light rain. He didn't have a coat, just a faded denim shirt layered over a blue tee, but the cold didn't bother him.

Soft drops drizzled from the sky and hovered in a layer of mist above tufts of brown grass. The rain collected in puddles that ran down toward the orchard and the garden and finally to the trees that edged the south side of the farm.

The main house sat to the west of the pavilion and south of the horse stalls, facing an old road that cut through the valley. The house was white, or had been once, with faded black shutters and a wraparound porch with square posts. The steps off the front and back sagged to one side. Cam cut across the pavilion, weaving through the picnic tables to the back porch. Avoiding the tilted steps, he gripped the railing and pulled himself up. The wooden boards threatened to snap under his weight, but he figured if they still held Mama Lucy, he would be fine.

The slop bucket sat out on the porch by the back door instead of inside where it was supposed to be. *Stupid kids*, Cam frowned as he scooped the thin metal handle into his fingers. *A stray dog could've gotten to this out here.* The bucket was only half full, the orphans fighting even more than the pigs for every scrap of food, but a half-eaten apple sat on the top of the corn husks and rotten beans.

His stomach growled at the sight of the fruit, reminding him that he had given half of his dinner to Peter, and he briefly wondered who had thrown out the rest of a perfectly good apple as he picked it out of the bucket and took a bite. It was old, withered, and the best thing Cam had eaten in seven months.

When he was done, he flicked the stem off of the porch and poked his finger into the bucket, stirring the slop to see if he would find an apple core, or maybe even part of Mama Lucy's chicken leg.

I know you've been stealing from my cellar, Mama Lucy had

accused him. Cam glanced up at the door to the house. He wasn't the one who had been stealing, but he had been making plans to run away again, careful plans that involved cutting out his tracking chip and disappearing into the early spring mist, miles away from Mama Lucy and beyond the reach of the Regulators who had caught him the first two times he tried. Plans that had changed when Peter arrived.

It wouldn't have mattered if Mama Lucy had stuck the boy in the row of horse stalls with the other little kids, but she had put Peter in the pig shelter with Cam. It made him wonder if somehow the sludge of a woman suspected he was getting ready to run.

She doesn't care about immunes, Cam told himself, but the truth was that she hated them. *No,* he corrected himself, *she loathes us.*

The door to the house was mostly gray, a few flakes of white paint clinging to the weathered wood. He had gone inside nearly every morning to get the slop bucket for the pigs, but for months the only thing he had taken was a pair of kitchen scissors so that he could cut his hair. He had stayed out of Mama Lucy's way, trying to be invisible. Now she was accusing him of stealing from her cellar.

Might as well make it true, Cam wiped the slop off his finger. *Time for some unleveraged trading.*

Since his parents died three years ago, Cam had survived on stealing. His older brother Dom called it 'unleveraged trading,' saying that they were trading for what they took, only they never left anything in exchange.

The knob squeaked even though Cam turned it slowly. The house stood hushed, like it was waiting for something or someone, everything gray and two dimensional in the thin morning light. Taking off his boots, Cam tiptoed to the door that led under the stairs, the knob loose and broken. He had to wedge his fingers along the casing and pull the door open with his fingertips. Damp and cold, the cellar air smelled like dust and onions. Loose dirt sprinkled the old cement steps, powdering Cam's toes as he felt his way down to the bottom.

The basement had a small window, the glass crusted with years of rainstorms and wind. After a few heartbeats, Cam's eyes adjusted and his jaw fell open.

Bags of onions, apples, turnips, and potatoes hung from the rafters. Metal shelves hugged the cement walls, cans of everything from olives to ravioli stacked in neat rows.

"Whoa," Cam exhaled and ran his hand over a bag of onions. "Mama Lucy, you've been a bad girl." He *tsked* and shook his head. "No wonder you have arm flab. You've been holding out on us." He picked up an old oat sack that had been dropped on the floor and filled it with apples and potatoes and cans of beans. "And here I thought the only things I would find were moldy oats and your oversized underwear." He grabbed an apple and took a bite, a drop of juice running down his chin.

"That's more than just a snack. Going somewhere?" Tara melted out of the shadows between two of the wire shelving units.

"What are you doing down here?" Cam hugged the bag to his chest and stepped back, bumping his ankle into the bottom stair.

Tara chuckled, "Me? What are *you* doing down here? If Mama Lucy caught you stealing her potatoes, she'd wring your neck like you were one of the chickens."

Cam swallowed his bite of apple, "You're the one who's been stealing."

She shrugged, "Maybe."

"Why?" Cam studied her, the marked half of her face hidden in the shadows, her eyes wide and luminous in the half-light.

"Why not? Mama Lucy certainly doesn't need it. She has more than just arm flab, and this stuff rots down here while we go hungry."

"She feeds you and your brother more than she feeds the rest of us."

Tara held up an apple and a can of pineapple. "You think this is for me, don't you?"

Cam stared at her. *You steal food and Mama Lucy thinks it's me. If it weren't for you and your mutant brother messing things up, I would be invisible,* but he didn't say anything as he held his eyes steady with hers.

She shrugged, "Figures you would think that."

So this is where she got the apple for Peter? He wanted to ask her about the night before, but he had made a pinky promise. "If you don't eat the food, what do you do with it?"

"Nothing, right?" She reminded Cam of his promise by the pavilion as she stepped out of the shelves and stood in front of him, "Let's make that our motto. Nothing."

"Okay," he nodded. "That goes for both of us, right? You're doing nothing and I'm doing nothing? We were never here?"

She nodded, "Nothing."

It was harder to think with her standing so close. Beautiful. "Well," he shrugged and swallowed. "Nice talking to you."

"Nice talking to you?" she broke into a low laugh, "Was that supposed to be a conversation?"

Suddenly, Cam felt awkward. "Well, it was kind of a conversation, you know, like two humans talking to each other."

Her eyes narrowed. "Like humans?" She flipped her braid behind her shoulder, "Like I'm not human because I'm a mutant?"

"No," Cam shook his head. "That's not what I was saying."

She looked up as the floor above them groaned, "Mama Lucy's awake. Better get out of here before she catches you." Then she cut her finger across her throat, "Like a chicken, and that's mine," she grabbed the bag out of Cam's hands.

He watched her go up the stairs. *Oh, great, the first time I actually talk to her and I've pissed her off. Maybe she'll be glad when I'm gone.*

The floor groaned again. Cam tucked in his shirt and dropped two apples down the front, where they pooched out above his belt. Mama Lucy had said the Scouts would be coming soon. He would be back for more that night, and then he would be gone and free of the Stalls forever.

He took the stairs two at a time with his bare feet, pushing the creaky basement door open just enough to sneak out the back of the house with his boots in his hands. The slop bucket was right where he left it, but it had picked up another apple core. He slid off the porch, careful not to splash up too much mud, and headed out into the rain.

A flicker of movement in the gray light of early dawn caught his eye. At first he thought it might be Tara, but it was Peter hugging the post, his bright hair darkened by the rain.

Cam stopped and gave the boy a scolding look, then waved at him to follow. *I'll be gone soon, and somebody will have to slop the pigs and take care of the horses. Might as well be Peter.* He swung the bucket in rhythm with his steps, the mess of scraps sloshing as his boots sucked in and out of a thin layer of mud. Peter scurried behind him, splattering the back of Cam's pants as he tried to keep up.

A single cloud moved over the sky, absorbing the light, but the rain had slowed to a drizzle.

Still a winter sky. Cam hoped it would be cold enough to freeze the ground that night, making it harder for his boots to leave tracks.

He didn't want to leave Peter. The boy arrived the night Cam had planned to cut out his own tracking chip and run away across the snowless, frozen ground to the old roads. Cam knew he couldn't go home, but there were plenty of empty houses, some of them burned long ago, that would make suitable shelter. And beyond those he had the mountains.

But Peter complicated things. *Damn Mama Lucy, and damn her mutants.* The apple Cam had eaten in the cellar sat like a lump in his stomach, heavy with guilt. He couldn't be sure what Devon or Mama Lucy might do to Peter if he disappeared and left the small boy behind.

But the Scouts are coming soon, Cam argued with himself. Maybe as early as tomorrow, and I'm sure they'll take Devon. Maybe Mama Lucy will get whatever it is that she wants and they'll leave Peter alone to take care of the horses and the pigs and to play with the other kids without being called names.

He stopped outside the pig run and waited for Peter to catch up. The young boy ran the final three steps to the fence and hopped onto the bottom rung, smiling as he shivered.

Cam held out the bucket, the plastic tub swinging on its metal handle. "Why don't you throw it in?"

"Really?" Peter's eyebrows shot up. He grinned wider now, a missing front tooth leaving an empty space in his smile.

"Grab it on the bottom like this," Cam helped Peter get a grip on the bucket, "and your other hand here," he gave him the metal handle, "so that when you chuck it in the trough you don't get it on your hands."

Peter looked serious now, focused. The bucket was half as big as the small boy but only half full. Bracing his foot against a post, Peter tossed the slop through the fence rungs. Some of it landed on the fence, some in the trough, and some on Peter's boots. He hopped down and frowned, the bucket hanging from a limp arm and rolling against his leg.

Cam ruffled Peter's hair and patted him on the shoulder. "It's okay, little man. I did that my first time, too." *And Dom ruffled my hair the same way and called me 'little man.'* Cam thought again of the words his brother had always repeated, words that had become a sort of mantra for him. Be invisible, be strong. The nightmare flickered.

"Yeah, I guess," Peter's teeth had started to chatter. His face was pale in the cold morning, freckles dark against his white face. It reminded Cam of yesterday when Peter's face had turned white, then red, and then purple as he hung in the air from Devon's hand.

I know I promised you, Peter. Devon will leave you alone after I'm gone, and Mama Lucy, too. Cam picked up the bucket. "We'd better get you inside before you get sick."

"I'm fine," Peter said quickly, clenching his teeth. "What's in your shirt?"

"Something for the horses, and you need to get warm, and dry, so stop talking and go get into the hay." Cam gave the boy a little push, but Peter stayed planted by the pig fence.

The boy hung his head and pulled his jacket sleeves into his fingers. "How come you're not cold?"

Cam shrugged, "Dunno. Just not cold."

Peter looked up, his eyes round. "Are you a mutant?"

His face flat, Cam answered, "No. You're an immune,

and we share a stall. They only put mutants with mutants." Like *Devon and Tara.*

Climbing up on the railing, Peter came up to Cam's chin. "Why are mutants so special, anyway? They just seem like everybody else to me." He thought for a second, "Well, a little meaner, maybe. And their faces are messed up."

"You mean the mark?" Cam leaned against the fence.

"Yeah, the red patch kinda here," Peter waved his hand around his eye.

"Their mark. That's how you know they're mutants." Cam said.

"Well, I wouldn't want to be a mutant if it meant that I would have to look like that." Peter seemed warmer now that he was moving around, though his teeth went back to chattering as soon as he finished talking.

Cam shrugged, "They don't all have them on their faces. I think Mama Lucy's a mutant, but I've never seen her mark." *It's probably lost somewhere in those folds of fat.*

"Is that why she has that ugly scar on her face?" Peter asked.

"That scar is because she's been to Salvation, not because she's a mutant."

"Why did she ever come back here?" Peter cranked his head to look at the house. "She's mean."

"Sometimes they get sent back. I don't know why."

Peter turned back to Cam. "I wish the Scouts would take her when they come, and leave us a nice lady instead."

"I don't think Salvation wants her back, either." Cam ran his fingers through his hair.

Peter shook his head and watched his foot swing. "The lady at my day care was nice. What about the lady at your day care?"

"I didn't go to a daycare." Cam answered, watching the pigs fight for the meager slop that Peter had managed to get into the trough.

Peter thought about Cam's response for a moment, then looked at the older boy in awe. "You had parents?"

"I did," Cam's chest grew tight as the nightmare pressed against his ribs, "I had parents and an older brother."

"Are they dead now?" Peter asked.

"My parents died in the Second Wave, like yours," Cam said.

"What happened to your brother? Did the Scouts take him away?" Peter asked softly.

Cam kicked the empty bucket toward the pavilion. "No, little man, he died of the plague like everybody else, a rogue strain. And it's not the Scouts who burn the dead, it's the Regulators. The Scouts collect the mutants for Salvation, remember?"

Peter hopped off of the fence and hugged himself, shaking with the cold. "Mama Lucy said the Scouts will be coming soon. I hope they take Devon away."

Cam nodded. "Me, too, little man. Now," he pushed Peter toward the pig shelter again, "get warm. I'll come for you when it's time to line up for breakfast." This time the small boy obeyed.

Cam cradled the apples in his shirt and turned toward the horse lean-to where the two mares stood side by side in their rough shelter.

He took a step, and the nightmare bloomed.

CHAPTER 3

Scout

Ten steps. Cam stumbled for five of them to the fence that defined the horse corral, the logs roughcut and tied together with wire stolen from an abandoned farm. Three more steps brought him to the lean-to, and two more steps to the mares themselves.

Ten steps of mud. Ten steps of cold rain. Ten steps of remembering and pain.

Dom.

The horses snorted and huffed as he squeezed between them, clinging to their thick, sturdy necks. He turned his face into a tangled mane and took a deep breath of horse. He squeezed his eyelids tight, hoping to force the nightmare—no, the memory—back into the darkness where he could forget it again.

I'm sorry, Dom. The memory stabbed at him from inside, threading through his veins. *I'm sorry I wasn't invisible, but I'm trying to be strong.*

He buried his face deeper, his nose flattened into the horse's thick neck muscles. The mare stood still, as if she knew what Cam needed, and the other softly nudged him between the shoulder blades.

They remember, too. They know. They were there when the Regulators came and burned the house with Dom still inside. But that wasn't the part of the memory that caused Cam pain, that constricted around his lungs and made him scream in his sleep. *He was alive. The Regulators burned the house when Dom was still alive.*

The memory twisted and bloomed.

Their house had been a simple brick ranch, brown and boring. The front windows had been smashed out, jagged shards of glass catching at blankets as a late summer breeze sucked them through the empty spaces. Cam had hung the blankets when Dom got sick so that he could move his brother into the living room where there was better access to water, and out of the bedroom where their parents had died.

The rot inside Dom's body had started to ooze from a sore that had opened on his throat, bloody green puss leaking out of it.

Just like Mom and Dad.

Cam had settled his brother on the couch, every towel he could find layered under Dom's body to soak up the puss that he knew would come. Torn sheets lay stacked in neat squares next to a bucket of water on the coffee table. Cam had been cleaning the greenish stuff as it leaked out of Dom's body for only a few hours when he heard the horses.

Just as he looked up, the door had burst open and three Regulators came into the house to drag him out, two of them cornering him while the third tackled him to the kitchen floor.

"Dom!" Cam had kicked and screamed, trying to twist out of the Regulators' grip. Two of them pinned his arms and razed him over the coffee table, scattering the carefully arranged rags over Dom and onto the floor.

All Dom could do in answer was blink, the puss gurgling from the hole in his flesh as he turned his head slowly to watch as the third Regulator kicked Cam in the gut to shut him up and shove him through the door. Outside they had strapped him to a board, gagged him, and laid him down in the back of an old military truck. He never saw the flames, but he smelled his house burning.

Now he stood in the horse shelter at the Stalls, breathing in the scent of horse, of home, and letting out the scent of frost and mutants and memories. A large nose nudged Cam's elbow, then pressed into his hip. He stood up and wiped tears from his eyes, surprised because he hadn't been aware he was crying.

Sparta, a reddish bay with a white blaze on her snout, blew a spray of hot air onto Cam's chin. Cam turned his face into the other mare's pale golden mane and rubbed the moisture off. "Guess you guys aren't fooled. I bet you can smell these apples all the way from Mama Lucy's cellar."

Crix, the golden mare, worked her lips on his hair and collar while Cam untucked his shirt. He caught the apples and held them out. Crix knocked one to the ground and followed it as it rolled a little through the dirt and hay, while Sparta sniffed and gently nibbled the other off of Cam's palm.

"Apples for the mutants and horses. The rest of us are sucking up sludge for breakfast, lunch, and dinner. Did you know," he lowered his voice in Sparta's ear, "that if you can sneak yourself into the basement, there's a hoard of apples down there? And onions, if you like those. I'm sure you'll fit through the door because Mama Lucy does, but be careful on those stairs." He scratched her ears and swallowed back the memories that no longer pressed but still clung to the surface of his awareness. Sparta and Crix had been there when Dom died. They had been there to watch the house burn.

They knew.

He pulled a chain out of his pocket. Two square tags, stained with soot and blood, hung heavy in Cam's hand. He cupped them in his palm and read the name etched into the metal.

Dominic Landry.

Boot steps splashed across the field to the pavilion as the orphans woke and left their stalls for more tasteless sludge. Cam's stomach sunk as he remembered the promise he had made to Peter to get him before breakfast.

A set of steps broke out into their own rhythm, coming quickly with a thump slosh toward the lean-to. Peter clambered over the low corral fence, rolling his belly over the top log and almost dropping himself into the mud. He hung on with both arms until his feet found solid ground, then rushed up to Cam. Face flushed, freckles standing out against his cheeks, he fought for breath.

"Hey, little man," Cam shoved the tags in his pocket and braced Peter by the shoulders, "I'm coming."

With round eyes, Peter stuttered, "R-Regulators."

Cam's heart pounded, his eyes following the kids across the yard as they filed into line. Mama Lucy stood on the porch, patting her broken spindle against the palm of her hand. Next to her stood a man in the green and tan military uniform of the Regulators.

Cam rubbed his fingers over the scar at the base of his neck where the Regulators had inserted his tracking chip seven months ago, after they had taken him from his home and burned Dom alive.

He hated Regulators.

Peter's breath settled, but the young boy clung to Cam's leg. Cam looked more closely at the Regulator. *Why is there only one?* They never went anywhere alone. Both times they had chased him down and brought him back to the Stalls, there had been three. Cam would expect to see at least two of them.

But one? Something was wrong.

Cam willed his heart to slow and forced himself to think. *What would Dom say?* But the answer was always the same. *Be invisible. Be strong.*

Cam patted Peter on the shoulder, "We just have to stay calm and do what we normally do. Blend in. Mama Lucy will notice if we're missing, so we'll get our breakfast and sit down by Jake and suck down whatever they slop in our bowls." He bent down to look Peter in the eyes, "Don't look at them. If you look at them, it gets their attention. Keep your eyes down. Got it?"

Peter nodded and whispered, "Why are they here?"

Glancing over his shoulder, Cam shrugged, trying to be calm for Peter's benefit. "Either someone ran away, or someone got caught stealing. It wasn't us, so no big deal, right?"

Peter's face relaxed, "Right."

He took Peter's arm and led him toward the pavilion, keeping the boy on the side away from the man on the porch. Only a few orphans were left waiting for sludge when Cam and Peter tacked themselves to the end of the line. Cam kept his eyes down, stealing glances at Devon and Tara and the stolid man in the uniform.

The Regulator stood stiffly, his hands behind his back pulling his shoulders tall and square as he scanned the orphans. He nodded at something Mama Lucy said, then gave his attention to the mutants. While most of the orphans kept their heads down, trying to be invisible, Devon stood tall and smiled directly at Mama Lucy and the man on the porch.

Regulators returned runaways and administered punishment for stealing. As far as Cam could tell, nobody was missing. That left stealing, and from the look on Devon's face, Cam had a sinking suspicion the mutant knew about the cellar.

It wasn't me. I only took two apples. But Devon wouldn't care about that. *How would he know? Did Tara tell him?* Cam found the blond girl in her usual place by the side of the house, watching her spoon as she stirred it around in her bowl.

Once they had their food, he pulled Peter to the table in the corner of the pavilion where Jake sat hunched over his bowl like a starving, wild animal.

"Hey," Cam nudged Jake with his elbow as he sat down, then helped Peter climb onto the bench. "What's the Regulator doing here?"

"What are *you* doing here?" Jake glanced at him through the side of his eye. "I thought you would be gone."

"Not yet," Cam looked at Peter to see if the small boy was listening. "Tonight."

"Well, I hope your careful planning pays off, because that's not a Regulator," Jake shifted his eyes to the man on the porch, "that's a Scout, and he has an acquisition order."

Cam looked up at the porch. Mama Lucy held a finger out toward him and Jake, the fat on her arm swinging in the early morning light. As the man turned to see what she pointed at, Cam saw the red sash on his right shoulder that identified him as a Scout rather than a Regulator.

He should have been relieved, but instead his heart raced again and he felt sick. Nobody would accuse him of stealing, but a single Scout with an acquisition order could do even more damage. *I was supposed to be gone.*

"I hope the Scout takes the Evil Emperor Mutant with him when he leaves." Jake muttered, pointedly avoiding any acknowledgement of Mama Lucy's finger or the Scout's penetrating gaze. "Maybe someone in Salvation will teach

Devon a lesson he'll never forget. You know, a lesson like what knives and swords do to mutants who are too big for their extra-strength britches."

"Be quiet, Jake. He's looking at us." Cam drew shapes on the top of his sludge, watching the colorless mush slowly sink back and erase the lines. *Be invisible.*

"Cam," Jake leaned close and whispered, "Mama Lucy is taking Tara and Devon to the house. They're leaving, Cam. The Scout is going to take the mutant twins away." He squirmed on the bench and scooped a heaping spoonful into his mouth.

"Did the Scout come alone?" Cam risked a glance around the Stalls. *There has to be more. Where are they?* He looked at the pig yard and the horse shelter, then scanned the stalls where the orphans slept.

"I haven't seen any others," Jake shrugged and took another bite.

Be invisible. Cam swallowed a mouthful of sludge and looked at Peter, who sat rigid on the bench, his head cranked around as he watched the Scout pace the tables in the pavilion.

"Hey, Peter," Cam put a hand on the boy's shoulder, feeling the bone through his oversized coat, "don't look at him. It'll just get his attention."

Untwisting, Peter looked at Cam with wide eyes. "Do you think he'll pick me?"

"No, no," Cam gave the small shoulder a squeeze and tried to smile. "You're too young. Just stay by me and you'll be okay, I promise."

The red head bobbed up and down, "Okay. Is he really taking Devon away?"

"I think he is, little man." Cam kept one eye on the uniform.

"Really?" Peter's legs swung under the table.

"Really, now sit still and finish your breakfast." Cam also dug into his bowl, taking a big bite and nodding at Peter, who copied him. He listened to the boot steps on the packed dirt under the pavilion, like a heartbeat, *one, two, one, two.*

Then they stopped. He saw the boots, laced tightly over green pants, through the gaps in the weathered table.

"Cameron Landry?"

Cam's heart skipped and he met the Scout's blue eyes. The face was younger than he expected, smooth and winter pale under the stiff brim of a worn hat. *He's not any older than Dom would have been. And not very big, either.* Pushing himself up, Cam unwound himself from the bench and table.

"Yes?" he kept his eyes steady.

The Scout looked over at Jake, "Jacob Lee?"

Jake must have nodded because the Scout met Cam's eyes again. "Come with me."

Blood rushed to his ears and Cam clenched his hands. "No," he took a step back.

A heavy hand landed on his shoulder and a gruff voice asked, "Where you going, son?"

I knew there had to be more than one.

CHAPTER 4

Acquisitions

Cam shivered.

But it wasn't because he was standing in the medic room of the main house with no clothes on. He shivered because they were all staring at him.

Well, they were staring at both him and Jake, who was also standing in the middle of the room with his hands over his groin.

This is humiliating, Cam shuddered and kept his eyes on the mountains through the window. He concentrated on making out the peaks and snow through the mist left by the morning's rain, but the two men in uniforms and Mama Lucy were hard to ignore.

The Scout stood in front of Cam with a piece of paper. "Says here you're a stray."

Mama Lucy glanced briefly at the Regulator before answering for Cam, "Found at home when his brother caught a rogue strain, parents dead from the Second Wave. He's been tagged but won't wear the chain." She sniffed, "What do you want him for?"

The Scout ignored her and addressed Cam. "They found you when your brother died?"

Cam bit the inside of his cheek and met the Scout's eyes, "He wasn't dead."

"Says here he was dead. Also says you've run away. Twice."

The Scout popped his finger against the sheet of paper in his hand.

Cam stared at him, feeling like his skin was being peeled away and his heart exposed to all of the eyes in the room.

"Twice," the Scout pushed his finger into Cam's shoulder.

"You don't need to go poking." The Regulator swiped the Scout's hand away. "You can see every damn inch of him. He's got the same parts as the rest of us. And no mark." The man was grizzled and gray, with deep lines etching his eyes and mouth.

Mama Lucy glared at the Regulator from the doorway, her beady black eyes twitching with the gray man's every move. For the most part, the Regulator ignored her.

The Scout looked at the Regulator with an even expression. "I have to make sure there's no mark. It's my job."

"Fill the order. That's your job, not poking at boys." The Regulator had a rough voice, like gravel. "Let's go."

"I want my tags." Mama Lucy settled her weight in front of the only exit from the room.

The Regulator gave her a grim look, "We're here to fill an acquisitions order, not grant your wishes."

She pinched her lips and scowled. "My tags, Colter."

Mama Lucy knows him. Cam studied the brand burned onto the Regulator's right cheek. It was an outline of an eye with two chevrons on each end. A ragged scar ran from the middle of the brand to the old man's chin, cutting through a week's worth of gray stubble. *I bet that's a scar from the arena.*

The Scout stepped back into the corner, watching the exchange between Mama Lucy and the Regulator with a wary look. Cam glanced at the twins where they leaned against a wall by the door, Devon watching smugly and Tara staring at her feet, the door, the peeling yellowed wallpaper—anything but the arguing adults and the two naked boys in the middle of the room.

Jake sneezed.

After an annoyed glance at him, the Regulator met Mama Lucy's glare. "It's Officer Smith."

"Not to me." Her eyes narrowed, "You have your tags. I can see that chain like a leash around your neck. Are you going back?"

"I'm fulfilling an acquisitions order. The rest of it is none of your business." Officer Smith put his hand on his belt, where a taser hung in a worn leather case.

"Then tell me this, Colter," Mama Lucy emphasized the name and pointed at Cam, "Why that one? He's chipped but he didn't code, no tags. He's not supposed to exist." She dropped her arm and her beady eyes burned at the Regulator. "Why was he put here to sleep with my pigs? Are you collecting him for Winters?"

Cam's fingers felt numb. *Are they taking me to shoot me? Burn me?* Suddenly he wished he *had* been caught stealing. He glanced at Tara, who met his eyes and blushed. *I just needed one more day.*

The room waited in silence for the grizzled man's response, then the Scout stepped in between Mama Lucy and Officer Smith. He looked young and undersized between the doughy woman and the thick-chested Regulator, but he straightened his uniform and cleared his throat.

"Two mutants," the Scout waved at the twins, then at Jake and Cam, "and two immunes."

"One immune and one no-code." Mama Lucy interrupted.

The Scout glared at her, "Two immunes. Once we get him tagged at the outpost, Cameron will be an immune. No mark, no questions. End of discussion."

"I want my tags released," Mama Lucy stretched her arms across the doorway, the porch spindle gripped tightly in her hand. "No tags, no acquisitions."

"Stand down, Ms. Malin." The Scout straightened his hat.

"Or what, boy?" Her arms flopped to her sides and she took a step toward the Scout. "You gonna taser me? You gonna tell on me? Who's gonna come here and get me?"

"Enough of your drama, Malin." Smith huffed.

"My drama, Colter?" *Mama* Lucy gave the grizzled man a crooked smile. "Once we were on the same side. Thought maybe you'd understand, being that we were both banished. I guess I was wrong."

"You've been wrong about more than one thing, *Mama* Lucy." Smith gave her a final stare.

The Scout cleared his throat and shifted his weight. "Time to go."

Mama Lucy tested the young Scout with her beady black eyes, then sniffed and moved aside so that the doorway was clear.

"Now you're being reasonable." Officer Smith nodded toward Cam and put his hand on his taser. "Get them dressed. We leave in five minutes."

Five minutes? Cam kept his face flat until Mama Lucy left. *Peter.* He grabbed his pants and slid them on, rolling the cuffs and sliding on his boots. He pulled his tee shirt on and grabbed his long sleeved shirt. Jake was still trying to get his second leg in his pants when Cam ran out the door.

Mama Lucy caught him at the bottom of the stairs, snatching his arm and pulling him into the kitchen. She slammed him against the wall.

Peter. Cam struggled against her grip, but stopped when

she pressed the rusty blade of a knife to his throat.

"Boy," her voice was raspy, desperate. "I need you to do something for me."

Cam shook his head, "Why would I do anything for you?"

She chuckled, the motion shaking the fat under her chin. "Because of a precious little boy with freckles and red hair. Peter, right? What's he gonna say when you're gone? When you leave him here? Who will be around to save him if he falls in the river, or maybe gets caught up in some barbed wire?"

"You can't—" Cam started to argue, then caught the feral glint in her eye. She was deadly serious. "Why? Why would you hurt him?"

"I've been waiting for this. I want my tags. I've served my sentence and I want to go back, but the bastards think they can play with me. Well, I'm gonna make up my own rules to the game, and you're gonna help me."

Footsteps echoed down the stairs, and the back door slammed shut. *Jake.* Cam realized he was completely alone in the house with Mama Lucy.

"They're taking you to Salvation, where the Houses rule." Her breath was hot on his cheek. "Them blond twins? They're the pretty ones. They'll get the gold and the jewels and the cheers. Immunes are just rats, left to fight over their scraps. And you?" She turned the blade of the knife until it dug up under his jaw. "You're not anything, an accident. You're not even supposed to be alive. That Regulator's as dumb as a headless chicken trying to smuggle you into Salvation." She reached in to her dress and pulled something out.

Cam caught the glint of metal in her chubby hand before she pressed a small disk into his palm.

"That's your ticket to living, boy. You listening?" Spittle

clung to the corner of Mama Lucy's thin lips.

He swallowed and nodded, the blade cutting into his skin.

"Good. That's a coin, special. You're gonna go to Salvation, find someone for me before the others find you. Got me so far?" Mama Lucy's breath came in little excited huffs.

Cam nodded again, watching beads of sweat crawl past the black eyes. His heart hammered in his ears.

She continued. "There's a man, old but strong, the oldest man you'll ever see. Takes care of the horses for one of the Houses. Simple man, white hair and a row of pretty teeth. Goes by the name of Adam. Give him the coin, but don't let another soul know about it, especially that Regulator. He works for the other side. Can't trust him." She studied Cam for a moment, searching for something. "Can't trust anybody."

He held still, willing himself not to tremble under the sharp edge of her gaze, and hoped she would find what she was looking for.

"Promise me."

"I promise," Cam wheezed out past the blade that pressed into his throat.

"If you don't deliver the coin, you understand what will happen to Peter?"

"Yes."

"A lot of people will be looking for you once they know you exist. You're going to be keeping a lot of secrets, boy, and I'll be keeping an eye on your little friend. One year. I will know by the spring thaw if you've done it." She snatched the knife away and smoothed the front of her dress. "Better get yourself out there. Colter's the suspicious type, got something planned for you, don't he? But we don't need him sniffing about our business, understand?"

Cam shook his head and slipped the coin into a pocket on the side of his cargo pants and zipped it closed. When he looked up, Mama Lucy's expression softened and she frowned.

She nodded toward the door, "Tell him good-bye. Make it sweet, might be the last kind thing that boy ever hears."

Peter. Cam bolted before she could change her mind, the weight of the coin in his pocket and the sting under his jaw both reminders of the pact he had just made. *I promise.*

Outside, he scanned the field for Peter. The other kids were scattered in small groups, playing games or fighting. He saw Peter by the chickens, curled up against a coop post and poking a small stick into the mud.

"Peter!" Cam jumped off the porch and a strong hand yanked at his arm.

"Where do you think you're going?" The Regulator's voice grated along Cam's spine.

Jerking loose, Cam took two steps back. "I just wanted to say goodbye to someone."

"Looked like you were going to run," he settled his hand over his taser, like he had done to warn Mama Lucy.

"Not going to run," Cam swallowed.

"Cam!" Peter barreled into Cam's legs.

"Hey, little man." Cam crouched next to the small boy and wrapped his arms around him. Even through the thick coat, Cam felt Peter's sobs.

Peter looked up, sniffing and wiping his sleeve across his nose. "Cam, you promised."

"I know I promised, Peter. I promised to take care of Devon though, too, so it looks like I can only keep one promise at a time." Cam pointed at the Regulator, "See that man right there?"

Peter nodded, tears streaking over his freckles.

"That man is here to take Devon away, but he has to take me away, too. So I have to go now, but I'll come back for you. That's a new promise, okay?" Cam watched Peter for a nod, but the small boy only sobbed. He wiped his thumb across Peter's cheek. "Hey, little man, I need you to be big right now. You know the horses? I need you to take care of the horses. Can you do that for me?"

Peter opened his eyes and sucked in a breath. "Uh-huh," he nodded.

"I need you to talk to them every day, scratch their ears and give them apples. Sparta likes them still green, before they drop from the tree," Cam's throat tightened and he blinked back tears.

Taking a deep breath, Peter stood up straight. "I'll take good care of them, I promise."

"Pinky promise?"

Peter smiled, "Pinky promise."

"You know if you break a pinky promise, you'll die, right?" Cam peaked an eyebrow, matching Peter's smile.

"Right."

Cam rustled the boy's red hair. "That's my little man."

Smith cleared his throat. "This is all very touching, but it's time to go."

"Bye, Cam," Peter choked back a fresh sob as the Regulator grabbed Cam's arm and pulled him toward the front of the house where the other three orphans waited by a faded green truck.

Smith shoved him toward the others, hard enough that Cam stumbled until he caught the edge of the truck bed. The Scout stood near the cab, pulling on leather gloves and fussing with his uniform.

Devon stood with his arms folded, looking almost bored, but Tara and Jake both watched the two men nervously.

Cam shifted his eyes to the tasers on their belts. *You're not even supposed to be alive.* Mama Lucy's words pinched at the back of his neck. *Then why didn't they kill me? What do they want with me?* The coin in his pocket pressed against his leg.

The Scout scanned the group with a warning. "I am Scout Brian Carrigan of Denver Depot 112, and you are now my acquisitions. You will ride in the back of the truck. You will address me as 'sir.' You will not ask questions," he looked directly at Cam, "and you will not run away or Officer Smith will be forced to shoot you. Do you understand?"

Devon grinned, "Yes, sir."

Tara dropped her eyes to the ground, and Jake jammed his hands in his coat pockets. "Yes," he answered in a small voice.

"Yes, what?" the Scout raised an eyebrow.

Scared, Jake glanced at the Regulator, then looked to Cam for help.

Cam seethed. *This guy is barely older than we are and he's talking to us like we're five years old.* He was starting to hate this young Scout almost as much as he hated Devon. Cam cleared his throat and stood up tall, pretending to straighten a uniform, "Yes, sir, Scout Brian Carrigan of Denver Depot 112, sir."

Carrigan scowled, "Do you think this is a game, acquisition?"

Devon shoved Cam's shoulder. "He likes to be a nuisance. I'll take care of him."

"You'll get in the truck," Smith growled at Devon.

The blond mutant met the Regulator's glare with his own, then hopped over the tailgate. Tara followed reluctantly, and

Jake took a moment to get his foot settled on the bumper, his hands shaking as he braced them on the tailgate and pulled himself up.

"You're next, acquisition," Smith pushed on Cam's shoulder.

Spinning around, Cam shoved the older man away. "Don't touch me."

"Likewise," Smith grabbed Cam's wrist and twisted his arm.

Cam swore as the Regulator pinned his shoulder to the ground and pinched a set of cuffs on his wrists.

"Cam!" Peter ran out from behind the house, Mama Lucy on his heels.

"Peter," Cam could only grunt, the Regulator's knee pressing hard on his back.

"Get back here, you little runt!" Mama Lucy screamed. The world spun as Smith plucked Cam off the ground and tossed him in the back of the truck. His head smacked against the window and the Regulator settled next to him against the cab.

"Peter," Cam scooted toward the tailgate. *What will Mama Lucy do to him?*

His shoulders screamed when they were wrenched back by the cuffs. The engine rumbled to life and the truck lurched forward, tilting sharply as it pulled onto the road. Cam watched the Stalls shrink as the truck picked up speed. Mama Lucy followed them with a warning gaze, holding Peter tightly by the arm as the small boy screamed Cam's name.

You promised.

CHAPTER 5

Consolidated Resources

The pain in Cam's shoulders eased when he stopped pulling against the cuffs. Officer Smith let go as soon as the Stalls faded from sight.

Devon squinted at Cam from where he leaned against the wheel well. "Miss your little friend, Pig Boy?"

"Shut up, Devon." Cam snapped back.

"I bet Mama Lucy gets hungry and bakes him into a little porky pie," the blond boy chuckled.

This time Tara snapped at her brother, "Shut up, Devon." It was the first thing she had said since Mama Lucy collected them in the main house for the inspection of the Scout.

If you don't deliver the coin, you understand what will happen to Peter? Mama Lucy's threat echoed in Devon's words. Cam's throat tightened. *I understand, Mama Lucy. You made me promise.*

Devon kicked at his sister, "What do you care, Tara? It's Pig Boy and his little Sty Fly, the scum of the Stalls."

"What did he ever do to you?" Tara pulled her knees up and hugged them to her chest, but there was no way she could get out of Devon's reach in the few square feet of the truck bed.

"What did he ever do for you?" Devon pushed his bare foot into her shin, and she kicked back at him.

Jake gave the Regulator a pleading look, "Aren't you going to do something?"

44

Beside Cam, Smith huffed, "What would you like me to do?"

This time Devon kicked Jake. Cam curled his fingers into fists and strained lightly against the cuffs, testing them. The links stretched and he stopped. At least he was strong enough to get out of them if he needed to.

Jake's eyebrows went up, "Maybe stop the Evil Emperor Mutant and his twin sister from killing each other? Or us? Or killing us accidentally while they're trying to kill each other?"

The Regulator folded his arms, "Do I look like your mama? Or a daycare lady? Somebody to kiss your boo-boos and keep the boogieman away?"

Jake rubbed his shin, "I just thought that you would be orderly, you know, have rules and give orders and stuff."

Cam felt the Regulator laughing more than he heard him. *Jake's a fool to think that this guy cares about us at all. We're just a list of names to him. Except me.* Cam looked at the man's crooked smile through the corner of his eye. *There's something else he wants from me.*

Officer Smith raised an eyebrow. "I have an acquisitions order. That's the only 'order' I care about. I deliver you to Salvation, I get something I want. End of trip. End of story."

"What is it you get?" Jake asked.

Shut up, Jake. Be invisible. Cam wanted to tell his friend, but he sensed Smith's agitation and didn't want his own situation to get worse than being in handcuffs, so he kept quiet.

Devon kicked Jake again. "Stop asking stupid questions."

"Stop kicking my acquisitions," Smith leveled Devon with a look, then shifted his gaze to Jake. "Fortunately for you, son, all Salvation wants from you is a strong back. They don't care much about how bright you are, as long as you can work." He pulled a hunting knife out of his belt and inspected the blade in the morning sun. "And there are those in Salvation who have a simple solution for a slave who won't learn to keep their mouth shut." He pointed the knife at Jake, "They just cut out your tongue."

Jake snapped his jaw shut and craned his neck to watch the road feed out behind the truck. Tara looked sick as the Regulator slid the knife back into the leather sheath on his belt, but Devon just leaned back against the wheel well with his usual smug expression.

The road was rough, but it was only a few miles to the outpost. The truck sped up and slowed down, popping over old chunks of asphalt and dipping into holes full of rainwater from the early morning's drizzle. They passed a few abandoned homesteads with bare trees creeping into the fields and weeds choking out fences and vining up walls.

As they approached what was once the main street of a small town, the road smoothed out and there were a couple of streetlamps still standing, embedded in uneven chunks of cement. The outpost itself was a large stone structure that looked like it had been some kind of city government building before the First Wave of the plague.

The truck shuddered to a stop in the middle of the yard next to the building. Three other trucks sat parked in a neat row, their bumpers inches from the mortared stone. Covered with an even layer of gravel and clear of weeds, the yard was well maintained. The entire outpost was surrounded by a chain link fence that looked like it had been patched together from pieces off abandoned farms.

Devon braced his hand on the edge of the truck bed to jump out.

"Stay in the truck," Smith warned.

The blond boy narrowed his eyes at the Regulator, but settled his weight and folded his arms. Tara hugged her knees and stared at the holes in her pants.

Squirming, Jake raised his hand halfway. "Uh, I got to pee."

Smith frowned and pulled Cam to his feet.

Carrigan came around the back of the truck and pointed to the side of the yard away from the outpost building. "The latrine is over there."

Jake squinted, "That old shed?"

"No, not the shed. The latrine is behind the shed," the Scout answered Jake and motioned for Cam to get out.

Watching the hunting knife on Smith's belt as he hopped out of the back of the truck, all Cam saw on the other side of the shed were brown weed stalks as tall as his chest.

Jake frowned at the tailgate, "Alright."

Smith landed on the gravel right behind Cam. The two military men ignored the acquisitions and glared at each other.

"This is my protocol," Carrigan straightened his hat.

Glancing at the taser on Carrigan's belt, Cam's throat tightened and his heart sped. *It's a gun. He must've switched it in the truck. And Mama Lucy said I should have been shot and burned.* Cam pulled on the cuffs, feeling the links stretch a little more.

Then Smith grabbed his wrists and shoved him into Carrigan. "Be quick."

"Of course," Carrigan answered.

Smith folded his arms, "I'm already waiting."

The Scout tugged Cam toward the front of the building, the gravel crunching under their boots.

"Where are we going?" Cam asked, his mind on the gun.

The Scout ignored him and pulled his tags out of his shirt.

The main door was on the south end of the building. A metal plate was bolted to the heavy solid wood, identifying it as Outpost 216. Carrigan passed one of his tags over a small black bar next to the door. The lock clicked and Carrigan pushed on the heavy wood.

"Sir," Cam breathed out.

Now Carrigan looked at him, the Scout's blue eyes reminding Cam of Dom. "New tags. You won't get past Denver without proper identification."

Cam followed the Scout inside where it was warm. They stepped into a large entry where a hallway cut the building in half, dark brown doors punctuating its length. A desk occupied the right side of the room, flanked by two metal filing cabinets and a flag that Cam recognized but couldn't exactly place. The Scout moved a chair out of the way and pulled Cam down the hallway to the third door on the right and knocked.

Footsteps echoed through the floor and the door cracked open. A dark brown eye and tight black curls squished through three inches of space. The eye moved back and forth between Cam and the Scout.

"Scout Brian Carrigan of Denver Depot 112. Acquisitions order. I need tags."

"Been expecting you. Where's your Regulator?" The eye asked.

"With the others," Carrigan answered.

"He come from Denver with you?"

The Scout didn't respond to this question as quickly as he had the first. "Yes."

The door swung open. The eye belonged to a slightly built man, no older than Carrigan, with a wild head of black curls and khaki pants. He held out his hand. "Officer Darren

McCall, Outpost 216, located pretty much at the edge of the world." He pointed his thumb over his shoulder at a thickset man with an unruly black beard and a stain on his shirt. "That's Barnes."

I know them, Cam realized.

Carrigan gave McCall's hand a single shake and a curt greeting. "Officers."

McCall dropped into a wheeled desk chair, his tags clinking as he slid over to a set of screens that stretched the length of one wall. "How's our favorite runaway?" he asked Cam.

Then Cam remembered. He remembered the smell of the fall air blowing through the broken windows, carrying a scent of the pus oozing out of Dom's sores. He remembered the crunch of the Regulators' boots on the gravel walk as they dragged him out of the house. He remembered Dom screaming his name as the flames licked at the bricks. These were the Regulators who had snatched him from his home and left it black and smoking with Dom still inside. He pulled against the handcuffs and felt a link pop. He was free.

"How'd Mama Lucy treat you?" McCall's brown eyes watched him.

Peter. The reminder hit him like ice water and he froze, tucking his hands behind his back. *If I don't make it to Salvation, Peter could die.* It was the first time he had allowed it to form a thought. *Peter could die.* Cam straightened his spine and glared at the black curls. "Fine."

The Regulator named Barnes stomped over, his bulbous nose stopping within an inch of Cam's face. A scar cut through the man's bushy black eyebrow and ran like a white, ropy worm up across his forehead and into his hair.

Cam watched the man's nostrils flare, beads of sweat

popping up on the thickset Regulator's greasy upper lip.

"Remember me, boy?" Barnes oozed the words.

Cam caught a flash of memory, the man's sausage fingers pinching into his bicep and the pain of the taser biting into his back. "Yeah, I remember you."

Barnes pointed to the scar on his forehead, "Gave me this, you little bastard. Remember that?"

Cam pinched his lips and met the Regulator's eyes. *I remember the greedy look in your eyes when you tased me. I remember you setting my house on fire. I remember the way you laughed before the world went black.*

Carrigan cleared his throat, "Step away from my acquisition, officer."

The thick man's dark eyes flitted to the Scout. "You don't need tags for this one. You need an iron box." The floor creaked under Barnes' weight as he slowly stepped back, his eyes locked again on Cam as he folded his arms and leaned against the wall.

McCall locked his fingers behind his head and leaned back in the chair. "So you want tags? You know he didn't code, right? We got him chipped, but didn't see the point in making tags with no code. Sent the info into Central, but nothing came back until you showed up."

Carrigan gave the Regulator a tight smile, "He has no mark. My orders are for tags that code for an immune."

"If his blood won't code, I don't have anything I can use to make him tags." McCall's face remained flat but his eyes hardened.

He knows something isn't right. Cam could almost feel the tension ripple through the three men in the room.

Carrigan smoothed his jacket. "I need the tags. I don't care if you have to steal them off of one of the bodies you burn."

McCall's eyes followed Carrigan's hand as he ran his fingers over the handle of the gun on his belt. McCall nodded, "Got it."

The chair wheels clicked on the floorboards as they rolled through some well-worn grooves to a table that sat under the window. McCall grabbed a black box off of a larger rusty metal box with 'TOOLS' stamped across the front. Large jars lined a deep windowsill, the late morning sun illuminating the different shades of glass and giving distorted hints of their contents. A series of monitors hung on the wall across from the door, their screens dark and gleaming. The rest of the room was clean and military, with a bed on each side that had blankets tucked around the mattresses so tight Cam thought he could skip rocks on them.

But he was most interested in the jars. One of them looked like it contained coins like the one Mama Lucy had given him. *Answers,* Cam hoped.

Carrigan pulled his fingers off of the gun and folded his arms, looking satisfied that the Regulators were following orders.

McCall popped the top open on the black box, then grabbed a jar off of the windowsill and thunked it down on the table.

Tags. It was a jar full of shiny new tags, the mass a lump of silver-gray through the curved glass.

Digging in the jar, McCall dug out a pair of the silver metal slices hooked together with a tiny metal ring. He set them down and pulled the black box toward him, flipping the top open. "You'll need to take those cuffs off of him," McCall continued working while he spoke to Carrigan, pulling out an assortment of small stainless steel instruments.

I need answers, Cam held his wrists together as Carrigan

inserted the small key and unlocked the cuffs. Cam caught the first side in his fingers to keep it from clattering to the floor as the Scout pulled off the other half and realized they had been broken.

Holding his breath, Cam watched as Carrigan took both halves of the cuffs and hung them on the other side of his belt from the gun. Cam disliked Carrigan, but he hated the Regulators even more, and for a moment at least, he and the young Scout were on the same side.

Time to play nice. Rubbing his wrists, Cam stepped over to the table and pointed his chin at another jar. "What's in that one?"

The Regulator glanced up, "Coins," then returned to arranging the things on the table.

"Can I see them?" Cam held up his hands. "Just curious."

"What are you up to, boy?" Barnes growled.

Cam relaxed his face, trying to look as innocent as possible, and showed his empty hands to the other Regulator. "Never seen them before, that's all."

McCall pulled the jar down from the sill and dumped it out on the table. Coins jingled into a small mound, a few tinkling onto the hardwood floor. Cam picked one up that looked like it was the same size as the one in his pocket, a silver piece with a diameter half as long as his finger.

"Silver dollar," McCall talked while he finished arranging his tools. "Found it in a dead guy's pocket."

Ridges edged the perimeter, some smoothed with age. A lady's face was stamped on the front, a crown that said 'Liberty' and what looked like stalks of wheat in her hair. The back of the coin had an eagle clutching arrows and a branch. Between the eagle's wings were tiny fancy letters.

"In God We Trust?" Cam rolled the coin in his fingertips.

"Who came up with that?"

McCall's eyes lit up, "Some random guy from ancient times. Look at the date on that thing," he pointed at the lady's face as the coin stilled on Cam's palm.

"1921."

"Yeah, like a century and a half ago," McCall picked up one of the shiny steel instruments, a tube with a needle on it, "and there are coins a hundred years older than that." The Regulator turned in the chair and reached for Cam's wrist.

Cam dropped the coin and threw his arms up and away from the man's reach. "What are you doing?"

Carrigan stepped to the side, cutting Cam off from the door, and Barnes pulled out his taser.

McCall's eyes hardened. "Gotta take some blood to code the tags."

"I thought I didn't code."

"You don't, but I need your blood for identification in the tag. Salvation wants to keep things pure. Chips for tracking, tags for id."

Glancing behind him at the door, Cam lowered his arms and shifted his weight from one foot to the other.

Barnes waved his taser up and down and grinned. "Going to run? I've chased you down before, you filthy stray. Go ahead. Let's see how far you get this time."

A beep drew Cam's eyes to the monitors on the wall, now lit up with brown and green maps, a bright dot pulsing on one of them.

"Already tracking you," McCall waved the syringe. "Itty bitty needle? Or do I need to have Barnes over there hold you down?"

"I'm not afraid of the needle. I don't want to be like you." *I'm not invisible anymore, Dom, but I'll try to be strong. For Peter.* Cam's chest tightened and he took a deep breath to clear his head and stepped up to McCall, careful not to look as the Regulator tied a rubber strip above his elbow and tapped on the crease. Cam's tension eased slightly when he saw Barnes lower the taser and he weighed the risk of asking more questions. *I don't need to ask more questions, I need to ask the right ones.*

The needle pinched as it went in, and Cam fished through the coins with his free hand. "Where did you get all of this stuff?"

"The coins?" McCall asked, watching the blood in the syringe.

"Everything." Cam scanned the wall of screens. His dot was pulsing steadily like it was connected to his heartbeat. "I thought fancy gadgets like this were gone with the First Wave."

McCall shrugged. "The First Wave killed a lot of people, enough people to force us to shut down worldwide industry and shove us back a few centuries, but the plague virus doesn't kill *things*, not even the worst rogue strains."

The Regulator pulled the needle out and placed a small white square over the hole. "Keep some pressure on that."

Holding his fingers on the gauze, Cam watched the Regulator insert the needle into a small silver box and empty the syringe.

Carrigan added, "We survive by consolidating our resources, collecting the things we need into a few places." It was the Scout's official purpose that Carrigan echoed.

Consolidated resources. That's what the acquisitions are. We're resources.

McCall chuckled, "What he means is that we steal from the living and rob the dead."

A screen on the top of the silver box lit up and McCall

wrapped the rubber around his own arm, his black curls bouncing as he pulled it tight with his teeth.

"What are you doing?" Carrigan asked.

"Confusing the scanner," McCall answered, and sucked in a breath as he jabbed the needle into his vein.

"That works?" the Scout stepped around Cam to get a better view of the silver box.

"The scanner's the easy part. Won't change the ID in his chip. If anybody checks it, it'll still say he's a no-code," McCall set the needle down and pressed another square of gauze to the dot of red that welled up. He used his teeth again to pop the rubber off of his arm.

"Can you change his chip?" Carrigan's weight came forward onto the balls of his feet.

Barnes stood up off of the wall. "We put 'em in, don't take 'em out. Might kill him if we're carving out part of his neck." His eyes gleamed at Cam. "I'd be willing to risk it."

Carrigan took a step toward Barnes. "Don't touch him."

Barnes scowled.

McCall repeated the motions with the silver box, this time tapping the top when it lit up. The box beeped and the Regulator picked up the blank tags and inserted them one at a time into a slot in the side, then tossed them at Cam.

They were hot. Surprised, Cam dropped them on the floor among the coins that had fallen off of the table.

"Careful," McCall's brown eyes looked amused.

Cam picked up the newly etched tags, then paused. *Answers.* He dropped to his knees and fished the coin out of his pocket, then pretended to pick it up off of the wooden floor and held it out to McCall.

"What kind of coin is this?" Cam asked.

The Scout snatched it from Cam's hand before the

Regulator could. "Skull and bones." He looked at McCall as he backed up, pushing Cam behind him toward the door, "Where did you get this?"

"I don't know," the Regulator's shoulders almost touched his black curls as he shrugged, "I collect coins. Could have come from anywhere."

Barnes rested his hand on his taser. "Probably found it on a dead guy."

Carrigan flipped it over and his eyes narrowed. He pulled his gun and pointed it at Barnes. "You didn't find this."

Barnes held up his hands and backed up into the wall. "I don't know what you're talking about."

"Winters," Carrigan answered, and pulled the trigger.

CHAPTER 6

Ashes, Ashes

Cam's new tags felt heavy against his chest, sticking to his clammy skin, and the chain rubbed on the back of his neck as the truck jolted them onto the road. He reached up and ran his fingers over the inch-long scar that marked where his tracking chip pulsed out a silent signal.

After Carrigan shot the Regulators, Cam had turned to the corner of the room in the outpost and retched. When he had looked up again, it had been to see Carrigan's gun shaking in his face. For several heartbeats they had been frozen in that room with the two dead Regulators. Then the Scout lowered his gun, his other hand shaking so badly that he dropped the chain for Cam's tags and the coin rolled into the blood pooling out from under McCall's shoulder.

Settled back against the cab again, Cam stared at a dark red smear on his pants that shook into a blur with the vibration of the truck. He couldn't remember exactly how the blood got there, but then there had been so *much* of it. His fingers curled around the coin in his pocket. *Pinky promise.*

The others in the truck were silent, even Devon, who usually wasn't afraid of anything. Jake stole glances at the gray haired Regulator and chewed on his cheek, and Tara hugged her knees to her chest, staring at the scenery.

Cam was glad for the silence, glad for the fear that the others had of the Regulator. *They should be afraid.* He pressed the tags to his chest. *We should all be afraid.*

His parents told him that Salvation had been an attempt to consolidate what was left of humankind, to bring them together in the name of ending the plague that had left them all scattered and grieving. For half a century Salvation had been collecting orphans and promising a cure that never came. That's the reason why his parents never had him chipped or tagged, a reason they hadn't understood in time for Dom.

Pressing his hand on his pocket, Cam reassured himself that Dom's tags and the coin were still there.

The truck shook and rolled over chunks of asphalt, the pavement veined with overgrown grass and weeds. The road had fared better than the sidewalks, which were now merely jagged slabs of cement pushed up by thick stalks of grass and thorn bushes. Cam saw three streetlights, one still with the glass over the dead bulbs.

We're almost there. Cam's throat tightened as they passed an old church, intact except for one wall that was missing most of its bricks. The hole in the building was clean, following the brick line, the bricks most likely picked off by Scouts as part of their 'consolidating resources.'

His house sat back in a field, a quarter of a mile off the road down a lane lined with trees. One story, made of brick, the windows smashed by Dom long before the Regulators broke down the front door. Dom had said he wanted them to think the house was empty and already sacked by scavengers.

Cam remembered thinking Dom had lied about Regulators coming to raid old houses to hide the fact that he was angry that their parents had died, that really all he wanted was to hurt something, to hear the glass shatter into sharp pieces like his heart. But Cam never said anything. Now that Dom was gone, Cam knew exactly what that anger felt like.

Home. The house had the same trails of soot as the other burned houses, flowers of black that bloomed out of the windows and doorways and hugged the rough texture of the brick with their petals. The roof was gone over the living room where Cam had taken care of Dom after the first sore opened up on his brother's neck.

They are dead, Dom. The house faded from view and Cam dropped his eyes to his hands in his lap. *They are as bad as you always said. They burned you, burned our home, burned everything, but the Scout shot them.*

His mouth tasted sour from the bile that had come up when the bodies crumpled to the floor. It had surprised him, sickened him, but what remained like a lump of guilt in his bowels was that he was so satisfied they were dead.

The road smoothed out and the truck picked up speed. They headed east, chasing the late morning sun. Next to Cam, the Regulator leaned his head back against the cab of the truck and closed his eyes.

While the other three stole glances at the officer, Cam found his eyes straying to the knife on the man's belt. In the tight space of the truck bed, it rested only inches from his hand. With that knife, he could cut the chip out of his neck and stop the pulsing light on the screen. With that knife, he could become invisible.

But he had made a promise.

"Our Pig Boy has some new jewelry," Devon said above the noise of the wind.

Cam pressed the tags to his chest and looked up. Devon leaned against the wheel well, his legs stretched across the bed of the truck with his feet next to Tara, who still hugged her knees. Jake sat by her, between the wheel well and the tailgate, his gangly legs squeezed awkwardly into a small space.

The mutant boy smiled when Cam looked at him, "Gonna go 'clink, clink' when he runs away from me."

"Be quiet, Devon," Tara hissed, her eyes on Smith.

"That old man's asleep," Devon said. "You think he's really gonna cut out our tongues?"

"He might," she bit her lip.

Devon shook his head, "No way. He has orders, and I don't believe that Salvation will pay full price for a mutant with no tongue, no matter what that Regulator says." He waved at Jake, "He might cut out his tongue, though. Nobody wants to listen to an immune."

Sludge for brains, Cam grew heated at the taunt toward Jake, but remembered what Mama Lucy had said and knew Devon was right. *They'll get the gold and the jewels and the cheers. Immunes are just rats, left to fight over their scraps.*

Devon stretched his hands behind his head, leaning back, and continued, "Salvation exists for mutants, built by mutants. We are worshipped over there, like gods."

Tara scoffed, "Who told you that?"

"Mama Lucy," her twin answered.

"Mama Lucy," Tara shook her head. "It's so hard to believe that she fought in the arena."

Jake sat up and stretched his legs a little, careful not to be too close to Devon but trying to get more comfortable. "I can believe it. She has a mean swing with that stick she pulled off of the porch."

The blond twins looked at him.

I knew he wouldn't keep his mouth shut. Cam held his breath. Worried about the threat to cut out Jake's tongue, he studied the Regulator, but it was hard to tell with the jilting of the truck if the rise and fall of the man's chest was the steady breath of sleep.

Devon chuckled. "I saw her kill a wild dog with that stick once. The ratty beast was after the chickens. You'd never know she could move that fast."

The Regulator didn't move. Jake smiled with relief and Cam exhaled.

Cam brushed his fingers under his jaw where Mama Lucy had held the knife. "She's faster than she looks."

Tara smiled, too. "She is kind of scary."

"Yeah, she is, with the extra chins and creepy black eyes," Cam added, encouraged by the way Tara's smile lit up her face.

"Somebody should take that porch spindle and beat her with it," Jake spanked the air with an invisible stick.

Tara laughed. Cam watched the loose strands of her golden braid float in the wind, thinking of that morning in the cellar and the way the gray light had illuminated her hazel eyes. She looked at him and winked, "I bet she'd share her food stash then."

"Food stash?" Jake's eyebrow shot up.

"Nevermind," Cam waved him off, "it's nothing." He and Tara said the last word together. He met her eyes, and her face flushed.

Devon scowled.

Jake squinted against the wind, "I never saw a mark on her."

Cam raised an eyebrow, "As if anybody'd climb up those skirts to look."

Instead of smiling, Tara looked at her brother's scowl and frowned.

Jake cleared his throat, "My grandpa was a mutant. He was from the House of the Kraken. His mark was here, over his heart."

"You had a grandpa?" Tara asked.

Jake nodded. "Like him," he pointed to the Regulator, "only not as mean. My grandpa was sent back from Salvation when he got hurt and couldn't fight in the arena any more. He had a scar like this." He drew a line across his body from his shoulder to his hip. "His left arm didn't work as well as his right, but he taught me how to do things, like play some of the arena games."

Devon scoffed, "Why would he teach you any arena games? You're an immune. You'll never step foot in the arena." He chuckled, "Unless they send you in there as the ball."

"He was my grandpa," Jake shrugged.

"Well, he was a waste of space like you if he couldn't fight any more. That's all there is in Salvation. Either you fight, or you're mutant meat. Nobody cares about the immunes. You guys are as easy to break as a chicken's neck."

"I could fight, if I had to. I could fight like my grandfather did." Jake set his jaw and met Devon's eyes. "He showed me how."

Cam swallowed, tasting the tension in the back of the truck. *Jake, shut up. Don't challenge him.*

Devon leaned forward and Cam saw the muscles in the mutant's arms shift and flex.

Tara glanced at the sleeping Regulator, then reached out and put her hand on her twin's arm. "Devon, don't."

Devon snapped his fingers around his sister's wrist and twisted her arm, shoving her back. "You know how easily they die, don't you sister? How easily they break? How easily they can *drown?*"

Tara's eyes pinched in surprise and pain.

"Let her go," Cam's heart hammered in his chest as he pushed himself off of the cab of the truck, only to be immediately slammed back by a thick hand.

In a heartbeat, Smith had Devon pinned back against the wheel well, the hunting knife cutting into the soft skin below the mutant boy's jaw. The tailgate had popped open with all of the moving and shoving, and Jake had nearly fallen out. Tara clutched the front of Jake's coat and pulled him back into the bed as if he weighed nothing more than the coat itself. As easy to break as a chicken's neck.

"You're out of line, son." Smith growled into Devon's ear as the truck slowed to a stop.

"Yes, sir," Devon breathed out past the edge of the blade. He swallowed, and a trickle of blood slid down his throat.

CHAPTER 7

Burned

Devon stared at him.

Cam held his gaze steady, determined not to flinch. Devon had the same hazel eyes as Tara, but they never lit up, never softened as hers did when she smiled or became thoughtful. They were always hard, cruel. *He blames me for Smith and the knife. He really thinks the Regulator was sleeping until I got up to stop him from hurting Tara.*

The sun hung low over the horizon, the evening rays on Cam's face. The rumble of the truck had been the only sound for hours. Even Jake had been quiet since Tara saved him from falling out, but he kept stealing glances at her when he thought Devon wasn't paying attention.

They slowed and pulled off onto a half-moon gravel shoulder. Smith hopped out of the truck while it was still rolling to a stop, his boots nearly as loud on the gravel as the truck tires. He popped the tailgate open and pulled Jake out by his coat, setting the boy on his feet like he was a child's doll, then waved at the others to follow.

Cam hopped out last, clearing Devon by a few inches and stepping over onto the other side of the Regulator where Jake stuffed his hands in his coat pockets. The way the mutant boy had been staring at him through the last stretch of the drive gave Cam more than his usual reasons to stay away.

"Time to set up camp," the Regulator's hands rested on

the weapons that hung from his belt. Cam noticed that, like the Scout, he had also replaced his taser with a gun. Cam had been too focused on the knife to worry about what was attached to the Regulator's other hip.

Carrigan was restless, agitated. Cam stole glances at the Scout while he paced around Smith and the truck. *His hands are shaking,* Cam saw as Carrigan fumbled to open the truck door.

The Scout brought out a knapsack and tossed foil-wrapped bars at each of them. "Rations."

The bar was hard and tasteless, and far better than the sludge Cam had lived on at the Stalls.

While they ate, Smith pointed and barked orders while Carrigan returned to the cab and pulled out sleeping bags. "You," Smith waved at the twins, "set up the sleeping bags over there and find rocks for a fire pit. And you," he pointed at Cam and Jake, "firewood. Looks like you might find some decent scrub around that ridge."

The ridge was in the opposite direction from the camp, a rise of pale sand that crested like a wave in the fading light. Sagebrush dotted the sand, with a few stunted juniper trees twisting above the horizon and into the twilight.

Cam shrugged and headed toward the ridge, Jake on his heels. As they approached the base of the rise, Smith yelled out behind them.

"Acquisitions!"

They paused and looked back.

The Regulator's gruff voice echoed, "Watch out for predators."

Jake raised an eyebrow at Cam. "Predators?"

Keeping his voice low, Cam turned. "Those two are the predators." He dug the toes of his shoes into the soft sand

and worked his way to the top. Small, pathetic branches lay scattered among the sagebrush and trees.

Struggling to keep up, Jake tugged on Cam's shirt. "Wait up."

Cam slowed for his friend. When they reached the top, Cam looked back at the truck where the two men were talking, and beyond that to where Tara and Devon hunted for rocks, the sleeping bags left in a rumpled pile.

Panting, Jake sucked in a few deep breaths. "Have you seen any sign of animals? Dogs? Bears?"

"Bears?" Cam raised an eyebrow at his friend.

"Yeah, bears," Jake surveyed the sagebrush. "My grandfather was killed by a bear."

"I know," Cam chuckled to himself. "You've told me a million times."

"Well, it's true. He was out in the orchard at sunset. Bear came out of nowhere, tore straight through his heart." Jake raked his nails over his coat.

"Look where we are," Cam looked out on the other side of the ridge. "Why would a bear be here?"

"Because we're here?" Jake shrugged. "I don't know, but we got to stick together, especially since it's getting dark."

Cam put his hand on Jake's shoulder, hoping to settle his friend. "Alright. We'll stick together. Just don't tell me that bear story again."

"Deal," Jake nodded.

He's worried about bears when the real danger wears a uniform. But Cam would rather have his friend worry about a simple threat like wild animals until Cam understood exactly what the danger was. He still needed answers.

Cam's chain weighed on the back of his neck as he bent over and picked up a twisted piece of wood that weighed as much as a flake of straw.

A few feet away Jake held up a ragged piece of sage bark. "This isn't going to burn very long. Why'd they send us up here for firewood? There would be better stuff over where Tara and the Emperor of Evil are playing with rocks."

Cam stood and looked at the men by the truck. "You're right."

"I am?" Jake dropped the bark.

"Yeah, they're keeping us separated."

The wind picked up and rustled the junipers. Startled, Jake sucked in a breath and jumped, bumping into Cam's elbow.

"It's just the wind," Cam said in a low voice.

"Sorry," Jake straightened his coat.

Then Cam heard something else, something carried on the wind. He motioned for Jake to be still and held his breath. Voices, men's voices. He could hear the Scout and the Regulator talking down by the truck.

"Shhh," he exhaled.

Jake nodded, his eyes wide.

"...shot them. They had a coin from Winters," Carrigan's voice shook.

That name again. Cam slipped his hand in his pocket and curled his fingers around the coin. *Winters.* It was familiar, but he wasn't quite able to place it.

"How do you know it was from Winters?" Smith's gruff tones were easier to pick up than the Scout's higher pitched voice.

"It was a Death's Head with a snowflake on the back. The boy found it on the floor. What's going on, Colter?" the Scout's voice went up a pitch and Cam strained to make out his words.

"Where's the coin?" Smith held out a hand.

Carrigan stepped back and shook his head, but the wind stole his words.

Smith folded his arms, muscles tensing beneath his tee shirt.

Cam swallowed. *He's angry.*

The wind shifted back and Cam caught their words again.

Smith pointed at Carrigan. "Keep an eye on the boy. You get us to Denver and your part is done."

"What if they know something there? I can't kill all of them," Carrigan had a tremor in his voice.

Smith let his hand fall to his gun. "Can't? Or won't?" Carrigan shifted his feet.

"What are they saying?" Jake whispered, his breath hot on Cam's ear.

"Shhh," Cam warned.

"I can't hear them. What are they saying?" Jake nudged Cam with his elbow.

Cam glared at Jake, "They're talking about bears."

Jake backed away and frowned, "Real funny."

Then Cam heard something else. "Jake, don't move."

"Stop mocking me," Jake sounded angry, but what Cam was listening to was a low growl, feral and hungry, from the other side of the ridge.

Jake took a step back. "I'm not making fun of you, Pig Boy, like the fact that you had to be hauled away from the Stalls in *handcuffs*. Did you want to stay there with Mama Lucy?"

"Don't move!" Cam hissed, his heart pumping.

He heard Jake swallow.

A snarling blast of fur and teeth shot out of the dark,

knocking Cam to the side and pinning Jake by his shoulders. Even in the dark, with his blood pumping, Cam could see that the dog was mangy, fur matted over skin and bones, and it had Jake's forearm in its mouth. Blood ran down like spit from between the animal's teeth while Jake screamed, twisting under the gray beast.

Gripping the dog's throat, Cam tore him off of Jake. They fell into the brush, Cam wrestling his legs around the dog's belly and hugging its neck close enough so the beast couldn't reach him with its teeth. The animal smelled like piss and rot and fought like a demon, raking its back claws down Cam's belly and thighs.

He rolled on top of the dog and pinned him against the sand, his knee hard in its gut as he twisted the head around until he felt the neck pop. The dog twitched and went limp. Cam leaned on his arm, his other hand braced in the dirt, the metallic scent of blood mingling with the smell of the dog.

Jake. Cam turned to see if the other boy was alright when the sound of a gunshot cut off a growl and turned it into a sharp whimper. His gut jumped as a ball of blood and fur crunched on a bush by his face, followed by a stream of light.

It was another dog, a bullet wound through its chest, which rose and fell once, twice, then stopped. The light flashed over Cam, then settled on Jake. The boy sat in the sand, gripping his arm to his chest while blood soaked his shirt.

Smith handed Cam the flashlight and tried to pull Jake's arm away from his chest to look at the damage. Jake resisted for a moment, but the pain and blood won and he went limp.

Pinching the flashlight between his legs, Cam slipped off his shirt. "Here, use this," he held it out for Smith.

Smith glanced at the gashes that razed Cam's chest and

snatched the shirt. "How bad?"

Cam pointed the light at Jake's arm. "I'm fine."

"Well, your friend needs more than just a tee shirt." Smith scooped Jake off of the sand, the boy's gangly legs flopping awkwardly as the Regulator half slid, half walked through the sand to the bottom of the ridge and over to the back of the truck. Carrigan had the tailgate down with a medical kit rolled open on one side and Smith laid Jake down on the other side.

"I'm going back. They could have been part of a pack." Smith pulled out his gun and headed back.

Tara ran up to the truck and gasped. "What happened?"

"Dogs," Cam answered.

The Scout grabbed the flashlight out of Cam's hand and gave it to Tara. "Hold that for me. You," he pressed a tinder kit into Cam's hand, "start a fire. It'll help keep them away."

I heard the dog. I heard the growl. Cam continued to stare at the blood soaking the shirt wrapped around Jake's mangled arm. *I wasn't fast enough.*

"Snap out of it," the Scout smacked his face.

Cam blinked, blushing when he saw Tara glance at his bare chest, then sucked in a breath as the sting of the slap followed.

Moving pulled on the gashes, but he bit his lip and made himself feel it, made himself focus on the pain as he walked toward the cottonwood trees that flanked the east side of their campsite. *I did this. This is my fault. I wasn't fast enough.*

Larger rocks formed a ring on the gravel, the sleeping bags surrounding that, but he needed firewood. The ground beneath the trees was mostly bare, packed dirt with some sage and cactus spotted between the trunks.

He quickly found some deadfall, mostly finger thin

branches that snapped easily in his hands, and a couple of bigger branches that might burn for an hour or more. *Enough to start a fire, but it will take a lot more to burn through the night.*

He arranged the smaller branches within the ring of stones and fished the tinder kit out of his pocket. He slid out a match with his fingertip, flipped it on his zipper, and cradled it in his hands as it caught. The smaller branches caught after some coaxing, then the breeze picked up and blew on the flame. Cam pulled one of the smaller branches out of the fire, the end of it in the flame, and watched the tongues of heat lick at the torn tip of the branch.

Stepping into the golden glow, Devon chuckled. "Nice fire, Pig Boy," his voice was low, grating.

Cam stood up and took a step back, the flame on the end of his stick sputtering. "Devon."

The blond boy held a thick section of branch in one hand, the end of it torn and jagged, much heavier than the wispy deadfall branch Cam held in his. Devon smacked it against the palm of his hand before he plunged the end of it in the small fire.

"When I heard gunshots, thought maybe you had been caught trying to run away." He grinned, the flames highlighting his teeth and raking shadows along his mark and over his eyes. "Thought that maybe they went and put a bullet between those pretty blue eyes, but I guess they saved you for me." He pulled his stick out of the fire and watched the flame cling to the wood, hungry. "Seems you've been making friends with my sister."

Cam watched Devon in silence.

Devon didn't care, didn't wait for an answer. He put his stick back in the fire and continued. "She can't have friends, though, Pig Boy. You see, she doesn't deserve them. She deserves to suffer."

You deserve to suffer, but not Tara. And not Jake. Cam kept his eye on the mutant boy, watching the tension ripple in his throat, then started when a shot echoed from the ridge.

Devon glanced behind him, then laughed. "They might put your little friend down now that he's damaged goods, but don't worry. They won't shoot you, Pig Boy. Oh no, little piggies go to the butcher." He stood as another shot rang out.

Cam glanced up at the truck. Tara held the flashlight steady, but the cab blocked Cam's view of Jake and the Scout.

Devon swung the branch across the top of the fire. Cam scooted back, the jagged end grazing his belly button. It pulled him off balance. His feet shuffled and he fell back, catching himself with his hand on the gravel, the stick sputtering out as it rolled away on the gravel. Devon jumped over the fire and pushed Cam flat on his back, pinning a knee onto his chest.

The burning end of the branch sparked across Cam's eyes and he smelled the stink of singed eyelashes. He pushed up on his legs, trying to unbalance the mutant, but Devon leaned on him harder, pressing into the gashes left by the dog.

"Do you know what they do to us when we get to Salvation? What they do to slaves, even Pig Boys?" He ground the flame out in the gravel next to Cam's head where the new set of silver tags strung out from his throat, the smell of dirt coming from the hot rocks. Sweat beaded on Cam's forehead as blood pumped through his body. He searched the gravel with his hand, looking for something big enough to smash against Devon's face.

The blond boy lifted the stick out of the dirt, the end glowing orange. "They brand us, like this." He dug the end of the stick into Cam's bare chest, over his heart. Pain shot from the tip of the branch up through the side of Cam's neck.

He arched his back and sucked in a scream, curling his fingers around a fistful of gravel.

Devon's eyes flickered as the flashlight shone on his face.

Cam smashed the gravel against Devon's marked cheek and twisted to the side. Devon's knee slid off of his bare belly and the blond boy landed on his side, almost rolling into the fire.

As Cam stood and backed away, Smith pulled Devon to his knees and twisted his arm behind his back, the gun to his head. Tara stood by with the flashlight, her face ghostly white in the contrasting shadows.

"Seems like we're having quite a misunderstanding, son. I thought I made it clear that you were to keep your hands off of my acquisitions," the officer leaned down and spoke directly into Devon's ear. "Are we clear now?"

Devon swallowed and nodded, glaring at Cam with a promise.

The throb of the burn washed over the sting of the gashes, Cam's lungs stretching his chest to take in the chill night air.

Looking at Cam, Smith waved the gun toward the truck. "Go get cleaned up."

As Cam passed by Tara, she caught his hand.

"What happened?" She whispered, keeping the flashlight on her brother.

Cam squeezed her fingers and pulled away, "Nothing."

CHAPTER 8

Sticks and Stones

The scream stuck in his throat.

He sat up, the sky still dark enough that he could see the stars. Blinking, he looked at the others around the pile of blackened logs. The Scout stirred, but he did not wake.

The Regulator was gone, his sleeping bag rolled up.

Cam's heart pounded beneath the burn and gashes on his chest, more of a dull ache than the throbbing sting that had followed him to sleep. He reached over for the zipper of his sleeping bag and realized he was holding Dom's tags. The metal was warm, the edges leaving lines on his palm and across his fingers as he dropped it on his lap and stretched his hand.

Watching the others, Cam slid out of his sleeping bag and stepped out onto the gravel with his bare feet. The morning smelled clean, a breeze still blowing through the sagebrush that dotted the low hills.

He glanced toward the ridge where the first glow of sunrise erased the night along the horizon. As he rolled up his sleeping bag, he glanced at the others. Carrigan's fingers curled loosely around the grip of his gun, his breathing growing shallow. Devon and Tara lay on their sides, facing away from each other. In the half light of the early spring morning, Devon looked younger, innocent, and Cam looked away. The burn on his chest proved otherwise, and the sight of Devon sleeping like that seemed somehow wrong.

Cam tied up his sleeping bag and left it in the gravel. Jake groaned as Cam stepped over him, his face pinched together, and Cam's empty stomach clenched.

The wind shifted and brought with it the stink of blood and fur and piss. Cam lifted his chin toward the rise where the dogs had attacked. A gust picked up and Cam wrinkled his nose, the half-healed gashes across his chest and belly shivering in the wind. Carrigan had saved the bandages for Jake's arm, cleaning Cam's wounds with basic antiseptic and some salve and telling him not to let the sleeping bag stick too much.

He couldn't see Smith anywhere. Tiptoeing around the fire, Cam paused as he crept by Tara. She had taken her hair out of its braid, the long strands waved out in a golden mass under her head.

The sand that made up the ridge was soft and unsubstantial under Cam's feet, kicked up where they had climbed in the dark. As he approached the top, his stomach dropped and turned.

One dog lay in the sand, its head twisted up to its shoulders with its snout facing away from its forepaws, dried blood matted under its chin. *A male*, Cam noticed. The body of the other dog, a female, twisted awkwardly in the sagebrush that had kept her from hitting into Cam when she was shot, her front feet caught up in the twisted branches.

Mates.

In the sand down the far side of the ridge was a small heap of dark fur. *A puppy.* Cam looked around. There had been two shots last night. *Where is the other?*

He found it, stretched out beneath the sagebrush that had broken the fall of its mother, its head half gone. It was more of a golden color than the first, harder to see against the pale sand.

A paw twitched on the female and Cam fell back a step. He watched her for a moment as her chest rose and fell, a small whimper lost as the breeze shifted. He climbed to the top of the rise, rounding the sagebrush on the other side of the dead male, and looked at her face. Her nose twitched, sniffing, and she blinked her eye open and whined. The bullet hole went through her ribs but must have missed her heart, blood and fluid dribbling down the sagebrush branches and into the dirt. Along her belly, her teats were swollen.

Cam's heart sped. *There might be more.* Smith had said he searched the ridge for a pack. *Only puppies, and he still shot them.*

With his back to the camp, Cam scanned the basin below the ridgeline. It was mostly barren sand and sagebrush, but to the west, shadowed from the rising sun and cut into a curve of the same swell on which he stood, was a crop of rocks, pockmarked and spotted with lichen, and underneath that the dark shadow of a hole.

Their den. Cam looked at the dog. *Maybe she won't have to die alone, like Dom.* He heard voices and glanced behind him at the camp, the sleeping bags all fanned out around the dead fire. The Scout crouched next to Jake, unwinding the bandages from his arm while Tara helped, and Devon poked at the black logs with a half-burned stick.

And still no sign of Smith.

Taking a deep breath, Cam reached his hand toward the dog's head. She growled, baring her teeth, but didn't move. He finished circling the bush to face her spine where he thought he could get a grip and have a better chance of lifting her without being bit. He had to push the male dog back to have enough room to plant his feet, the head flopping grotesquely as the stiffening body rolled over in the sand. Bile burned at the back of Cam's throat as he crouched and slid his arms under the shoulders and hips of the female dog. She growled but didn't turn her head or bare her teeth.

He lifted her easily. She snapped, her teeth twisting back and clamping shut an inch from his eye. He nearly dropped her, but she went limp and whined and he managed to stand. The sand was soft as he climbed down, hugging the dog to his chest. She was skinny, her hip bones sharp against his forearm, and she didn't seem to weigh any more than a month old piglet even though standing she would have been able to put her paws on Cam's shoulders.

Halfway down the ridge toward the crop of rocks, he slid, landing on his butt. The dog stayed still but whined, her legs flopping a little as he heaved himself back to his feet. The final stretch to the opening in the rocks was easy and quick. Cam laid her down in the shade of the hole and backed a few feet away, careful to be downwind.

He heard a whine first, then a nose peeked out of the shadows, pink and twitching. It tested the morning air, then a pair of dark eyes and two fuzzy paws crept out of the hole.

Slowly, Cam sunk to his knees. "Here, little guy," he coaxed.

The puppy growled and backed into the shadows.

"It's okay," Cam inched back, "I won't hurt you. Come on."

The nose appeared again, then the black eyes and pointed ears, one of them torn at the tip. The pup sniffed and whined, inching out with its belly to the ground until it nudged the bigger dog's nose. The female lifted her head and whimpered.

"There you go, little guy," Cam inched forward and the female growled. "Alright," Cam held up his hands. "I get it.

I'll stay right here, I promise."

The female laid her head back down and the pup licked her muzzle. Her chest rose and fell twice, then stilled.

Cam reached his hand out toward the pup. It sniffed and whimpered, but didn't back away. His fingers only inches from the twitching black nose, a gunshot cracked and blood sprayed across his arm. Cam fell backward in the sand and the pup landed in the shadows of the crevice, red splattering the rocks around it.

No. His lungs fought for air, his breathing fast and shallow. Behind him, Smith slipped his gun in the holster and headed up the ridge. Cam looked at the pup through tears, then at the Regulator, then the pup. *Why?*

He scrambled to his feet and up the ridge, anger burning the tears away. He closed the distance on Smith as they reached the gravel and pushed his shoulders with both hands. Smith lurched forward, catching his balance with a step, then spun and caught Cam's chin with his fist.

Cam landed on the gravel, the palms of his hands peppered against the sharp rocks. *Why?* He jumped up and shoved the Regulator again, shouting, "Why? Why did you do that? It was just a puppy!"

Smith grabbed him by both shoulders and pulled him to the back of the truck where Jake lay in a daze. "Do you see that?" Smith asked through gritted teeth. "That is why I killed it, killed them all. You want to give those pups a chance to do this again?" He grabbed the back of Cam's neck and swung him around against the bed of the truck. Smith pinned a hand on his chest, pressing the tags into his sternum and stretching the flesh. The gashes stung and Cam winced involuntarily.

"We're surviving here," the Regulator growled in his face,

the scar across his cheek pulling at the man's eye. "Killing is not an 'if,' it's a 'when,' and you better learn quick when to kill, or you'll end up in worse shape than your friend." He pushed hard on Cam's sternum and stepped back. "Get in the truck. All of you, in the truck."

"At least it didn't die alone." Cam said, his head hanging and his eyes on his feet. He brushed the palms of his hands, looking at the scrapes left by the gravel.

"What?" Smith spat.

Cam met his eyes, his voice steady. "At least it didn't die alone." *Like Dom.*

"In the end, son, we all die alone. But if killing means we live," the Regulator sounded grim, his eyes narrow blue slits, "we gotta kill, or we ain't got a chance in this hell."

Carrigan handed Cam a shirt, big enough to belong to Smith, and put his hand on the door, "He's right, you know, about the killing."

Tara and Devon, who had watched silently while the Regulator dragged Cam to the back of the truck, got in. Devon smiled triumphantly at Cam as he jumped over the tailgate, but Tara moved in slow motion, weighed down by a pained frown. Cam reached out to touch her shoulder, then saw Devon's smile shift to a glare and pulled his hand back. *She doesn't deserve friends.*

Bundled in a sleeping bag, Jake moaned as they settled in the truck. Cam looked at him as they drove, his friend's face pale except for the fever that flushed his cheeks. Jake was helpless now, and Cam wondered how long Smith would let him live, how long it would be until he shot the boy like he had shot the puppy.

I'm sorry, Jake. I should have been listening for what was in the darkness. But in his mind he saw Dom and heard the Regulators break down the door. *I'm saving Peter, but at what cost?*

Beside Cam, Smith sat perfectly still like he had before, but this time his eyes were open, his hand resting on his knife.

You better learn when to kill. Cam had a sinking feeling about what lie in wait for him in Salvation.

The road followed a river, the sun climbing and sparking off of the water. Devon slouched against the wheel well and dozed, and Tara had her knees pulled to her chest, watching the scenery go by. Cam caught glances of her hair as it pulled out of its new braid and trailed in the wind, but his eyes were drawn to the boy in the sleeping bag, the only friend he had ever had.

"Is he going to make it?" Cam asked. He hated the Regulator, but the man with the gray beard was the only one who had any answers.

Smith folded his arms and leaned his head back against the cab. "Two days in a train, then six to cross the ocean. It's a long trip for someone who might die before we reach the depot."

"We're crossing the ocean?" Tara sat up and looked at Smith.

Smith sounded amused, "Where exactly is it you think we're going? Over the river and through the woods?"

She shrugged, "Salvation."

Smith chuckled. "Salvation is half a world away, girl, on another continent. Gonna take more than a little truck ride to get there."

Who in Salvation wants him? Mama Lucy had asked the Regulator. *Who wants any of us?*

"Why does Salvation ship us over there? Why bother?" Cam glanced at the knife on Smith's belt, thinking of Barnes' offer to cut the chip out of him. *Might kill him if we're carving out part of his neck.*

Smith looked at Cam with sharp blue eyes. "Why not just leave a hoard of orphans to fend for themselves, right?" His expression became amused. "Somebody figured out that you're worth more as child labor than as dog chow. Or in her case," he nodded at Tara, "worth more as entertainment. Worth enough to ship across the ocean to play their little games."

"You're a mutant, aren't you?" she asked. "You fought in the arena."

Smith nodded.

"What kind of games?" she hugged her knees.

"The kind where people get killed. Even though no one is supposed to die, someone always does." He smiled, the scar on his face pulling his mouth up into a crooked, mocking grin.

Killed, Tara mouthed the word and turned back to the scenery, squeezing her knees to her chest. Her bare feet were dirty, the nails jagged past the frayed hem.

She's afraid of where we're going. Cam felt the same fear, the fear of what might be, what might happen, but he choked it down and focused on one thing. *Peter.*

The road wound through a narrow canyon, sharing what space there was between the cliff walls with the river.

It's beautiful, Cam watched the sun on the water. The cliffs were the color of Tara's hair, shades of gold and copper that veined along the uneven cuts in the rock. He had only ever known the mountains at home, the snowcapped peaks that he had stared at out of the window of the medic room of the Stalls while standing naked next to Jake for the Scout's inspection. The thought made him homesick, not for the Stalls, but for *home.*

He turned back and met Tara's eyes as the truck rocked hard to the right and she slammed into the side with her shoulder.

The truck squirreled to a stop, the low screech of metal scraping the asphalt. Below them, on their left, the ground dipped down to the river, the slope spotted with new spring grass stretching out of last year's matted brown stalks. To the right, the cliff met the road, the steep side towering forty feet above them.

The door popped and Carrigan hopped out of the cab, his hat in his hand. He slapped it against his leg and tossed it in the window. "Dammit!" he slammed his hands against the hood, sending an echo across the rocks. Bracing himself against the truck with both hands, he stared down at the pavement.

As he rounded the bed of the truck, Cam saw it. A rockslide had covered the pavement, filling in several feet of the narrow road between the river and the cliff face.

Smith walked up and whistled.

"Water," Jake croaked.

Tara looked at the boy in the back of the truck and frowned. She looked at the Scout. "Do you have a canteen? A water bottle? Something I can get him a drink in?"

The Scout looked at her over his arm. "Who?"

Her shoulders tensed. "Jake. You know, the one who might be dying right here in your truck. He's asking for water."

Carrigan waved down at the river. "There you go. Water. Throw him in for all I care. I've got bigger problems," he pointed behind him at the pile of rocks that covered the road.

They stared at each other for a few heartbeats, glaring.

Devon rolled his hands into fists and stepped menacingly

toward Carrigan.

The Scout took a step forward.

Smith's voice echoed off of the rocks. "Carrigan, check ahead to see how the rest of the road looks. Half a mile or more."

The Scout took another step forward.

"Now, officer," Smith shifted his hand toward his gun.

The Scout snapped his eyes to the Regulator. Cam watched the younger officer's jaw flex before he answered.

"Yes, sir," Carrigan picked up his hat and walked away.

Devon folded his arms and watched the Scout pick his way through the rockfall.

Before they left the Stalls, Cam would have mistaken Devon's tension for caring, but now he knew better. *He thinks he owns her.*

Smith squinted up at the sun, then surveyed the rocks.

Jake groaned.

Tara stretched her arm into the bed and pressed her hand to his cheek.

Smith turned his squint on Tara, "Take him down to the water. You can wash his bandages while these two clear the rocks," he waved at Devon and Cam.

The mutant boy stretched. "Looks like we get a little alone time, Pig Boy."

Cam's stomach turned. *Devon and rocks.*

Looking at her brother and then Cam, Tara bit her lip. As the Regulator stuck his head into the truck for the medical kit, she folded her arms and cocked her hip. "You don't think I can move the rocks? You think they're too big for a poor little mutant girl like me? Gotta have the big, bad boys do the hard work while I play at nurse?"

Smith slowly pulled himself out of the cab and looked at

her. "Got an attitude, don't you, girlie?"

"Yes, sir," she nodded, emphasizing the last word. "I'll even do it with the puny immune."

Digging out the medical kit, Smith slammed the door and stepped toward Tara. "Go ahead, knock yourself out."

"I will."

Puny? Cam glanced at his arms. He wasn't as tall as Devon, or even Tara, but he hadn't thought of himself as puny. Even if Tara was stronger because she was a mutant, he was still bigger than she was.

"Puny Pig Boy," Devon chuckled as Cam went by, then let out a hard exhale as Smith slapped the medical kit into his gut.

Jake groaned as Smith picked him up and carried him down the steep slope to the river.

Giving Cam a warning glance, Devon followed the Regulator.

"Puny?" Cam watched Tara pick up a rock the size of her head and swing it past her hip. It landed short of the water, kicking up dust and grass before it rolled and splashed over the edge of the bank.

"I thought it added drama," she looked down to where Smith set Jake against a boulder and carefully unwrapped the bandages.

"Now Devon's going to wash bandages. That could add drama." Cam surveyed the rocks and picked one, a boulder the same size as the one Tara just threw down the hill, and slid his hands under it. The bottom was cool, out of the sun that hung a little to the east where they'd been headed before running into the rockslide.

Tara passed close to him as she selected another boulder. She smelled like sweat and gasoline exhaust and morning mountain air.

"Watch this," she winked. Hugging a boulder to her chest that was too large for her to even wrap her arms around, she pushed up with her legs, her face turning red. She walked the giant rock to the edge of the pavement and dropped it on the slope. Picking up speed as it rolled, the boulder brushed past Smith and splashed him as it fell into the river.

"Watch it!" Smith stood up and turned to yell at them, a bloody strip of bandage hanging from his hand.

"Sorry, sir!" Tara smiled and waved at Smith, then turned her back to him. She threw her hands over her face, laughing.

Cam chuckled, "Not bad."

"I think I just made him wet his pants," she smiled.

Cam realized he was staring at her and shook his head, "You might want to be careful. I'm pretty sure he knows how to kill people."

She laughed, low and soft, and shrugged, "I don't think he's that bad."

"He shot puppies, Tara," Cam lowered his voice, serious. "I'm not sure he wouldn't shoot one of us."

"He's keeping Devon in line. And besides, you're too busy watching the knife on his belt to see anything else that he does."

"Is it that obvious?" Cam asked.

"Yeah," she picked up a rock the size of her fist and tossed it back and forth. "What are you planning to do with it if you get it? You're not going to hurt anybody with it, are you?"

I'm going to keep my promises. "They have guns. Seems like a good idea if we have something."

"I don't think you have to worry about Smith. I'm not sure, but I don't think he even is a real Regulator." Tara spun on the ball of her foot and chucked the rock. It bounced off of the cliff face on the other side and plopped into the river. "At least he answers our questions. Sort of."

I don't think that makes him any less likely to kill one of us. It just means he doesn't really have to play by the rules. Cam hugged his arms around another large boulder and sent it down to the river. His chest felt raw underneath his shirt, the claw marks chaffing. "What about the other guy? Carrigan?"

"He's definitely a Scout," she answered. "Too insecure not to be."

At least she has some sense. He hadn't liked the Scout from the beginning, but the scene in the outpost made him sick every time he thought about it.

He watched as Smith unwound the final bandage from Jake's arm, the fabric soaked with blood. Jake sunk to his side against the boulder, a rag of a human form.

Tara came up next to him. "I'm sorry, Cam."

"I wish the dog had attacked Devon." He hadn't meant to say it out loud.

Tara frowned. "I didn't think it was a good idea for Smith to leave you with Devon to clear the rocks."

Cam huffed, "You know, I was actually pretty stoked to spend the next couple of hours with your brother and rocks. What could go wrong?" He gave her a sideways smile, then grunted as he chucked a rock against the opposite cliff face.

Tara picked up a rock in each hand, "You don't really need anybody to protect you from Devon." She chucked one and then the other across the canyon, breaking off small pieces of the yellow stone that showered into the water.

"Because I always get away?" Cam scoffed. "Because I'm faster and stronger than the mutant boy?"

Tara turned, her arms dangling at her sides, "You're fast

enough, strong enough," she wiped a sheen of sweat off her brow, "and you're smarter than he is." She found another rock to throw, tossing it from hand to hand. "Why do you think he chases you?" She threw it and found another. Cam watched, her muscles bunching beneath her shirt, her arms tan and smooth as she wound back for the throw.

"I thought it was because he hated me." Cam admitted, his smile gone.

"He wasn't always like this," she kicked a rock this time. It rolled past Smith into the river, and earned her another scowl from the Regulator, "He used to be kind, but now he hates everybody. You, me. Life. He likes...," she looked down at her feet as she searched for the word, "hunting. He chases you because you're the hardest to catch."

Hardest to catch? Me? Cam thought back over his months at the Stalls. He had spent so much time hiding from him that he hadn't really noticed if Devon paid much attention to the other orphans.

Until Cam got a stall mate. "Then what about Peter?"

She met his eyes, the sun striking her pupils so they looked translucent. Pinching her lips together, she looked down at the group by the water and folded her arms. "We had a brother."

Cam paused from where he had been trying to get a grip on another boulder as what she said sunk in. He stood and brushed off his pants, then stepped next to her by the edge of the asphalt and held his breath, waiting.

Devon lay stretched out on the bank with his eyes closed, face in the sun.

She half-turned to talk to Cam, but kept her eyes on her twin. "Like Peter, freckles and reddish hair. He died before our parents did, in the Second Wave. He was five." She swallowed.

Cam exhaled. *A brother. That explains the apples.*

"That was when I got this ugly thing," she placed her hand on her mark and closed her eyes. "They died and I became a mutant."

Cam cleared his throat. "My brother died, too."

Opening her eyes, Tara walked back toward the rocks. "What was his name?"

"Dominic." Cam followed her. "He was older. It was just the two of us after our parents died. Then he caught a rogue strain." *And I ended up at the Stalls.*

Grunting, Cam chose a boulder the size of a truck tire and hauled it to the edge. Breaking into a sweat, he dropped it and let it roll down. The early spring day was getting warm, the sun high and the heat reflecting off of the cliff. A breeze blew his shirt against the burn and gashes on his chest, where it stuck to the soft skin with his sweat. He winced and pulled the fabric away as he walked back to the other side of the road.

As he stretched his arm down for a smaller rock, Tara wrapped her fingers around his wrist and pulled him up.

"Can I see?" she whispered, glancing over to make sure they were far enough above the slope to the river that Smith and Devon couldn't see them.

"See what?" Cam gritted his teeth. *She knows.*

Staring at his chest, Tara frowned. "I want to see what Devon did to you. And I know it wasn't nothing." She looked up.

Cam swallowed and nodded. "You were watching."

"Holding a flashlight doesn't exactly require my full attention. Besides," she tugged his shirt up, "I couldn't stand to look while Carrigan cleaned it out with antiseptic. It made me kind of sick. That kid's arm is pretty mangled."

She held his shirt up and gently traced her fingers over the claw marks that covered his chest and belly, then around the circle that Devon dug into his chest with a burning stick. Goose bumps prickled beneath his sweat.

"Why didn't you scream?" she asked, her fingers still on the burn.

Cam swallowed, watching her face as she studied the wound, her lashes brushing her cheeks. "I don't know." The breeze picked up and brushed her hair over her shoulder, and Cam sucked in his breath as her fingers traced his collarbone and picked up his tags.

"Cameron Landry, immune," she looked up at him. "I thought the Scout called you a no-code."

He swallowed, "Smith thought it would keep me from having to take my clothes off all the time so that they could check for a mark."

Tara blushed and bit her lip.

He reached up and touched her face where the mark painted it the color of early strawberries. She dropped his tags and stepped back, startled.

Cam let his hand fall back to his side. "You're beautiful, you know. I thought so the first time I saw you. Even with the mark. It doesn't make you ugly."

She gave him a smile, her eyes round and sad. "I wasn't talking about the outside."

CHAPTER 9

Inventory

The mountains cast shadows as the sun waned behind them. Cam knew he should be worried about where they were going and what the coin meant, but he couldn't concentrate on that at all. All he could think about was Tara's fingertips brushing his skin as they traced his half-healed gashes, cool on his sweaty chest, and the million shades of gold in her hair when the sunlight caught it.

And that she had a brother who died. Not the heartless blond twin who called Cam 'Pig Boy' and burned him, unfortunately, but a little brother with freckles and reddish hair like Peter.

As they cleared the mountains and entered the suburbs of a large city, the terrain looked like home: burned roofs, broken windows, bricks stolen from the walls of dead houses to be used somewhere for the living. Gradually the houses grew more condensed, and crumbling strip malls with overgrown parking lots interrupted the empty neighborhoods.

In the city, more and more debris littered the road. The truck slowed to veer around fallen streetlamps with shattered lights, rubber tread from tires, frames of doors missing the glass. Cam even saw a doll, her head peeking out from under part of what he guessed was a chair. Through the shadows and light of the tall cement buildings, the sun streaked across the doll's painted eyes.

I've seen this before, Cam realized. *I've seen this in the newspapers.*

His mother had collected old newspapers and magazines along with a few books even though his father thought it was a waste of time. They fought about it, but she insisted that she teach Dom and him to read. She wanted them to know about the world and about what happened. He saw a picture like this in one of them, with the broken things in the street after people realized what was happening and why they were all getting sick.

And that they were going to die.

A magazine had called it a 'great tragedy,' but looking at the toys, parts, and shattered glass that still littered the street half a century after the First Wave of the plague, Cam thought that they hadn't understood the situation at all.

It hadn't been a great tragedy, it had been the end.

Jake groaned. Cam almost missed the sound with the rumble of the truck.

Cam leaned over, "Jake?"

"Where are we?" Jake looked at Cam with clear eyes, though his face was pale and a little gray.

Tara turned to Jake. "You've been slacking. None of us got to sleep all day."

Jake managed a smile, but Cam could see pain in his friend's face.

Carrigan stopped the truck and killed the engine.

Smith barked orders as the others climbed out. "Stay tight to the middle of the street. Avoid dense vegetation. And keep the Scout in sight." His hands rested on his belt, close to his weapons.

"Where are we going?" Jake asked again, wincing as he adjusted his coat.

Carrigan glowered. "Sir."

"Sir," Jake repeated.

"Denver. This is where you catch the train," the Scout answered, then spun on his heel and walked decidedly into the maze of the tall cement buildings.

'You'? Cam noticed. *He's not going with us. But what about the Regulator? I hope we're leaving him behind, too.*

Gritting his teeth, Jake took his first few steps, then settled into a slow but steady pace through the twisted metal and shattered glass. The bandages on his arm peeked out from the bloodstained gashes in Jake's coat sleeve, and Cam could see blood soaking through.

Tara glanced back and waited for them to catch up, jerking her arm out of Devon's grip when her brother tried to pull her along with him.

Devon scowled, then jumped onto an old cement planter with a tree growing in it, swung on a branch, and landed in the middle of a shattered section of wall. The scattered remnants of the world became his mutant playground.

Jake looked up at the walls of cement, gaping square holes where glass used to be. "I bet all of the people left in the world would fit in one of these buildings. We could live here, in one place, and start over."

Tara's gaze flitted between her brother and the shadows.

Jake kept talking, as if the sound of his voice would keep the unknown at bay. "This place is a mess. It looks like a mutant came through here on a bad day. Look at this," he kicked at a rusty bike wheel and stumbled. Cam caught him, the boy little more than a rag doll beneath his thick coat.

Behind them, Smith had his knife in his hand, watching. Jake shook himself away from Cam's support and hugged his arm to his chest. "We could fix this stuff up and use it again."

The sun set and twilight cast a gray shadow as they

rounded the corner of a seven story building, the street closing in. Cam swallowed and listened for things that might be prowling in the dark, hungry.

Jake shuffled along, his voice drowning out the sounds of the spring crickets. "My grandpa said that's what they did in Salvation. They collected people and fixed up the old stuff and made a new city out of it."

"Shh," Cam warned him.

Jake glanced over, his eyes wide, "Do you think there are wild dogs out here?"

"Shh," Cam hissed.

"Do you hear them?" Jake looked around and tripped. This time Tara kept him from falling, but she bumped Jake's arm and he swore.

"Jake, be quiet." Cam pleaded. *Why can't he ever be quiet?*

"Do you think it's a bear?" Jake halted.

"Shut up!" Cam's shout echoed off of the dead city. "Shut up! If you could have just kept your mouth shut, I would have heard the dogs. I would have heard them coming. But you won't ever just shut up! Dammit, Jake!"

Cam sucked in a ragged breath. He could feel the others staring at him, their silence worse than Jake's constant jabbering.

"Dammit, Jake," Cam whispered. "I would have heard them coming." He kicked at something metal, and it skipped across the street with a clang.

Jake nodded, his face ghost-pale in the deepening night, then sunk his head and shuffled on. Tara looked at Cam for a heartbeat before moving on with the other boy.

The train depot was a tall building with grand arches on the face, set back from the road behind a yard lined with pavers, broad sections on the sides dotted with trees and grass. In contrast to the ruin of the city, this building was in nearly perfect condition.

Fires burned in pots out in front of the first two columns, the orange flames casting a glow up the giant stairs to the main doors. In the gloom, at the edges of the light from the fires, a sign arced above the building. The name *Union Station* curved at the top, with the slogan *Travel by Train* underneath the numbers and dials of a clock.

The Scout waited for them in the street, standing stiffly in the fringes of the firelight. When their small group had gathered, he led them to the wide staircase, "Stay in the yard. I'll be back."

Cam looked for Smith. The Regulator stood at the edge of the pavers, facing the street with his knife at his side.

Hairs pricked on the back of Cam's neck as shadows moved among the columns. He caught a face, then a thick neck and shoulders that looked like they had been borrowed from a bull cow.

"Well, looky here. New toys," the voice was younger than Cam expected.

Kids, Cam realized as four more of them stepped into the firelight.

A girl, tall and slender with dark skin and a rope of black hair, elbowed the thick boy as she pushed her way to his side. Her eyes settled on Jake with an emphasized pout, "It looks like one of them is broken."

"Wild dogs," Tara said.

"Immunes," the thick boy shrugged, as if that one word explained everything.

"The rest of you are mutants?" the girl raised an eyebrow, the question landing on Cam with a smile.

Cam stepped closer to Jake, but before he could answer,

Devon did.

"Those two are both useless immunes. We're mutants," he put his hand on Tara's shoulder. "Twins."

She ran her eyes up and down the twins. "I can see that." She held out her hand to Cam. "Myla."

He shook it, hoping that the warm firelight would hide his blush from Tara. "Cam, and this is Jake."

Myla reached her hand out to Jake, but he just looked at her with a flat expression, so she swung her hand back and smacked her friend's chest. "This is Austin. His skull is really as thick as it looks."

Austin looked at Tara with a crooked smile. He had something tucked under his arm, but Cam couldn't quite make out what it was. Tara returned an uncertain smile, "Tara, and Devon."

Devon shifted his weight back and forth, restless as he looked at the group standing behind Austin and Myla. "Those guys immunes?"

Myla chuckled, "Nah, they only let the big kids stay out late. The immunes are all inside where they can't get damaged. We're all mutants."

"We're getting ready to start a game. Wanna play?" Austin asked the twins, pulling out what had been under his arm and tossing it back and forth between his hands.

"Play what?" Devon's eyes narrowed and scanned the group of kids standing in the paved yard.

Austin grinned, "Live or Die. It's the game we'll play in Salvation." The object in his hands stilled and he held it out. It was a skull, a few bits of meat still drying on the bone.

"Is that from a dog?" Jake's voice wavered.

Austin shrugged, "I don't know. We needed a ball and we found this over there." He pointed toward the trees that flanked one side of the paved quad.

Jake sucked in his breath as Smith flushed three deer out of the trees and they bounded through the firelight and out into the darkness.

Carrigan stepped out of a set of tall glass doors onto the wide steps that stretched across the front of the building.

The acquisitions fell silent, waiting.

He nodded out toward Smith, then looked at the four who had come from the Stalls. "Time for inventory."

Jake's face was a mix of relief and pain as he climbed slowly to the doors. Cam took a step to follow, looking back at the group of mutants, and Myla.

She winked at him. "Maybe they'll let you come back out to watch."

Tara frowned at the dark girl, and Devon scowled at Cam.

Following Carrigan inside the building, Cam stuck close to Jake. *I don't think the most dangerous things out here are the dogs.*

The building smelled a little musty but mostly clean. Rows of seats stretched through the main hall, with square blocks dotting the floor and black screens hanging from the ceiling. Cam imagined what it had looked like when it all worked, the bustle and noise of people hurrying to go somewhere, shoes tapping the marble floor times a hundred as the sounds all echoed against the stone walls and the high windows.

They walked down a hallway where the steady glow of an electric bulb spilled out of what had probably once been an office for missing bags or rental cars. Cam could only guess since all of the signs were gone. One wall was all windows and stared out into the main lobby of the ancient train station. A service counter cut a line across the room.

"Damn Regulators," Carrigan mumbled before he smacked the counter with his hand.

The man on the other side jumped to his feet, knocking his chair into the wall. It took several heartbeats for him to register that there were people standing in the room.

"Carrigan," the man stumbled over the syllables. His hair was a wild mess of dark brown, too long and unkempt, and he had been snoring before the Scout startled him awake.

"Keller," the Scout replied.

While the man fussed behind the counter, Cam found his eyes drawn to their reflections in the glass.

Smith stood behind them in the doorway and watched, his hands folded across his chest. Compared to the Regulator behind the counter, Smith looked hard and disciplined. The man Carrigan had called Keller was sloppy and overweight and reminded Cam of Barnes back at the outpost. *Stupid and careless.* Cam shuddered, *Maybe he'll end up dead, too.*

Keller stood up and placed his scanner on the counter, then looked at the Scout. "Started wondering if you'd show," the man ran his hand over his face, groggy. "Mutants?"

"No, two are immunes. Had a request for laborers." Carrigan stood stiffly.

Nodding at Smith, Keller frowned. "Who's that?"

Cam watched Smith's reflection. *Keller's never seen him before.*

Smith stayed quiet and Carrigan answered. "Officer Colter Smith."

"I thought we sent Jones with you," Keller's eyes narrowed.

"Jones went north with someone else," the Scout swallowed, a bead of sweat escaping from under his hat.

Keller didn't seem to notice. "We've had quite a mess with the paperwork. Damn recruits who can't read." He picked up the scanner. "Alright, step up. You first, honey?" Keller leaned across the counter to grab Tara's tags off of her chest and she snatched his hand and twisted it backwards.

"Don't touch me," her voice was steady, dark.

Across the counter, Keller swallowed and nodded, shaking the pain from his wrist.

In the glass, Cam saw Smith smile.

"It's late," Carrigan said. "They all have tags. Do you really need to check them?"

"I guess not those two," he waved at the twins, careful not to look too long at Tara. "Pretty obvious they're mutants. So they're the immunes?" Keller pointed to Cam and Jake.

Carrigan glanced at Smith, then answered. "Yes, sir."

"What's with all the blood?" Keller asked.

Blood? Cam had forgotten about the splatters that smeared his clothes. He had only worried about Jake, how he had failed to protect his friend.

"Dogs," Smith answered this time, stepping in front of Cam. "Attacked last night. No fever, but he needs new bandages."

Keller's frumpy head nodded and disappeared into the room behind the counter, returning with a tackle box like the one Mama Lucy had in the medic room at the Stalls. He slammed it down on the counter and scowled. "Any sign of rabies?"

"No," Smith shook his head and helped Jake slip his jacket off. "Had a litter of pups, though."

"I meant in the boy." Keller frowned.

"No, no sign of rabies," Carrigan answered quickly, pulling off his hat.

Cam stepped back and Devon shifted restlessly, then watched with gruesome fascination as Smith pulled Jake's coat off and slowly peeled away the bandages, each layer getting bloodier. Finally, Cam looked away, sick, and caught Tara looking at him in the reflection of the glass that faced the dark lobby.

As he smiled at her, she blushed and turned away. Cam watched for a moment, hoping she'd glance back, but she didn't. Instead, he found himself looking at his own reflection. He *was* a bloody mess. His hair was cropped short, matted on one side with dirt and blood and more splattered his shirt and pants. He wished he had jumped in the river and washed off when he had the chance. Blinking, he was surprised that even in the ghostly version of himself standing in the glass, he could see the blue of his eyes.

I've gotten taller, he realized when he saw that the hems of his pants only bunched up on his boots instead of dragging on the ground. *And I'm not puny,* he squeezed a hand on his bicep and nodded at his reflection, then dropped his arm. *I look like Dom.*

Jake's breathing sped up. Cam turned away from the windows and forced himself to look at his friend's arm. The skin was pale, the pink flesh bled out, and the arm looked thin. Cam could even see a small piece of the bone where the muscle and tendon had been torn out. He could smell Jake's sweat, the scent of stress and fear and raw flesh mixed with antiseptic as Smith dabbed a small bottle onto a strip of gauze, and had to fight to keep his stomach from heaving up bile.

I wasn't fast enough. Cam felt even worse for yelling at Jake. *This is my fault.*

Keller's nose pinched up at the smell. "You should have put him down."

"I'll be fine, really." Jake's voice shook. "I can make the train, and the ship. I can work. I'm strong, you know, for just an immune. My grandpa taught me--"

Smith put a hand on Jake's shoulder, silencing him.

Jake swallowed and nodded.

Carrigan smoothed out his jacket and put his hat back on his head. "I'll make the decisions about my own acquisitions. Mess hall?"

"Down the hall to your left. Might be some food left." Keller watched the Scout leave with Devon and Tara, then his eyes traveled over Cam. "Heard rumors of a no-code. Expect Salvation would pay a pretty penny to whoever can get their hands on that one."

Cam's throat tightened and he watched Smith. The Regulator kept a flat expression as he wrapped clean gauze around Jake's arm. By the look on his friend's face, Cam didn't think Jake could hear anything through the pain.

"Hadn't heard that yet. A no-code, huh?" Smith's gruff voice seemed to take up the empty space in the room. "Sounds like a fairy tale to me. I've been alive a long time. Ain't been a no-code since the First Wave."

"Well," Keller sniffed and hitched up his pants. "Wish I were younger. I'd go hunting for sure, set myself up for a life of luxury on the other side of the ocean."

Cam forced his breathing to stay steady. *What am I?*

Smith snipped off the final stretch of gauze and dropped the scissors in the med box. He stood and gave Keller a curt nod. "The only thing you'll find on the other side of the ocean is a pretty way to die."

CHAPTER 10

Broken Things

"Man, look at that kid. Makes me feel like we got cheated getting the human sized mutants instead of that double serving of muscle." Jake's eyes followed Austin.

Cam sat with Jake at the top of the steps in front of the train depot by one of the brick columns. Fires burned in metal barrels, lighting the corners of the paved quad.

"You want bigger mutants? We can't handle Devon and that kid's twice the size." Cam spooned a bite of the venison hash the Scout had found for them in the mess hall.

Austin tossed the skull they were using for a ball back and forth in his hands, explaining to Tara and Devon the rules of a game that he claimed they would play in the arena once they reached Salvation.

"Hey, boys," Myla walked over. She had narrow black eyes and caramel skin like Jake, her long legs stretching out from a pair of shorts. "Did your daddy say you could come out and play?"

Smith hovered in the shadows, peering into the trees and the darkness beyond the glow of the fires.

Cam wasn't sure what to say. "Hello, Myla."

Jake gave the mutant girl a lopsided smile.

She sat on the step next to Cam and waved at Tara when the blond girl scowled. "Is she your girlfriend?"

Jake nearly choked, wincing after he coughed up a piece

of meat.

"Um," Cam stalled. "I don't think so."

"You're not sure?" Myla raised an eyebrow. "Should I ask her for you?"

"No," Cam answered quickly.

Jake sighed, "You could ask her for me."

Myla stretched out her legs and looked past Cam at Jake. "I'm pretty sure I could guess what her answer would be."

Jake went back to his venison hash, his bowl pinched between his knees so that he could stir it with his good hand, his mangled arm slung close to his chest. A new coat, requisitioned by the Scout, hung on his shoulders.

"We're all from the Stalls," Cam explained. He found himself torn between meeting Myla's mischievous black eyes and Tara's scowl.

"What's with her brother?" Myla followed Devon with her eyes as the blond boy snatched the skull from Tara's hands. He looked over to make sure Myla was watching before he tossed the ball behind him to one of the other mutant boys.

Cam rubbed his hand over the burn on his chest. "It's a long list."

"He's the mutant Emperor of Evil," Jake added. "He dipped Cam's head in a river a few days ago."

Myla chuckled, "So I take it you guys don't like him much."

Cam gave her a half-smile. "He's about as much fun as sticking a fork in your eye."

"Alright, I'll keep that in mind," she stood. "Time for a little game of Live or Die. Too bad you guys are too fragile to play." She joined the others as Austin designated teams.

Without the distraction of Myla, Cam took a closer look at Jake. The boy's eyes sunk in above pale cheeks, and his hand shook as he lifted his spoon to his mouth.

Cam frowned, "You look like you might be better off inside."

"I want to see this." Jake set his bowl down and leaned his good arm on his knees. "This game was my grandfather's favorite part of being in the arena. It reminded him of being a kid before the First Wave, going out and playing with other kids." Jake set his empty bowl on the cement step next to him. "He tried to teach me some of it. He'd throw me a ball that he made out of some of our old shoes. I wasn't very good at catching it, but it was fun anyway."

A spattering of mutants faced each other in two groups across an invisible line that cut the quad in half, eight of them divided into teams of four.

Cam took a bite and kept his eyes on the mutants as they set up to run through some plays. Of the eight on the makeshift field, three of them were girls. Tara hopped from foot to foot behind Devon, nervous uncertainty straining her face. On the other side, Myla stood still, but tensed and released the muscles in her arms. She was the same height as Tara, with a long black ponytail instead of a blond braid. She had her eyes trained on Devon, but Cam sensed she tracked Tara out of the corner of her eye. There were a few other mutants, the smallest of whom was a girl with a mess of brown curls.

Cam glanced over at Jake. His friend watched the mutants intently, sadness and pain etching lines on his face.

The game started with what looked like a wrestling match, Austin and Devon locking shoulders and Devon losing ground. The skull rolled unevenly out behind him and the small girl snatched it up and hugged it near her waist.

The boy who had been hanging back with Tara tackled the girl. The skull-ball rolled at a strange angle on the pavers while half of each team locked arms and shoulders, the other half waiting to see where the skull would come out of the mess. Myla got it and ran across and between the firepots on the other side of the yard from where she started. She raised the skull and smiled.

A dog barked from somewhere out in the skeleton of the city. Jake gasped, then gave Cam a nervous smile. "What if I don't go?" he asked in a hoarse whisper. In the undercurrents of his voice, Cam could hear Jake's desire to see what his grandfather had seen, to be what his grandfather had been. Even though Jake was not a mutant and would only be able to pretend, it would be enough to go to Salvation and see the games and the gladiator fights.

"I'm sure you'll go." Cam answered. *And if they don't let him go?* His stomach turned with the memory of the dead Regulators at the outpost. *He knows I'm a no-code.*

"I don't know, Cam. The Regulator here asked why they hadn't put me down, like I was a lame horse." Jake stared at his bandaged hand. "I can't even move my fingers."

The mutant teams reset in their original positions. Tara's face was more determined now, while Myla's still held the shadow of a smile. The game started again and Tara got the skull this time, running along the steps by the columns. Myla sprinted to cut her off. Tara's boot planted on the step directly below them as Myla lowered her head and tackled her.

Cam jumped to his feet and pulled Jake by his coat. Tara flew up into the column, dropping the skull as her face sliced open along the corner of the stone, several of the bricks crumbling under the impact. Stepping back, her heel caught the step that Cam and Jake had been sitting on and she fell backward. Cam caught her, blood running down her face. She had dropped the skull after she hit the bricks, but the teeth had left their mark on her forearm.

He felt her tense and exhale before she pushed herself away, jabbing an elbow into his rib and glaring at Myla. He caught Devon's eye and quickly wished he hadn't. The blond boy clenched his jaw and shot a warning look at Cam.

Cam swallowed and found Smith in the shadows. *At least the Regulator keeps Devon from doing any real damage.*

"Hey, you okay?" Austin asked, reaching for Tara's face. She knocked his hand aside, "I'm fine," and swiped the blood from her cheek, smearing it across her jaw. The cut ran below her eye and through the middle of her mark.

Austin gave Tara a low whistle and a smile. "I knew you were tough enough to play with us."

"I didn't think I had a choice," she met his eyes.

He shrugged, "Well, you kind of have a choice, live *or* die." He chuckled.

Tara glowered at him and returned to her starting position, arms above her knees, weight on the balls of her feet. The others nodded and set up.

Before Cam sat back down next to Jake, he caught Smith's eye. The old mutant nodded once and turned back to watching the group in the quad.

Jake pulled his knees to his chest and wrapped his good arm around them while his other rested in his lap. "I think whoever named the game Live or Die was being honest about it. That cut looks bad."

Cam nodded. *You're fast enough, strong enough,* Tara had said to him when he made fun of himself for hiding from Devon. *Does she think she's fast enough? Now that she's facing other mutants?* He had seen the fear in her eyes behind the glare she gave Myla.

Jake moved a little closer to Cam. "Do you ever wish you were a mutant?"

"No," Cam answered quickly.

"I do. My grandpa talked a lot about being a gladiator in the arena, about the way the crowd cheered and called his name. He said the crowd liked blood, and they let you win if you gave it to them. He was lucky he didn't die." Jake pushed the toe of his boot into the step below them. "He told me that most of all. That he was lucky he didn't die."

The ball rolled out and the boy with the big nose playing next to Tara picked it up. This time Devon pushed the play over toward the steps and the columns. The big-nosed boy went out of bounds, but he had passed the point where Cam and Jake were sitting and he stayed out of Devon's reach. The players on the field lined up in a mob and the small girl threw the skull in over her head. Devon caught it and ran back toward the other end.

Austin's shoulder caught Devon in his sternum, knocking him sideways and backwards. Devon dropped the skull and caught himself on the steps with his hands, his face coming down next to Jake's knees. Jake scooted up behind Cam as Devon pushed himself to his feet. The thick boy never even wavered, his hand out to help Devon to his feet even though Devon didn't take it.

Instead he turned and glared at Cam and Jake. "What are you looking at, Pig Boy?" he spat.

"I'm watching the game," Cam stood and backed away toward the doors. The others were coming over, gathering near the steps. "And I'm not 'Pig Boy.'"

"Yes, you are." Devon closed the distance and grabbed Cam's arm. He swung him back and Cam caught himself against the column. The bricks were rough on Cam's palms, the flesh already tender from hauling rocks, and they smelled like blood.

"You will always be a Pig Boy," Devon snorted.

"Let him go, Devon." Jake said behind him.

"Shut up, Jake. That dog should have ripped out your throat." Devon growled.

Strong enough. Cam braced his hands against the column and pushed.

There was no resistance. He turned and Austin had Devon by the tee shirt, twisting it under the blond boy's chin. "We don't fight with immunes. We don't play with immunes. We stick with mutants. Do you understand? They're not made like us. Too easy to damage."

Devon narrowed his eyes at Cam but nodded at Austin, who let the blond boy go. The shadows shifted and Smith stepped into the uneven glow of the firepots, the flicker emphasizing the deep scar on his face. "Time for lock down. Mutants by the mess hall. Immunes, follow me."

Separate. Like the Stalls. He had explained it to Peter. Mutants and immunes don't share stalls. They don't share rooms. They don't share anything.

Keller and another Regulator waited inside the glass doors as the mutants filed into the building.

"See you on the train," Myla winked at him and joined the others, her long black hair flipping over her shoulder before she disappeared into the dark lobby.

Smith caught Tara's arm before she could follow the mutants. "Let's get that cut taken care of."

Her eyes went straight to the scar that wormed through the Regulator's gray beard, and she nodded.

He led them to the inventory room, where the lights worked and the med box had been left on the counter. Tara stood perfectly still while Smith cleaned the blood off of her cheek and pinched four little bandages over the parts of the cut that gaped open.

When he finished, Tara touched a finger to Smith's cheek. "Will I look like that?"

He backed away from the gesture and frowned. "Not as bad, but you'll have a scar."

She nodded and tears threatened.

Smith spoke to Tara, but his eyes flitted to Cam's, "Be strong."

Cam's heart froze. *Be invisible, be strong.* He stared at the Regulator, watching for something more, but the older man avoided his gaze.

She shrugged, "At least this way, people can see the scars."

Smith held her gaze for a heartbeat before he nodded. "At least."

They traded the smell of antiseptic for the musty odor of the train depot lobby. Cam tried to offer Tara a sympathetic smile, but she refused to meet his eyes. Smith sent her down the hall to where the mutants were sleeping and guided Cam and Jake to a room on the other side of the train station from the trading room. It was an old office of some kind, back on the other side of the main lobby and down a hallway.

"See you at 0500 hours," the Regulator closed the door.

The steel slab snapped in the frame and the lock clicked. A couple of sleeping bags and some other supplies had been tossed on the floor. The lights worked, and the room had an attached bathroom. Cam wondered if the mutants had a room like this, if they had to share, and he pictured Devon and Austin fighting over where to put their sleeping bags instead of celebrating the indoor plumbing. *A room full of egos.*

He flipped the sleeping bags out on the floor. Jake fought with his sling, so tired he looked like he was about to pass out and plant his face on the musty carpet. "Here," Cam helped him get his coat off and settle into his sleeping bag. In a few breaths, Jake was asleep.

Only one bulb glowed in the fixture above the sink of the small bathroom, but it was enough to see the dust on the mirror and the spider webs that clung to the corners. Pulling off his shirt, Cam sighed as the motion stretched his skin. The shallower scratches across his chest were already fading to scars, and his fingers tested the gashes around his belly button. Still tender, and so was the burn on his chest from Devon. Cam wondered if, like Tara's cheek, they would be scars by morning.

Do you ever wish you were a mutant?

No.

But if he were a mutant, at least there would be some peace in knowing what he was.

The faucet spit air before the water flowed enough for Cam to wash the blood off his arms and out of his hair. He hung his tags on the doorknob and stuck his head under the faucet, watching the water swirl red before it sucked down the drain. He used the shirt the Scout had given him to wipe the blood off his chest before washing it, too, and hung it to dry on a hook by the mirror.

As he reached for the light switch, he paused, staring at his wet hair and the drops running down his cheeks. He traced a line along one side of his face.

At least this way, people can see the scars.

In the dark room, the only sound was that of Jake breathing. Cam slid his sleeping bag zipper closed and settled his arms on his chest. The nightmare came for him, and he sunk into a pit of broken toys, a bent bike wheel, a baby doll looking at him from one eye.

Maybe we're all just broken things.

CHAPTER 11

Spiders

"I've seen this before," Cam stopped on the wide cement platform next to Jake as other acquisitions filed past them. The train sat still on the tracks, blue and white paint faded and chipped.

"You've been here before?" Jake asked. He was still pale and weak, worn from the pain, but he had kept down his breakfast and still wasn't running a fever.

"No," Cam shook his head. "I saw it in an old magazine. This same train, only the paint was new and people filled up this whole place," he glanced down the platform at the handful of acquisitions scattered over the cement. The cover of that magazine had pictured a man in a gray suit standing in front of a glossy blue and white train, waving to a crowd of angry people.

That man in the suit was the one who had started it all, who had made the plague in a laboratory and hadn't known how to stop it. And he left on a train, *this* train, waving to the people he had killed.

And now Cam remembered where he had heard the name that Carrigan said before shooting the two outpost Regulators. The man in the picture getting on the train had been Dr. Jayden Winters.

Jake winced as a kid coming onto the platform bumped into him, and Cam pulled his friend out of the way. About thirty more acquisitions had shown up that morning, wandering out on the pavers in front of the station until the Regulators herded them through the building and out through the other side.

Two Regulators stood at the doors to two of the passenger cars, Smith, and another who had helped bring the mutants in last night. They were dividing the kids into mutants and immunes and directing them onto the train.

"Where's Keller?" Jake asked in a low voice.

"I don't see the Scout, either. Maybe they're inside." *Or dead.* Cam's chest was tight as he watched the acquisitions get on the train.

The train platform was chilly under its white curving cover. A morning breeze snuck in from one end of the tunnel and tickled goose bumps through Cam's tee shirt. Next to him, Jake shivered in his coat and hugged his good arm over the bandaged one.

He stalled, waiting until the final few kids lined up outside of the car doors before pushing Jake in front of him. The other acquisitions were the same age as the group from the Stalls. Most of them wore tee shirts and cargo pants or shorts. A few had jeans on, and the immunes all wore a jacket.

Stepping onto the textured strip on the edge of the train doorway, Cam looked over at the mutant car and watched Tara follow Devon inside. The cut on her cheek drew a line from her cheekbone to her jaw, a jagged pink rope that cut her mutant mark in half. Although the blood had been cleaned off of her face, some of it stained the collar and the shoulder of her gray tee shirt. She looked at him a moment, the green-brown of her eyes flashing in the milky light before she turned away and disappeared into the train.

Myla followed the blond girl, turning to smile and wink

at Cam. He smiled back, then followed Jake into the car and looked around for a seat. Inside the light was dim and it smelled like sun-rotted carpet mixed with old body odor. He blinked, feeling his way into the aisle between two rows of seats. As his eyes adjusted, he scanned the assortment of immunes sitting neatly in pairs. They were a ragged lot, tangled hair sticking up and faces smeared with dirt.

A seat was open near the back. Cam pointed it out to Jake, but when they got there, they discovered that it wasn't empty. A small kid slouched back against the worn blue cushion, squinting down the aisle through a pair of dirty glasses.

Jake glanced at Cam, "Seriously?"

"Excuse me," Cam ignored him and waved at the seat. "Can we sit here?"

The kid's face lit up as he looked at Cam, his full cheeks almost making his eyes disappear when he smiled. "Go ahead."

Climbing over the kid's knees, Cam stood on his seat before dropping into it. Jake squirmed into the middle.

"Cameron Landry," he held out his hand.

The other boy gripped harder than Cam would have expected. "Alex Parker."

"This is Jake."

Alex held his hand out for Jake and waited.

Jake raised an eyebrow. "Did you miss something?"

The kid squinted at Jake's bandaged arm. "Oh."

The cabin stilled as all of the shuffling, squirming, climbing, and talking faded to an expectant quiet.

Smith stood at the front of the aisle and the door closed behind him. "Eight days to Salvation, two on the train and the rest on the ship. You have two rules: no killing anybody, and no doing something stupid enough to get yourself killed. Got it?"

Staring at Smith, the kids nodded. Someone sneezed, and Alex sucked in his breath, startled.

Gonna be a long two days if a sneeze scares this kid. Cam gave him an uneasy smile and the train lurched forward. It headed straight east, following the morning sun as the engine and then the passenger cars cleared the white dome that arched over the loading platforms. Smith sat in a seat near the door and appeared to get comfortable for the ride.

"I'm glad they gave us our own car, away from the mutants. Did you see that girl's face, the blond one with the cut on her cheek?" Alex sniffed and rubbed his nose with his sleeve. It reminded Cam of Peter, the small boy wiping his nose on his sleeve when it dripped in the cold mornings at the Stalls.

"That's Tara," Jake gave Alex a lopsided smile.

"Well, those mutants get too rough, if you ask me. Did one of them hurt your arm? Did they chew on it?"

"She's from the Stalls," Jake said.

"The Stalls?" Alex leaned in, as if his hearing were as bad as his eyesight. "I'm from the Schoolhouse. Not a bad place."

"Did they teach you stuff there? Like reading and math?" Cam asked.

"They didn't really teach us any anything at the Schoolhouse. They just sent us outside to play or feed animals. And weed. We had to weed a lot. But it did have a library." He sniffed again.

Jake scowled. "Are you sick or something? You keep sniffing."

"I have allergies," Alex rubbed his nose on his coat sleeve and sniffed again. "I don't see very good, either. Well, out of my right eye. The glasses work for my left eye. The Regulators at the train station found them for me." He pulled the glasses off of his face. "Pretty cool, huh? I'm hoping I get a new pair over in Salvation. They have glasses, don't they?"

Realizing that the dark streaks on Alex's coat sleeve were more than just dirt, Cam shifted in his seat to give Jake a little more room.

Alex rubbed his nose and squinted around the cabin. "So how did that mutant get her face cut?"

"Her name is Tara," Cam gave him a hard look, "and it was some game called Live or Die."

The train had picked up enough speed to make the bushes and grasses close to the tracks blur by in a streak of green leaves and gray bark.

"Sounds like some kind of gladiator game," Alex blinked. "Mutants are a strange lot. Do you know how they mutate? How they become stronger and faster than us?" Alex looked at Cam and Jake with his lopsided eyes.

"The plague changes them." Cam shrugged. "It changes all of us in some way or we die."

"The plague *bonds* with their DNA, and changes it, I guess," Alex hit the back of the seat in front of him for emphasis. The kid sitting in it turned around and gave him a dirty look over the top of the seatback. Alex slunk down and offered the kid an awkward smile.

Whispering, Alex leaned against Jake's good shoulder. "I don't think the mutants are human anymore."

Jake pushed Alex upright and gave him a stern look. "I think that you are one of the dumbest creatures I have ever known, and I've met a lot of chickens."

"I'm not dumb," Alex squinted at them. "I know a lot about stuff."

"Well, you don't know a lot about mutants," Cam shook his head.

Alex nodded, his glasses slipping down his nose. He

pushed them up and squinted at Cam with his right eye, his left eye open and dark behind the dirty lens. "I spent a lot of time in the medic room. It had pictures."

Cam huffed, "Of mutants?"

"Um, diagrams and stuff. Of people." Alex looked at Cam. "I like to ask a lot of questions. The medic finally gave me a book to look at. I think he was hoping I'd leave him alone."

"I understand how he felt," Jake said.

Alex thought about that for a moment.

Cam asked, "Did it work? Did you leave the medic alone?"

"Sort of," Alex shrugged. "I still had questions about the pictures. He seemed really happy when the Scout picked me as an acquisition."

Jake took a breath, but before he could say anything, Cam added, "Jake's grandfather was a mutant."

Alex's eyes grew big, "They can breed?"

Jake turned to Cam, "You had to pick this seat. With this kid."

Cam shrugged, "He talks a lot, but he's harmless."

"Yeah, but if my arm wasn't dog hash, I might not be." Jake scowled, and Cam read pain in the lines that pulled at his face.

Jake turned back to argue with Alex, something about mutants and bears, and Cam looked toward the front of the train car at Smith. The Regulator leaned against the door, his arms folded across his chest and his eyes half-closed.

No, Tara was right. He's not a Regulator. Regulators are nothing more than bullies, and Smith is too calculated. He wants me alive, but for what? Cam pictured Mama Lucy, the sweat beading down her face as she held the knife to his throat. Can't trust him. Can't trust anybody. But the words that Smith spoke to Tara were Dom's words. *Be strong.*

And Dom was dead.

His tags pulled on his neck as he thought of the ship that would take him across the ocean to a different world, to a world of slaves and gladiators and the unknown. He wanted to know what it looked like, what it smelled like. He wanted to know what it would take to survive.

I promise, Peter. He curled his fingers over his pocket and felt the curve of the coin and the square edges of Dom's tags.

The mountains shifted to smaller hills and then stopped altogether, flattening into a brown stretch of nothing. The sun angled in through the windows as it crept up in the sky and left the horizon behind.

Yawning, Cam leaned his head against the window and closed his eyes, warm sunlight on his forehead and cheek. He meant only to pretend, but as Alex and Jake droned on, the hum of the train on the tracks lulled him to sleep, and he dreamed.

It was a memory of Dom, lying on a couch with the wind blowing against the blankets that covered the windows. The floor was moving, and Cam stumbled with a bucket of fresh well water, spilling some. He watched it pool at his feet and run toward the open door and off the edge of the threshold. Then he saw that the door was a train door, not the wooden door of home, and outside of it the ground streamed by in a blur. Dropping the bucket, Cam tore the blankets off of the windows. The air rushed in, catching the smell of pus and rot and filling the train car with it.

Cam, the dream Dom gurgled and reached out a shaking hand. Cam took it, the skin cool and clammy, then screamed as someone grabbed him and pulled him out of the train door.

He landed on a slope of tall grass and rolled down to the edge of a stream. As he stood and brushed dirt and rocks from his palms, the train disappeared into a stand of trees. *Dom!* He took two steps up the slope and heard a grunt closer to the trees, then a soft whinny. Rather than hike up to the tracks, Cam ran along a riverbank, the sound of the horse lost in the rustle of the breeze through the tall grass. He saw Crix, hooves kicking the air as she wheezed. Blood spattered her golden main, a bullet hole through her right chest muscle. When she heard Cam shuffle through the grass, she swung her head and tried to get up, but fell back down, limp, blood pumping from the wound. *Hey Crix, easy girl,* Cam cooed and smoothed his hands over her neck.

He heard a click and turned around. A familiar figure stood above Cam, the sun behind her head and flattening her face into a black shadow. She pointed a gun at the mare's head. You want things to be fair, huh? Mama Lucy's voice said as the gun went off. Cam stood to fight and a hand grabbed his shoulder.

He jumped up, hands balled into fists, and blinked at Smith's blue eyes and weathered face.

"Hey, son," the gruff voice prickled at the base of Cam's neck. Uneasy eyes looked at him over the seatbacks, the other immunes' grimy fingers pulling on the cushions.

"I'm okay," Cam swallowed. "Did we stop?"

"More acquisitions," Smith backed out into the aisle. He had almost been standing on top of Alex, who was curled up in his seat, hugging his knees and leaning as far away from Cam as he could. Jake wore a worried, pained expression, and Cam could tell from the indentations on his friend's face that he had been sleeping.

Cam dropped into the worn cushion.

Alex stared at him through the dirty glasses, his right eye squinting and his left as round as it could go. The boy slowly uncurled, keeping his eyes on Cam as he slid his feet back to the floor.

Stretching his fingers, Cam looked out of the window.

Trees threatened to choke the tracks, their dark spring leaves close enough that Cam could reach out and touch them if only he could open the window. *Those leaves are like shadows in the sunlight.*

A couple of the kids wrestled over a ration bar, and Smith racked his hand across one boy's ear, telling him to get smart about it or he wasn't going to survive the ship because somebody would kill him for being stupid.

A girl got up and walked down the aisle, giving Cam a funny look as she went by. She was tall but thin and flat chested, and Cam only guessed that she was a girl because she had a head of long ratted curls. She shoved Alex on the shoulder as she passed, "Hey, Puddles," then slipped into the tiny bathroom at the back of the car.

Alex hung his head over his lap and mumbled something.

"Who was that?" Jake asked.

Alex mumbled again.

"What?" Jake elbowed him.

Raising his head, Alex frowned. "That's Hannah. She's from the Schoolhouse, too."

"I like her," Jake leaned back and cradled his arm.

"Why did she call you 'Puddles'?" Cam glanced at Jake, who raised his eyebrow.

"Well," Alex picked at his favorite thread, "sometimes I have accidents at night."

Hannah came out of the bathroom and ignored them as she returned to her seat.

Jake watched her for a moment, then turned to Cam. "Accidents? Can we trade places? Or I'm finding a new seat."

Still picking at the thread, Alex kept his eyes down.

Cam glanced through the train car. With the new acquisitions, the seats were nearly full. He pointed toward the front. "You could share a seat with Smith. I'm sure he'd like that since he doesn't have many friends."

"Are you trying to get my tongue cut out?" Jake's eyes pinched together with fear.

"No," Cam frowned, "I'll trade."

The train started to move as they shuffled, and Cam had to hold on to Jake to keep him from falling on the kids in the seat across the aisle. The boy's black eyes were dim.

"Sleep," Cam whispered in his friend's ear as he helped him settle in the corner by the window. Jake had to twist so that his bandaged arm didn't press into the side of the train car, and he leaned his head against the window and closed his eyes.

"Hey, Alex," Cam waited for the boy to look at him. "Did I say something? In my sleep?"

The lopsided eyes looked at him through the glasses. Alex pushed the frames up on his nose and sniffed. "You screamed out, 'Dom!' Then you stood up with your hands in fists. The Regulator thought you might hurt somebody." He wiped his nose on his coat sleeve and then scratched the side of his nose. "Are you crazy?"

Cam met the lopsided eyes and answered. "I don't know. I don't think so. I just have nightmares sometimes. Sorry, I didn't mean to fall asleep."

Sniffing, Alex nodded. His eyes shifted to the back of the seat in front of him and he found another thread to pull at. "I have nightmares, too. Just sometimes." He looked around, then leaned close to Cam and whispered, "I'm afraid of spiders. My nightmares are always about spiders."

My nightmares are always about Dom. "Well, I'll make you a deal. If I have a nightmare, you wake me up, and if you see a spider, I'll kill it for you."

Alex's eyebrows shot up. "Deal!" he smiled.

Sneezes and spiders. What's next? The boogieman?

This time Alex dozed off, snoring softly with his head back against the seat. Occasionally he sniffed and smacked his lips, then went back to snoring.

Cam watched the thick trees trail by, determined not to let his thoughts wander back to Dom. *Is Peter okay? Did he feed the horses? Did he brush them? Did they kill any more of the piglets?* His thoughts wandered from the Stalls to the wild dogs to the rockslide, then hung on the game he had watched the mutants play last night in the quad of the train station.

Thinking of Tara, he touched his fingers to his cheek, wondering what it would be like to have a mark, what she thought about the cut across her cheek. It had already left a scar.

Sliding his hand into his shirt, over the warm metal tags, he traced the burn on his chest. It was also a scar, uneven ridges of flesh evidence of the burning stick that Devon had used to put it there.

Will I see her again? After the ship docks in Salvation, will I ever see her fight in the arena? Against other mutants like Myla?

He thought of the dark girl, winking at him with her narrow eyes as she slipped into the train car. She had been aggressive, unforgiving as she tackled Tara into the brick post.

Cam folded his arms across his chest and closed his eyes. This time, he slept and did not dream.

CHAPTER 12

Ordinary

A breeze tickled his ear and he blinked his eyes open. Moonlight trickled in through the windows of the stopped train car, coloring the seats and the ratty heads shades of gray and black. The moon that had been absent when the wild dogs attacked now glowed as a curved blade amidst the stars that had followed him from the Stalls.

Even with a breeze slipping in through the open car door, the air was stale and smelled like the unwashed bodies that littered the seats. Cam sat up and Alex's face slid down his arm, smearing drool on his elbow. Cringing, Cam shifted the boy off of him and stretched to his feet.

The train car was nearly silent. Alex snored softly and smacked his lips, but Jake looked almost like he was dead, pale in the moonlight and perfectly still except for the regular rise and fall of his chest. The air that came in through the open door smelled fresh, inviting. *Be invisible.* Sliding off his boots, Cam braced his hands on the backs of the two seats and swung his legs over Alex. The floor of the aisle was ridged for traction and gritty with dirt. Sniffing himself down the front of his shirt, Cam wrinkled his nose. Dried sweat clung in a film to his back and his shirt was stiff under his arms, but at least he no longer smelled like blood.

He didn't see Smith in his seat. Squinting in the sparse moonlight, Cam crept down the aisle. As he neared the front of the train car, he heard a giggle.

Who's there? Cam looked around the train car. The sleeping acquisitions lay strewn throughout the seats, their bodies as limp as the coats puddled at their feet. Propped up against the doorway, Smith slept with his legs blocking the threshold. The Regulator looked uncomfortable, wedged into a corner between the door to the outside and a door that allowed access to the mutant car.

Cam took another look at Smith and reconsidered. *I guess I just slept for hours next to Alex, with his snot-covered coat. Maybe this wouldn't be so bad.*

Another giggle came on the breeze through the door. Cam braced himself to lean over Smith and peered around the edge of the doorway.

Long black hair and dark narrow eyes. *Myla.*

She smiled and waved for him to come out, playing with the long grass that followed the train tracks into the trees. Tucking his knees into his chest, Cam leveraged his hands in the doorway and swung himself outside, his tags clinking softly as he landed next to the tracks.

The breeze picked up for a heartbeat, cool and fresh, and ruffled through his thin tee shirt. It smelled like new leaves and starlight and fresh water. Sucking in a deep breath, Cam looked at Myla with a level stare. "What are you doing?"

She smiled and wrapped warm fingers around Cam's wrist. His heart jumped at the touch.

"Come on," she tugged him toward where the trees opened up around a lake.

Down the slope from where the train squatted on the tracks, Cam heard voices, low and careful. He twisted his arm out of Myla's grip and peered through the shadows. A group of kids stood in the grass, talking and laughing. He caught the moonlight off of Austin's broad shoulders and Devon's blond head.

"I don't exactly want to be the only immune out here with all of the mutants." He searched the small crowd for Tara, but couldn't make out her blond braid. "It's not likely to turn out well," he looked back at Myla, "for me."

"We're not hanging out with them." She turned back toward the water and picked her way through the grass down the slope, away from the tracks and the train and the Regulators. "We're going down here." She paused halfway down, did a little spin and, teasing Cam with a playful look, waved at him to follow. "Hurry before they see you."

Searching for a reason not to go, Cam couldn't find one. *I'm not breaking either of the two rules,* he shrugged and toed the ground, cool and damp beneath the straw of last fall's grass. *And Myla seems…fun.*

The bank was dense, wet dirt that sucked at his feet as he followed her past a stand of cattails. She stopped and looked back, shushing him while she watched and listened, then crept to a large rock that jutted out into the lake.

Myla climbed onto the rock and settled with her feet dangling in the water. She shifted and pulled her shorts up mid-thigh, swinging her legs to make her toes peek out of the water. Moonlight waved on the glassy surface, lighting the night with its glow. Cam stopped a few feet from the rock and shoved his hands in his pockets, not sure what to do.

"They won't find us here," she promised without looking at him. "I can't hear them, they can't hear us. Besides," her toes made a splash, "None of them really understand why I want to hang out with an immune."

Cam shrugged, "Why *do* you want to hang out with an immune?"

"A better question would be why do I want to hang out with *you.*" She turned her head around and peered at him over her shoulder. "Why do you think?"

"I have no idea," Cam didn't even try to puzzle it out. Dom had taught him about many things, slopping pigs and watching for Regulators and drawing the best water from the well, but he had never mentioned girls. He didn't think Dom had ever had the chance to see a girl as beautiful as Myla.

She looked back over the water, the scratch of moon reflecting down the middle of her shiny black ponytail. "What's your full name, Cam?"

"Cameron Landry."

"Well, Cameron Landry, I'm Myla Harris. I don't think the introduction we got back at the train station was quite proper. Austin doesn't like it when I'm friendly, especially with immunes. He always wants to play his game, anyway."

Cam shrugged and watched the breeze tease ripples on the lake. "He looks like he's pretty good at it."

"When you're playing with other kids who don't know the rules, it's easy to look like you're good at something. I mean, he's good, but we'll see how good he is when he plays in Salvation." She looked at him again and patted the rock next to her. "Sit."

Cam squished through the mud and half sat, half-crouched next to Myla, careful to keep enough distance between them that they wouldn't bump elbows or something awkward.

She looked at him and raised an eyebrow. "Really, you can sit on the rock. I don't bite."

No, you just run people into brick posts. But he scooted over, his arm touching hers.

Studying him for a moment, she laughed, low and husky.

"You don't talk much, do you?"

He shook his head and played with his tags through the buttons and thin cotton of his shirt. "I'm not used to new people."

"And I'm used to spending time with Austin. He's a mutant multiplied by an ego. You seem more..." she waved her hand in the air as she searched for the word, "practical."

"Practical?"

"Well, okay, ordinary."

Cam chewed on the inside of his cheek. "I'm not sure if 'ordinary' is much better than 'practical.' But thanks, I guess."

Myla sunk her face into her hands and laughed. "Sorry, I'm actually trying to compliment you for not being one of us." She looked up and shrugged. "Sometimes hanging out with other mutants gets old. All they want to do is chase each other around to see who runs faster or jumps higher. And all they talk about are the games. I just want to feel like a normal girl once in a while."

I wonder if Tara ever wants to feel like a normal girl, whatever that means. "Well, other than running faster and jumping higher, aren't you guys the same as us?" Cam leaned back on one hand and ran his fingertips across the gritty surface of the rock behind Myla.

She watched her toes dip in and out of the water, then rubbed her hands on her thighs and looked up at the moon. Her voice went low. "Austin says that we're different, that maybe we're not really even human anymore."

He thought of the way Tara's eyes looked as she told him about her dead brother. He thought of her fingers on his chest, warm and soft. And he thought of Devon, who burned him and called him 'Pig Boy'.

I don't think they're human any more, Alex had whispered on the train, but looking at Myla in the moonlight, with her feet hanging off of the rock, he thought they were all just motherless children.

"What do you think?" Cam asked.

"I think," Myla leaned back on her hands and gave Cam a lopsided smirk, "that I'd like to go for a swim."

"A what?" Cam's eyes rounded open as she climbed over him and off the rock. He rubbed his chest nervously, his scars itching.

With her back to him, she dug her toes into the mud and pulled her tank top over her head, then flung it behind her where Cam caught it against his chest. Her shorts followed.

Blushing, Cam looked at her in the moonlight, watching as she waded into the water. She was long and lean, the muscles between her shoulder blades flexing as she sunk waist deep and waved ripples into the calm surface of the lake with her long fingers. Her mark was the same tone as her skin and hard to make out in the silvery light, but it was there, covering her right shoulder blade. It disappeared into the water as she kicked off and swam out far enough to tread water.

Cam slid off the rock and stood on the bank, holding Myla's clothes, not sure if he was supposed to follow her. She turned around to smile at him again, the bottom half of her ponytail sucked into the water.

As much as he needed a bath, the knowledge that Myla was in there naked had him frozen to the mud, watching her swim and listening to the crickets behind him in the tall grass.

"Cam!" she shouted.

A hand pinched his shoulder and spun him around.

"Hey, Pig Boy. Come outside to play with the big kids?"

"Devon," Cam flinched at the sight of the light hair, more silver than gold in the thin light.

Laughing low in his throat, Devon pushed Cam onto his butt into the edge of the lake where the water lapped at the mud. It was cold, soaking through his shirt to his waist and halfway down his thigh.

"What do you want, Devon?"

"What is a pig boy doing out here with a mutant girl? Huh?" Devon crouched down, his hazel eyes narrowed under his eyebrows.

"I asked him to come," Myla splashed out of the lake behind him. Cam held up her clothes, the tank top and shorts dripping rivulets down his arm. She snatched them and pulled them on while Cam kept his eyes on Devon, as much to avoid looking at Myla as to keep his eye on the bully. The kid with the big nose from the game at the train station stood behind him, then Austin stepped into view, his arms crossed over his thick chest.

"Another pet, Myla?" Austin asked.

"He's a friend, Austin, not a pet." With her clothes on, the water ran down Myla's legs and into the mud. She put a hand on Devon's shoulder and tried to pull him up, but the blond boy stayed where he was, his face inches from where Cam sat in the water.

"We don't make friends with immunes, you know that. We stick with mutants. We play with mutants, we fight with mutants," Austin pinched his lips together and clenched his jaw, "we *die* with mutants."

"Those are your rules, not mine." Myla pulled on Devon again, but the blond boy didn't even blink. "I happen to like immunes. They're not as egotistical and rough, not always trying to be bigger and better than everybody. They just... are." She gave up trying to move Devon and offered her hand to Cam, instead. He took it, and she pulled him to his feet and twined her fingers in his.

Devon stood up with him, his eyes flitting briefly to Myla then locking back onto Cam. "Let her go."

Cam rolled the fingers of his free hand into a fist and tightened his jaw.

Myla reached back and squeezed the water out of her hair while holding Cam's hand more tightly. "What if *I'm* holding on to *him?* He can let go all he wants and I'll still have his hand."

Devon glanced at her, then pushed Cam in the shoulder, "You're fishing in the wrong pond, Pig Boy."

"Leave him alone, Devon," Tara stepped out from behind Austin.

Overly conscious of his hand in Myla's, Cam wondered how long Tara had been there. He offered her a small smile, but she kept her eyes on her twin.

Devon looked back at her over his shoulder. "Stay out of this, Tara. I'm getting sick of warning you."

Austin pulled at Tara's arm. "We got this, sweetie."

"I'm not a 'sweetie.' She stepped away, her eyes pleading with her brother. "Devon, this is wrong."

Devon's eyes traveled up and down Myla's body, then settled on her hand holding Cam's. "I agree, this is very wrong. Myla should be with one of her own kind, someone strong like me, and Pig Boy should be at the bottom of the lake." He leaned forward.

Myla let go of Cam's hand and all he saw was the blur of her arm as she wrapped it around Devon's neck and flipped him onto the ground. She had him by the throat, her nose almost touching his.

"Leave my friend alone, blondie, or we'll have to talk."

Blinking, Devon smiled and reached up to touch her hair.

"Let's make it a date, Myla, but only me and you. I don't like people watching."

Breathing hard, the muscles in Myla's arm flexed as she released her fingers and stood up. "Come on, Cam. I'll walk you back to the train." She pushed her shoulder into Austin as she passed him, then picked her way through the mud, going back the way they had come.

As Cam walked by, Austin glared at him but didn't move.

There's something about me and mutants that doesn't mix. Cam pushed his way through the tall grass and up the slope to the train, watching Myla's wet ponytail swish against the back of her tank top.

He looked back once, and his stomach sunk when he saw Austin wrap his arm around Tara's shoulders.

The train waited, the line of cars like oversized white segments of a steel caterpillar. Myla stopped by the door to his train car, looking down the slope at the other mutants as they cut an angle back toward the area where Cam had first heard their voices.

"I'm sorry," she rubbed his arm. "Sometimes Austin can be pretty thick-headed about the way he thinks the world is supposed to be."

Cam nodded, noticing she didn't mention Devon, or Tara. "That's why you were looking for something 'ordinary.'"

"Practical is good, too." She smiled, then stretched in on her toes and kissed him on the cheek. Warm and soft, her lips reminded him of Tara's fingertips. "Good night, Cameron Landry."

Good night, Myla Harris. He watched her go in silence, then swung himself back into the train car, tucking his knees almost to his chin to make it over Smith's outstretched legs.

He settled in his seat and leaned his head back, watching

the sliver of moon. When the sun finally streaked the horizon, he dozed. He dreamt again of Tara and the rocks, only this time when she touched him, her fingers were the color of caramel.

CHAPTER 13

Signs

Train wheels turned on the tracks, their slow grate vibrating through the back of Cam's seat and through his skull.

The sun fought its way through the thick trees and filtered past the pink and red arteries of Cam's eyelids. He kept them shut as he wiped a little drool off the corner of his mouth and listened to the train car wake. Alex sniffed next to him, and someone poked at his shoulder. Blinking, he sat up.

Hannah smiled at him, her brown hair combed through with her fingers. "Breakfast." She tossed a ration bar on his lap. "Here's one for the broken kid," she nodded toward Jake and tossed another bar onto Cam's lap.

Alex raised his hand.

She ignored him and retreated down the aisle, handing out bars to the other kids.

"Hannah," Alex called after her. "I didn't get one."

She turned around and threw one at his head. It hit the back of the train car and fell on the floor behind the seat. "There you go, Puddles."

"Thanks," Alex said, and dropped to the floor. When he fished the bar out from under the seat, it was covered in hair and grit. He brushed it off and took a bite.

His glasses slipping down his nose as he chewed, Alex squinted through the lenses and gestured with his ration bar. "I can't wait to see the ships," he said around a mouthful of food. He chewed and thought, pushing his glasses back up and folding an arm across his stomach as he leaned toward Cam. "I wish we were already there. There were tons of books on ships at the Schoolhouse, with pictures. My favorite ship was really fancy, with a billion sails and even tiny little sailors manning the wheel thingy and the ropes." He paused to take a breath and swallow.

"I don't think we'll be on a ship that has sails." Cam knew little about boats, and what he did know he had picked up from his mother's magazines, from ads with pictures and slogans like 'Glamour on the Seas' and 'Escape to Paradise.' None of those boats had sails.

"Probably not," Alex agreed, nodding. "I wonder if it's solar power like the train. There's got to be a lot of sunshine out in the middle of the ocean, right?" Alex sniffed and took another bite of his ration bar. "Or maybe it's an engine, a gas engine. I'd love to see that." He chewed for a moment. "Yeah, I'd love to see a real engine."

"I'd love to see you gagged," Jake interrupted.

"Oh," Alex's left eye got big, making the right one look even squintier by comparison. He shrugged and nodded, chewing. "A gas engine..." he muttered, looking up through the seats to the front. Smith looked at Alex until the kid lowered his eyes and played with the loose threads hanging off the seat in front of him. He stayed quiet, chewing on his bar and sniffing. Cam could almost see Alex's brain working up theories on how the ship's engine would work.

Jake seemed satisfied with the silence and leaned his face on the glass, nibbling at his food.

The trees past the window were a solid mass of green as the train sped down the tracks, its solar-fed engine gaining power as the sun climbed high enough to blaze through the trees. As Cam stared out the window past Jake, his thoughts wandered to the night before—Myla holding his hand and Tara watching him leave, Austin's arm around Tara's shoulders.

The girls were like the light and the shade, one gold and the other bronze. Dark skin and dark hair, Myla's narrow eyes shone with mischief, and she seemed somehow lighter than the girl made of gold. Tara's blond hair and tan skin smelled like summer and mountains, but something haunted her. Cam thought it had to do with more than just the loss of her parents or being a mutant.

The train shook as it curved on the track and the coin vibrated against the tags in Cam's pocket. He'd forgotten about it, caught up in navigating the whims of the mutants. He pulled it out as Alex started thinking out loud about engines again, whether solar or gas power would be better.

Cam pressed his forehead against the back of the seat in front of him and stared down at the silver disk resting in his palm. Blood smeared the metal, and as he recognized the image etched over the original design, Cam bit his lip. A human skull, the outline simple and clear, with bones crossed behind it. Around the edges, Cam could still make out 'In God We Trust' tucked in the lower left, though part of the phrase was covered by the ridge of the bone jutting out from beneath the grinning jaw. The edges of the superimposed image were black, as if the silver had been scorched.

Burned, like everything else.

He flipped the coin over. The grime carried to the back, which had also been changed. Cam didn't recognize the shape at first since it had not embedded in the metal evenly, but after a moment he recognized the symmetrical points of a snowflake.

"What's that there?" Smith's weathered voice grated

down Cam's spine.

He jumped and curled his fingers around the coin as he met the Regulator's wrinkled blue eyes. He could feel Alex and Jake staring at him.

"Nothing," Cam swallowed.

Smith gave him a grim smile. "I'd keep trinkets like that out of sight. I've seen people die in fights over pretty things."

Cam nodded and tucked the coin back into his pocket. He hadn't yet decided if he trusted the Regulator, but there was something about him that seemed genuine. *Be strong.*

Smith patrolled the aisle back to the front of the train car, scolding a pair of dirty-faced boys who had turned around to tease the girls behind them.

"He scares me," Alex stated.

Sneezes, spiders, Regulators... at least the Regulators part makes sense.

"What are you not scared of?" Jake sighed.

"Well," both of Alex's eyes squinted closed with the effort of thinking and he wiped his nose on his sleeve. "I'm not really afraid of you. You seem nice enough."

"I seem nice?" Jake raised his eyebrows.

Cam stifled a chuckle, his heart finally slowing down after the encounter with Smith. He looked at Alex. "How about bunnies? Or rainbows? Either of those give you the heebie jeebies?" Cam kept a straight face.

Alex looked at him with a lopsided stare. "Are you making fun of me?"

"No," Cam cleared his throat. "I just wondered if you imagined killer rabbits or man-eating leprechauns."

"Well," Alex considered it, "I'm not sure what a leprechaun is, but we had rabbits at the Schoolhouse and one of them bit me once."

"Only once?" Jake asked.

Alex thought about it. "Yeah, only once."

Jake chuckled, but Cam's face fell. "Once we get to Salvation, I don't think we'll get to worry about spiders, or rabbits."

Shaking his head, Jake shifted in the seat. "I hate being an immune. I could end up anywhere. I could end up digging trenches or cleaning toilets. I wish I were a mutant. At least then I would know that I was going to be a gladiator and play the arena games."

Cam searched his friend's eyes. *Even though nobody is supposed to die, somebody always does.* "And if you had to kill somebody? Could you do it? Could you go in there knowing you could die?"

Jake shrugged, his face drawn and pale. "I don't know about killing somebody, but it seems, sometimes, like dying would be easier than not knowing what's going to happen to you."

Alex sniffed, "I could kill somebody. If I were a gladiator, I'd fight with a sword and cut them all down." He swished and sliced through the air.

After a glance at Alex, Jake held Cam's eyes. "Could you kill somebody?"

The smell of blood twinged in Cam's memory. He had moments when he thought he could wring Devon's neck, feel the life pulse out of him and smile about it, but the memory of the dog's neck twisting and snapping in his hands made his stomach clench. He had wretched uncontrollably after Carrigan shot the Regulators at the outpost, their sightless eyes watching him leave with the coin he had pretended to find there.

He finally answered his friend. "I don't know, but I don't want to die."

Jake nodded and went back to looking out of the window, and Cam followed his gaze.

The train still sped through thick trees, the sun filtering down like it would on a ribbon of water, light on top and dark below the surface. Shifting from the trees outside to the glass, Cam's eyes wandered over his reflection in the window. His dark hair looked better with the blood and dirt gone, and he was glad that he had stolen a pair of scissors from Mama Lucy's kitchen to keep it short. When Peter had arrived with a nest of ratty red hair, Cam had cut it for him, too.

Or he would have looked like the stinking mess of orphans on this train.

The smell of the train car had grown rank over the past day and a half. Cam glanced up at the hair and dirty faces that filled the rows of seats. Smith caught his eyes, and Cam returned to studying his reflection.

Little man. Although Dom's hair had been lighter, more of a sandy brown compared to Cam's black brown, they both had the same intense blue eyes. *Landry eyes,* their mother always said, smiling at their father like there was some secret about having blue eyes.

Blinking, Cam sat back from his reflection and stared at the worn upholstery in front of him, wild strands of hair sticking out around the headrest. Next to him Jake had his eyes closed, and even Alex had fallen asleep. Cam was actually disappointed. He wanted a distraction now, wanted Alex to talk about his theories and ask what a wheel was or tell him that he was afraid of his own shadow.

As the train lulled him into thought, Cam found himself staring past Jake again at the trees through the window. His stomach growled and he wondered when Smith would come down the aisle with the lunch rations, scolding the kids again for leaving their coats lying around as the train car filled with their body heat.

The Regulator reminded him of Dom, skeptical and gritty, with eyes that saw everything. *Be strong, be invisible,* Dom always told him. *Be strong,* the Regulator had said to Tara.

Dom had once caught him sneaking venison strips out to a dog that had started picking off their chickens. Cam could have sworn Dom had been asleep, snoring in the next room, but as soon as Cam stretched a piece of meat to the animal behind the chicken coop, Dom had run up behind him and kicked the dog several feet out into the yard.

Dom had been tough, and he still died.

Shaking the memories, Cam focused on the blurred landscape outside the train. Once a wall of dark green shadow, the trees now backed away from the tracks and spread around burned suburban neighborhoods. First it was a house, then some kind of maintenance building, then several houses organized around carefully planned streets, the asphalt and cement flat and clean.

That was when he realized he was looking at people. Only a few at first, like the houses, then small groups out in the yards of their cul-de-sacs, with a few children even playing with old bikes and swings.

People. It was like a dream of the past, like the pictures from the old yellowed newspapers that had captions about school awards and neighborhood parks.

It was strange.

Cam shifted in his seat, sitting up to get a better view of the suburban stretch.

"Were those kids?" Alex asked over Cam's shoulder. His breath blew a little on Cam's ear, making it itch.

"Yeah, with bikes," Cam swatted Alex away.

"Weird," Alex leaned in and breathed on him again. "Do you know how to ride a bike?"

Shaking his head, Cam rubbed his ear and leaned toward Jake. *This kid has no sense of personal space.* "No, I don't know how to ride a bike. Besides, where we lived, all of the sidewalks and roads were in pretty bad shape. No place to ride a bike if we could even find one."

"Me, either." Alex said.

"I had a bike," Jake perked up. "My grandpa found it and fixed it up. I rode it in the field behind our house. He said that every kid should learn how to ride a bike and do a cartwheel."

"I wish I had a grandpa," Alex sniffed.

The trees closed back in alongside the train, blotting out the fairytale view of people outside of their homes.

Sitting back in his seat, Alex frowned. "My parents both died when I was little. They got pneumonia."

Cam turned to meet the boy's squinty eyes. "Really? Not the plague?"

Alex nodded. "Really."

"Hmph," Cam shrugged, "I thought everybody just died of the plague, either in one of the waves or from a rogue strain."

"Nope," Alex shook his head. "Just regular old germs. The plague has killed so many people that everybody forgets that there are still germs that kill people."

Cam looked at Alex's sleeve, where the kid had wiped his nose a million times during the train ride, and inwardly cringed. He scooted over as far as he could in his seat, glad that he was on the side of Jake's good arm. "Did you learn about germs in the books with the pictures?"

"Yeah, lots of pictures. Germs and diseases and what

they do to people. The plague is the worst, though. Nobody has really drawn pictures of it, but a couple of the kids in the daycare got it. I've tried to forget about it," he dropped his head. "I hated the burning part the most." Pinching his lip in his teeth, Alex shifted his gaze to the window. "Look at that," he pointed.

The trees broke again and a sign hovered above the landscape on a pair of poles. The original image had faded to nothing, the wood of the board warped at the corners, and somebody had painted over it in a dark orange paint that was also starting to fade.

"What does it say?" Alex asked.

"Can't you read it?" Jake's eyebrow went up.

"I can read," Alex said loudly, then dropped his voice. "I just can't see very good."

The sign disappeared behind them, replaced by more trees. Cam cleared his throat, "It said, 'Here they burned. Kill Jayden Winters.'"

"Jayden Winters?"

"Yeah," Cam thought of the picture of the man in the suit getting on the train, "he was the guy who made the plague, back in Denver where we got on the train. He left as soon as he knew what he had done."

Alex sat back in his seat and folded his arms. "Jayden Winters." He watched his toe press into the seat in front of him.

Jake leaned against the window, his eyes half-closed. "My grandpa wanted to kill him, but nobody could find him."

Have people forgotten? Cam's parents had made sure he and Dom knew what had happened, but Alex never had parents. Jake's grandpa had been there, and Jake never shut up about all of the things his grandpa told him, but how many of the other acquisitions didn't know?

Alex sat up straight. "I bet whoever comes up with a cure or a shot for the plague would be a hero. I bet that person would be made a king or something."

"The king of what?" Jake asked.

Cam thought Jake had fallen asleep, but the other boy lifted his head off of the window to give Alex a sideways glare.

Shrugging, Alex went back to picking at the thread.

Houses and buildings started replacing the trees again, and there were more people. Everything became denser and taller. *Consolidating resources*, Cam realized. *They consolidated people, too.*

The other acquisitions on the train grew restless, those in aisle seats leaning over the kids next to them to see what was outside the window. As they passed a house, Cam watched a little girl play with a doll. She was small, probably born after the Second Wave, and she held the doll like a baby. As the train sped by, her mother picked her up and pulled her away, but in the heartbeat of time that Cam had to see her, she met his eyes.

And she *smiled*.

Cam sat back in his seat and looked at his hands. Calloused from work, his palms were rough and red, the backs veined and his fingers long and scarred by barbed wire and fishing line and stealing. As he headed for Salvation with the other acquisitions, Cam wondered if he would ever smile like that little girl, if he would ever be happy.

If he would ever be allowed to *forget*.

CHAPTER 14

The Harbor

We're close, Cam knew he wasn't the only acquisition to feel it as the crowd in the train car grew more agitated, poking each other and moving around in their seats.

They reached the river, the afternoon sun behind them. It looked for a moment as if the train might sail above the water and cross in the air, but instead they dipped into a tunnel and a hush fell over the acquisitions. Cam heard Alex suck in his breath and hold it as long as he could before letting the air out in a soft explosion. Without the sun shining through the windows, the train car felt like a coffin and smelled like unwashed bodies and urine. It wasn't any cooler for being below ground.

"Wh-What are they going to do when the solar power dies? Like last night? The train stopped after the sun went down. Are we going to be stuck down here?" Alex's breathing was too fast and too shallow.

"I'm sure we'll come out somewhere. They can't trade dead slaves," Cam whispered loudly.

That didn't seem to help Alex feel any better because the kid shifted and groaned. "I think I'm gonna puke."

"Of course he's gonna puke," Jake mumbled.

Feeling around in the dark, Cam found Alex's head and folded him over into his knees. "Stay like that until we can get out."

Alex nodded in agreement, but Cam kept his hand on the kid's shoulder just in case. Up toward the front, another kid cried, and somebody else did throw up, the smell quickly making its way to the back.

Metal screeched against metal as the brakes grabbed the tracks and Cam's forehead pitched into the back of the other seat as the train came to a hard stop. A wave mumbled up and down the seats as the kids realized they were about to get off. Weak light trickled in from the platform outside of the train, enough for Cam to see Smith stand up at the front of the car.

"What we are about to walk through is not like the pretty rows of houses you just saw," Smith's voice was rough and nasal, like he was trying not to smell while he talked. "Manhattan Island. Stick close with me in your sight at all times. I want to make the dock before twilight, when everything that hunts gets hungry."

Dim lights spotted the stretches of cement outside of the train, a few bulbs blinking against concrete and tile, creating more shadows than light. One section of wall had crumbled enough that the steel frame supports showed through like excavated bones. A piece of cement the size of Cam's fist crumbled to the floor as the acquisitions filed out of the train car doors.

Gathered on the platform, the kids looked like ghosts in the blue-white glow of the low voltage emergency lights, their ratty hair like the fallen remains of halos floating above the crowd. The stale smell of cement and rats was a fresh relief after the rank stew of bodies in the train car. The mutants collected on the platform in their own mob, their Regulator younger and less severe than Smith, who hopped off the train and skirted the bodies pressed together at the bottom of a long, shallow stairway.

"Come on," he waved at them.

Cam looked at the signs that still hung tenuously to the deteriorating walls, directing train patrons to the upper floor to find the exit on Seventh Street. The orphans filed up the stairs in pairs, the second Regulator like a wedge between the two groups of acquisitions. Cam caught Tara's blond hair a few steps above him, the lights turning the gold into a bluish silver. He wasn't sure, but he also thought he saw Myla's dark ponytail bobbing up toward the main level.

The rest of the train station was dark. Smith cut a narrow path with a flashlight, the edges of the beam hinting at seats and columns and black message boards that would end up buried by rubble before there were enough people in the world to care. The group shuffled carefully, instinctively toward a square of late afternoon sunlight that fell in through a hole where some doors used to be.

Outside the air smelled like salt and growing things and warm cement. Clean. Cam closed his eyes and took a deep breath, then squinted into the evening sun. Like the walk to the train depot, the street was a jumble of asphalt, glass, and debris from the people who used to crowd the sidewalks on their way to somewhere when there was a somewhere. The Regulators spread out in the space between tall buildings, keeping the acquisitions from spreading out too far.

They're herding us, Cam thought of the dogs that helped keep the neighbor's cattle from crossing the river and wandering off.

"Where are we?" Alex blinked behind his glasses and wiped his nose on his sleeve.

"The Regulator called it Manhattan Island." Cam looked up. The building they had crawled out of curved in tall reflective rectangles, most of them with at least one hole and cracks webbing the glass. Dark vines climbed the walls and threatened to swallow the giant building in their waxy leaves.

So much waste, all these fancy buildings and wide streets so we could die.

"Well, if they leave the train under there, there's no way they'll ever get it out. It's solar powered, and that tunnel was long and dark." Alex pushed his glasses up and worked to keep up with Cam.

Nobody is meant to go back, Cam thought of home, and the Stalls, and Peter's tears as he watched Cam disappear in the back of a truck. *You promised.*

The tall buildings watched as the orphans picked their way through the broken remains of civilization. As they cleared the first block and turned west, the wind hit his face. It felt good to be outside where the air smelled like salt and sunshine. Instinctively, Cam tracked Devon and Tara out of his peripheral vision, the blond heads close together at the edge of their group. He also found Myla's dark hair behind them, and a spread in the crowd around Austin's broad shoulders.

As they left the darkness of the train station behind, the acquisitions spread out in the wide street, playing on the debris like Devon had before, the mutants challenging each other to races. Devon headed a group of mutants, almost ten others whipping out behind him as he wove his way down the broad street.

Having been cooped up for almost two days, even the immunes hopped up on chunks of asphalt and fallen light poles, playing versions of 'Simon Says' and 'Follow the Leader.'

Alex sniffed and watched Hannah, the pale, skinny girl who had called him 'Puddles.' She crawled under things, threw rusty chunks of metal through a few windows, and picked up a curtain rod as a baton. A handful of immunes followed her down the street, copying her cheers and shouts.

Cam nudged Alex forward. "Why don't you go with them?"

Alex shrugged and pushed his glasses up on his nose. "I don't think they'll let me."

"Sure they will," Jake pointed toward the group. "Just catch up to the end of the line."

Surprised at Jake's encouragement, Alex slowly nodded. "Okay," he headed toward Hannah's group at a slow jog.

"That was unusually nice of you," Cam said to Jake when Alex was far enough away that he couldn't hear.

Jake shrugged his good arm. "It was either that or listen to him sniff some more. I know you're all about the big guys looking out for the little guys, but sometimes you can be too nice."

Stretching, Cam sucked in a deep breath. "Alex isn't so bad if you learn to ignore his twitches."

"Be honest, Cam. That kid is mutant meat," Jake kicked something that might have once been a ball.

Farther down the street, Alex tripped over an old chair and scrambled to his feet to catch up to the others.

"He has potential." Cam hopped over a tire.

"Yeah," Jake shook his head, "the potential to contaminate the gene pool."

Cam jumped onto a streetlamp that had rusted through and fallen over, walking its length until it met the asphalt.

"You should go," Jake told him.

"What?" Cam didn't understand.

"You should go, like Alex. I'll be fine." Jake glanced over his shoulder at Smith, who had his knife out and prowled the edge of street. "I have the grouchy mutant Regulator and his little brothers to make sure that I'm safe from dogs."

Cam looked at Jake carefully, his bandage crusted with dried blood but his face less pale than it had been since the dogs attacked. "Okay," Cam nodded.

Stretching his legs, Cam caught up easily to Hannah's group, then got bored with their pace. He left the line and hopped onto a pole, balanced for a moment, then jumped over Hannah as she led her group through the middle of the street. His boots skimmed her ratty hair and she tripped over a rotting mattress, the rusty springs cutting into her arm.

Cam helped her up. "Sorry, you alright?"

Hannah grabbed her baton off of the mattress and patted it against the palm of her hand, like a skinny Mama Lucy with her porch railing. Her eyes narrow, she locked them on Cam. "How did you do that?"

"Do what?" he asked.

"Jump over me like that? I mean, they do it all day long," she waved her baton at the mutants who were leaping off the tops of sun bleached cars, "but most of us can't jump that high."

"Have you ever tried?" Cam shrugged.

She thought for a second, watching the immunes reorganize themselves behind a different leader and continue the game. "Yeah, I've tried to follow the mutants around. Can't do it."

Cam met Hannah's eyes. She was shorter than he was by at least a few inches, but she seemed to have a wiry determination. "Okay, see if you can keep up with me."

Hannah smiled. "Let's go."

The cars the mutants had been jumping on lined the sides of the road, parked bumper to bumper next to meters that read 'Expired.' Weaving his way to the side, Cam hopped over the trash, keeping it low and simple, his boots thumping on the pavement as he landed one foot at a time among the debris. Hannah worked to keep up with him, her knees poking out sharply through her pants. He glanced behind him a few times, watching her eyebrows pinch together in effort. She still held her baton, the curtain rod bobbing up and down as she used her arms for balance.

Red paint clung to the lower half of the first car, the hood and top more of a gray, rusty from the salt breeze that followed the acquisitions down the street. He leaped with two steps, first onto the bumper and then the hood. The bumper fell off of the car and clanged onto the road behind him as he jumped to the next car in front of him. He leaped down the line of cars, some of them already smashed in by Devon's gang.

Muscles flexing, Cam pushed and stretched, reaching for the clouds that spotted the late afternoon sky. As he pushed himself harder, he could jump from the front end of one car to the back end of the car two ahead of it, his tags swinging wildly and bouncing against his chest. A couple of times there was no car, just an empty stretch of road along the crumbling sidewalk and vines that pushed their way across the asphalt.

Crouching to jump down off the hood of a small truck, Cam's foot punched through to the engine, the metal folding in toward his ankle. He paused and looked for Hannah, scanning the line of cars past several of the mutants. He hadn't realized he had gone quite so far. The skinny girl had stopped a block back, bent over her knees as she fought to catch her breath.

Smiling, Cam carefully worked his foot out through the jagged edges of metal and hopped down. Pushing himself, running and jumping in the fresh air, felt so *good*.

"Well, well," a familiar voice mocked him from what would have been the middle of the road but was now a hill of trash, including another streetlight that had rusted through at the base and fallen over.

Devon slid down, sending a shower of rubble to the bottom. Behind him stood Tara, offering Cam an uneasy smile that stretched the cut on her cheek. A few other mutants paused as Devon closed the distance between him and Cam, then they shrugged and headed toward the water.

"Our good old Pig Boy. Did you get lost? I think you left your friend back there," Devon pointed at Hannah, who had straightened up and was slowly walking toward them. Smith followed behind her, his knife in his hand.

With Smith close, Cam could afford to play Devon's game. He clenched his fingers and gave Devon a steady look. "Miss me?" Cam spotted Myla and Austin trotting over from where they had been looking in through the broken display windows of a small shop. Others paused, some for only a moment and some waiting to see what would happen.

"You like jumping on cars, Pig Boy? Running? Do you think you're faster than me?" He locked his fingers together and stretched his arms in front of him, cracking the knuckles and squinted into the sun hanging over the water. "You and me, to the edge." He tapped the back of his fingers on Cam's chest. "What do you say? Gonna be a man about it?"

"And if I win?" Cam ran his eyes down the final stretch of asphalt and trash to the water.

Laughing, Devon glanced at Tara, and when he looked back at Cam, his eyes were bright. "If *you* win? Let's just see what happens."

He chases you because you're the hardest to catch. Cam nodded at Devon as Myla and Austin stepped up behind Tara. He knew his chances of winning a race against the blond boy were pretty much nonexistent, but it felt so good to be outside, to move, and he didn't think anything painful would happen with the Regulators around.

Be invisible, Dom always told him, but he couldn't resist the challenge.

"Let's go," Cam agreed.

Tara stepped between them and looked at Cam. "What are you doing?"

"It's just a race. You told me I was fast enough and strong enough. What could happen?"

Tara bit her lip, "Just...be careful."

Cam nodded.

Devon chuckled

Myla shook her head, and Austin frowned.

Cam tightened his boots and rolled up the bottoms of his pants, flexing his muscles and breathing in the salt air.

Devon swung his arms and jumped up and down. He winked at Myla, "Give us a start, yeah?"

Raising her hand, Myla gave Cam a slight nod before she sliced the air. "Go!"

Devon jumped halfway up the pile of trash, then ran up the broken traffic light pole to the top and jumped over two mutants. Leaping over the bottom of the trash pile that stretched toward the line of cars, Cam wove his way along the crumbling asphalt, jumping over what he could and often stepping on pieces of glass or metal. Legs pumping, the blood rushing through his body, it felt good just to be off the train.

The water stretched side to side as far as Cam could see, with a distant shoreline straight ahead across the wide river. The road he was running on connected to another that followed the edge of the island, an overgrown park in the corner of the two stretches of pavement. Devon plowed straight for the water, only a few steps ahead of Cam.

Putting his head down, Cam pushed harder and leaned into a dead run, keeping up with Devon but not closing the distance until the mutant pulled up and slowed to a jog as he approached the edge.

At least he's out of breath. Cam slowed down, too, taking a couple of final steps and stretching his chest to fill it with air.

Devon laughed and shoved Cam straight off the edge and into the water. The cold shocked him and he gasped, his mouth filling with a gritty liquid that tasted like the train car had smelled towards the end of the ride. He kicked to the surface and spit it out, shaking off his hair as a thick hand grabbed the waist of his pants and hauled him onto the road. Water splayed out on the ground, Cam coughing his lungs free of the murky stuff. A shadow fell on him as Smith cuffed Devon on the side of the head.

"Two rules, blondie. Take 'em or leave 'em. I don't make special rules for stupidity, so nobody in the water. You can't ever be sure they know how to swim." Smith glared.

Devon nodded, still chuckling, and jogged down the street to where a group of mutants waited. As he stood, Cam recognized the group who had been with Devon at the trash pile.

"Thanks," water dripped down Cam's face.

Smith glared at him. "For saving your ass?"

"For pulling me out of the water. You didn't save me. I know how to swim." Dropping his hand, Cam swept the water out of his hair and pulled off his shirt.

Smith looked carefully at the scar on Cam's chest from Devon, then he huffed and headed the same direction that Devon had just gone. His boots sloshing with every step and as he walked bare-chested behind Smith, Cam became very aware that Tara and Myla had almost caught up to them.

Austin was with them, scowling.

"I almost beat him, did you see that?" Cam stuffed his shirt halfway into a pocket as he pushed to keep up with Smith's determined strides. There was considerably less debris on the road along the water, but the asphalt was weathered down to the gravel base along the edge. "Pretty good for an immune, huh?"

Smith stopped and rested his hands on his weapons. "I saw you take up a bet with a mutant and end up in the water when you weren't looking."

The Regulator stood in front of a docked ship that soared a hundred feet or more above the water, whitewashed and rusty, and at least twenty times the size of the horse stalls where he had slept for seven months. A few of the windows were cracked but not broken through, though rust had eaten holes in the hull.

"Is that the ship?" Cam pointed.

Smith nodded. "That's her. She'll take us down the river and around the bottom of this island, then it's open sailing to Salvation."

Cam was sure the ship had once been new and shiny, the paint fresh like it had been on the train in the picture on the magazine cover, but now the faded white paint was streaked with orange like it had cried rusty tears. Everywhere Cam looked, something had been broken.

"Is it going to make it? It looks worse than the train." Scowling, Cam shuddered from the goose bumps that crawled across his skin at the thought of being trapped on the ship with Devon and the other mutants.

"She'll make it. But only once, and that's all we need." Smith paused and looked up at the hull.

"*The Princess Katherine,*" Squinting, Cam read the name

scrawled across the fading white. The script, once a crisp black, had an image scratched through the paint below it. A skull and crossbones stared at him through the paint below the ship's name, the metal it exposed dark with rot and rust. *Death's Head,* Cam swallowed and pressed his hand over the coin in his pocket.

Smith turned to the street, watching as acquisitions and Regulators made their way down the road toward an old cruise line terminal, the south half of the building nothing more than a pile of rubble. When he turned back, Cam met his eyes.

"We're the last shipment, aren't we? The last run of acquisitions to Salvation?"

Clearing his throat, Smith played with the knife hilt at his waist and nodded.

Cam hitched up his pants. "Why are we the last?"

Smith shrugged, his broad shoulders stretching the fabric of his shirt tight as he folded his arms. "It means that they've promised to trade something that we only need once."

"A cure," Cam said it as a statement.

"Not quite a cure. It won't change any of us who have already mutated, but an antidote of some kind, a shot that will turn a newborn into an immune."

A cure, Cam still thought of it that way. Not a cure for the plague itself, but a cure for the broken houses, the crumbling roads, the dead train that sat underneath an empty city. A cure for all of the burning.

A cure for orphans.

"Is it real?" Cam asked.

Smith gave him a hard look. "It's real."

CHAPTER 15

Princess Katherine

A hundred and nineteen orphans stood in two neat rows along a lower deck off the back of the ship. Smith paced between their lines, one line of immunes and one line of mutants, pinning his blue eyes on each and every acquisition as he barked out the rules of the voyage.

"You have two rules," he repeated himself from the train. "No killing anybody, and no doing something stupid enough to get yourself killed. We are on a ship. We will be in the middle of the ocean. That means do everything possible to make sure nobody ends up in the water. They could drown, or worse. Those who break the rules will be punished." He looked directly at Devon, who had plowed a kid off the dock the night before during a game of Live or Die, even after being warned about pushing Cam into the water.

The ship creaked and swayed, subtly but enough to challenge the hard biscuits and venison jerky the Regulators had given them for breakfast.

Smith took a deep breath and continued. "Sleep wherever you're comfortable, probably on one of the decks, although you might find a room in the ship that isn't full of rats if you want to spend the time looking. In the case of a storm, everybody goes below. Staying on deck during a storm is doing something stupid enough to get yourself killed, and that is breaking the rules." He stopped and clasped his hands behind his back, face toward the front of the ship and the rising sun. His knife and flashlight hung from one hip and his gun from the other, the weight of it pulling at the waist of his pants. "Two rules for five days."

It's like the Stalls, adults leaving us to our playground rules.

The late morning sky was the color of blue glass, beautiful above the rusting ship and the acquisitions standing uneasily on the deck. The sun made Tara's eyes more green than hazel when she looked at Cam, her face tense. His heart skipped as her hand went to her cheek to cover her mark and her scar, and she shifted her gaze to the river beyond the boat. She stood between Devon and Austin, with Myla farther down the line. Devon eyed the other acquisitions like a predator, sizing them up.

Myla caught Cam's eye and winked. His stomach flipped and his heart sped. He hardly knew the girl with the dark hair and the caramel skin, but she had an immediate effect on him.

Alex sniffed next to him, wrapped tightly in his coat and shivering. Cam didn't shiver, although his tee shirt was thin and too big and stiff from his dip in the river after his race with Devon the day before. On the other side of him, Jake didn't shiver, but the boy looked tired, the hollows under his eyes deepening. Cam put his hand in his pocket and ran his fingers over Dom's tags, the ridges of the coin scraping his fingers.

The ship shuddered and half of the kids stumbled to keep their balance as it slowly backed away from the dock and into the river current. The buildings stood like sentinels along the coast, tall and stern, their windows empty eyes that watched the acquisitions scramble to the railing and stare at the concrete and metal giants. To Cam, it was fascinating. Home had nothing like these buildings, with their layers of shattered glass and stone corbels, the vines creeping up their faces, each of them trying to be grander than the next.

What kind of world was this? Cam wanted to know more than what the magazines and newspapers had said. He wanted to know what it had been like to walk the smooth streets, passing people on their way to work and families out for a stroll in the park, or perhaps passing someone walking their dog.

People living without fear that death hovered, waiting for them around the corner.

Down in the water, the river rippled over its own buried treasures. Debris that had probably been pushed off the road or blown in by strong winds peeked up through the murky water. Most of it Cam couldn't see enough of to name, but he did recognize a television, a rusty bike, and a baby stroller with one wheel spinning in the current.

The other kids, mutants and immunes both, stretched themselves out along the deck railing, some of them pointing and talking about what they saw, the rest of them watching the edge of the world slip by.

Next to Cam, Alex sniffed as usual, and then a low groan rumbled from both his throat and his belly.

"Hey, man, you okay?" Cam leaned over to get a look at Alex's face. It was pale, reflecting the river water with a grayish green color. Cam directed him to the deck railing.

Jake wrapped his good arm around his bandaged one and followed, "We just spent two days on a train with this kid—you should know by now that he's not okay."

Shaking his head, Alex leaned over the railing and puked, biscuit and venison streaking the side of the ship past a couple of rusty holes.

"Alright," Cam held his breath as best he could and

pulled Alex back by his shoulders, looking around for a place to tuck the smaller kid where he could lie down without risk of rolling off the ship. The railings had probably once had glass in the spaces of the sturdy metal frame, but now a body could easily slide through and into the water.

A bench flanked the wall of the ship where the deck ended, and Cam laid Alex down where it curved along the lines of the vessel. "Stay here for a bit. I don't imagine they have anything particularly tasty planned for lunch."

Groaning, Alex turned over so that he faced away from the breeze and the sea. Cam pulled his glasses off and tucked them inside the boy's coat pocket, then returned to the railing where Jake waited. After the initial motion of the ship to get out of the dock and into the river, Cam had felt fine.

The ship passed under a bridge, a stripe of shadow crawling over faded white paint and gray deckwood. Returning to his position against the railing, Cam watched as the ship headed out of the mouth of the river and into the ocean, turning east toward the morning sun.

"The beginning of the rest of our lives," a girl's husky voice said behind him.

He turned to see Myla smiling at him. Behind her, other mutants milled around the deck, drawn toward Austin as if he had some special form of gravity. One of the Regulators had given him a real rugby ball, and he spun it between his hands. Cam thought the ball looked like a squashed pumpkin, but at least it wasn't the skull they had found at the train depot.

Half of the immunes were sick like Alex, leaning over the railing while they purged their breakfast, the rest of them either stared out into the ocean or skirted the gathering mutants, not sure what to do.

Clearing his throat, Cam gripped the metal next to where

it crossed his lower back. "Hey, Myla. Not wasting any time, are they?"

She stepped over and leaned her forearms on the railing next to him, the wind tugging her ponytail behind her. Cam noticed that Tara kept her distance from Devon as the mutant crowd divided into two teams, with a thick group of onlookers.

"No, that's all Austin does, all he cares about. The game, and his mutant rules." She took a deep breath of salty air, "You know what the other mutants are calling him?"

Jake leaned back on the railing next to Cam, "Let me guess, the Freakishly Large Log?"

Myla scoffed, "The *Bull*, like he needs any help with his ego. It just makes him want to play the game even more, especially now that Tara's watching. And he's taking it even further by naming the teams after the Houses in Salvation."

Tara? Cam bit his lip. He thought about Austin's arm around her shoulders when he and Myla walked away from the lake. The blond girl glanced over as if she heard her name, and gave Cam a shy smile, then frowned when her eyes shifted to Myla.

Jake huffed, "The Houses in Salvation? Like, the House of Evil, the House of Unnecessary Violence and Destruction, the House of Nightmares. Those Houses?"

Myla went around Cam to face Jake. "No, funny boy. The gladiator Houses."

Jake gave her a tight smile. "That's what I was talking about, the mutant Houses."

"You'll probably go to one of them, too," she poked him in the shoulder. "You'll be a House slave."

"Yes, a House slave. I'll sweep the floors and make the beds and wash your little gladiator panties," Jake poked

Myla back.

Cam cleared his throat, relieved that his friend was acting like his old self. "Maybe you'll get to wash Tara's little gladiator panties."

A blush washed through Jake's face and he dropped his finger. "I hadn't thought about that."

The mutants divided into four groups, each of them with some sort of captain choosing from those lined up along the railing. His eyes followed Tara as she joined Austin's team.

"Why aren't you playing?" he asked as Myla settled her arms on the railing again, her back to the teams.

She shrugged and twined her fingers. "I've had enough, I guess. I'll get to play it more than I could ever want once we reach Salvation. It's pretty much the rest of my life. Right now, I'd rather look at the ocean and talk to you, Cameron Landry."

"Because I'm ordinary," he smiled.

"Ordinary, yes. Very practical, in fact. Much more practical than some silly game." She turned so that she faced the same direction as Cam, studying the mutants as they set up. Those who weren't playing called out to their friends as the game began. The game started and the immunes left on the deck looked for a way out, even the sick ones heading for a staircase that led up to another part of the ship.

Myla waved her arm at the mutants, "Now, what did I say? All they want to do is see who runs faster and jumps higher."

"You run pretty fast," Cam glanced over at Alex to be sure the boy would be well out of the way, "and jump high. You always seem to know where everybody else is going to go."

Nodding, Myla looked down at her bare feet.

Blushing?

Devon and Austin had ended up on opposite teams, facing each other across the imaginary line. Driving into The Bull, Devon seemed to realize that his weight matched Austin's and he was learning to use his greater height to drive the other boy back when they locked shoulders. Austin played defense, a mutant wall, and Devon preferred the challenge of running the ball and the glory of scoring. Both of them bled from cuts on their heads, too intent on the game to care.

"Good run against Devon yesterday," Myla shifted her weight and held on to the railing behind her, pulling her shoulders back and making her collarbone stand out. She had a long, slender neck, the muscles playing delicately under her ear.

Cam swallowed and turned his eyes back to the game. "Yeah, it was."

"And probably the dumbest thing I've seen you do so far. You should stay away from him," Myla warned.

"I like her," Jake said, his eyes closed and face to the sun. "I've seen you do stupider things than race Devon, but it's only because I've known you longer."

"What's the stupidest thing he's done?" Myla asked Jake, her mouth twitching as she tried not to smile.

"It's a long list," Jake looked at her. "Sure you've got time?"

"I've got approximately five days," Myla smiled now.

Jake went back to sunning his face. "You're pretty cool for a mutant."

"Whoa, now," Cam cut in. "Are you guys becoming friends?"

Myla shrugged, her eyes tracking Devon as he threw a kid off his arm and drove another back with his shoulder. The blond boy looked at them and smiled, wiping a line of blood out of his eyes, smearing it across the pink mark on his face. Cam shifted against the railing, uncomfortable against the metal bar.

Myla nodded toward the game. "You're all from the same orphanage, right? You guys and the blond twins?"

"Yeah," Cam frowned. "Jake and the twins were there first. I only came seven months ago in the fall."

"Not with the Second Wave?" she asked.

"Nope." *Dom.* The memory rippled like the water and Cam pressed his hand against his pocket.

"Well, he sure doesn't like you for some reason," Myla shifted her bare feet on the deck boards, nodding again at Devon. "Did you do something to piss him off?"

Cam looked at Jake for a reply, expecting to see his friend watching Tara, but Jake had his eyes toward the upper deck where Hannah leaned over the railing. Smith was up there, too, with a scowl on his face. Shrugging, Cam pushed his toe against the boards of the deck and answered Myla's question. "I woke up breathing this morning. That always seems to make him mad, but that's all I've ever done to him. I don't know why he hates me so much." *He likes hunting.*

The boys on the deck had shed their shirts, the players glistening with sweat, marks showing on various parts of their bodies. The girls had at least shed their shoes and any layers, many of them in old, faded tank tops.

Glancing at Alex, Cam felt relieved to see that the boy was still curled against the bench in his coat, undisturbed.

"Well, I don't think Devon will bother you with Austin around. That Regulator who came with you guys seems to have his eyes on Devon, too. Just be careful, Cam. That boy has something wrong with him." She reached up and squeezed his arm. Her touch was as warm as her kiss had been the other night, the feeling of her fingers lingering after she put her hand back down on the railing.

The wind pricked through Cam's thin tee shirt, drawing goose bumps through the scars on his chest as he glanced up at the grizzled Regulator. Apparently drawing blood didn't break either of the two rules because Smith had not done anything to interfere with the mutants playing.

If they bleed this much when they play for fun, I wonder what it looks like when they're let loose in the arena. Most of the mutants had blood somewhere on them, either their own or someone else's. The game spread to their side of the deck, the kids who were lined up along the edge scattering as a boy holding the ball rolled toward them, his mark wrapping around his left forearm and his tags flying around his neck. Devon had pushed him, not even attempting to make it look like a tackle, and followed the boy over to that side of the deck. Myla had jumped out of the way and stood with her back against Cam's arm.

"Wanna play, Pig Boy?" Devon's grin looked like the skull on the coin. Blood smeared down to his chin and his mutant mark made his right eye appear to sink back into the socket.

Swallowing hard, Cam watched as Austin came up behind Devon and pulled the ball out of the blond boy's arms. After helping the kid that Devon had pushed to his feet, he pressed the ball against Devon's shoulder. "Let's go."

Devon shrugged him off, "I think he's waiting for his turn to play," his eyes shifted to Cam. "You ready to come in, Pig Boy?"

Pulling Devon around by his arm, Austin pinned the ball against his chest and pushed him all the way back to the middle of the deck. "You're wasting time, Devon."

The blond boy narrowed his eyes at Cam, then shoved Austin's arm away. "Don't touch me."

The Bull ignored him and yelled at the rest of the players to reset in their positions. Devon followed, glancing back once over his shoulder at Cam, then up at Smith.

He knows Smith's the only Regulator watching us, Cam's throat tightened.

"I told you," Myla settled back against the railing to watch, "There's something wrong with him."

We had a brother, Tara had said at the rockslide. "I think something happened to make him that way," Cam said, then regretted it. *Why am I defending him?*

"Like what?" Jake asked. "Like he was dropped on his head as a baby?"

Myla laughed, but Cam frowned. "Never mind."

"Maybe having a mark on your face affects your brain," Jake joked, but Myla's face fell.

She stood up from the railing, her shoulders stiff with tension. "The marks don't really change us, not really. We're still people, you know."

Jake avoided her eyes.

The ball went into play and Devon grabbed it and drove into Austin, pushing the shorter boy away from the railing and toward the wall of the ship section that held the upper deck. Large metal hooks, secured over the white paint with rusting screws, stuck out like empty arms. All of the kids on the deck paused and stared when they realized Devon wasn't going to stop. At first it looked like he was aiming for the space between two of the hooks, but then Austin's head smashed into the metal and the thick kid the others had named 'The Bull' crumpled to the deck floor.

The wind whipped past, bringing with it the sound of

the ship cutting through the water. Several heartbeats passed before Smith jumped down from the upper deck, almost landing on Devon, who was standing over Austin with the ball. Shoving the blond boy out of the way, the Regulator checked for a pulse.

Myla stared at the whole scene in disbelief. With her eyes round and her hand over her heart, she sprinted to where Smith had Austin on his feet, the boy's arm around the grizzled Regulator's neck. She took Austin's other arm and helped Smith walk him slowly around where Alex lay by the bench and back to another part of the ship.

As the three of them disappeared, they left a trail of blood from the back of Austin's head on the deck boards, the sticky liquid shining a bright red in the noon sun.

Turning around, Devon tossed the ball and caught it again. He pushed through the kids who had been playing when he nailed Austin against the hook, gathered now in an uneasy press of onlookers.

He came straight to Cam.

His hazel eyes seemed oddly bright as he paused a few feet away and twisted the ball in his hands.

Myla's earlier statement echoed in Cam's mind and his heart jumped. *There's something wrong with him.*

Devon spun the ball on one hand, "We need a replacement player. Austin got a little owie and had to leave the game. What do you say, Pig Boy?"

Cam glanced around for Tara, then met Devon's eyes. "You did that on purpose."

Devon grinned and flexed his chest muscles, the sun throwing the marked and bloody half of his face in shadow. "Did what? We were just playing a game."

"You pushed Austin into that hook on purpose," Cam

stood up straight.

"Cam," Jake's voice was shaky behind him.

"Maybe I did. I wanted to give you a chance to play. You're always watching us, waiting for your turn with the mutants, show us how fast you are, and Austin didn't want to give you your chance." Devon tapped the ball to Cam's chest. "I'm just making things *fair*." The grin stayed.

Looking at the crowd, Cam saw a mixture of reactions. Some of the other players looked worried and frightened, others seemed excited by Devon's aggression, and a few just had blank looks on their faces, as if nothing were going on at all.

Then the crowd rippled and spit out Tara, her face tense and angry. "Devon, what are you doing?"

The blond boy turned and pinned his sister with a stare, eyes blazing. "Hey, sis," he spit the last word, "I'm just inviting the Pig Boy to play a little in our game. You know, good old fashioned sportsmanship."

Tara's eyes shone even more hotly than her twin's. "You don't have any sportsmanship, Devon. Not an ounce of it. All you have is hate."

Pressing the ball against her chest, Devon pushed his sister back into the crowd. "Stop interfering, Tara. Cam's a big boy. He can decide on his own whether he is going to man up and play, or if he'll just be Pig Boy." Devon turned back to Cam. "What's it gonna be? You gonna play? Or you gonna go whine about it to your little friends?"

Golden fingers wrapped over Devon's shoulder and pulled him back. "Devon, don't."

The blond boy grabbed Tara's hand and twisted it back at the wrist, turning and pushing her down to her knees. Pain pulled the fresh scar across her mark into a second smile, and she let out a gasp. Devon growled at her, "I said, stop interfering."

He thinks he owns her. Tara's gasp wrenched at Cam's gut and his heart pounded blood through his body, curling his fingers into fists and tugging at the muscles along his spine. *Tara, what are you doing?* He wanted to jump on the blond boy and gouge his eyes out, or break his neck like he had done to the dog. Devon pushed harder on his sister's wrist, his face twisted in a warning.

Cam clenched his teeth, "Let's play."

Dropping Tara, Devon stood up straight and grinned again. Cam closed the distance, looking up slightly into Devon's hazel eyes. Nearly matching Devon in height, Cam realized he had grown even more than he thought when he saw his reflection in the glass at the depot.

The mutant pressed the ball into Cam's chest, his hazel eyes excited.

No, Cam's heart stopped for a beat, then pounded beneath the tags that rested against his chest, *not excited. Hungry.*

"Alright, Pig Boy." Devon backed up and headed to the start position, pushing himself past Tara and parting the crowd like he was ripping the seam in a pair of pants. The other players looked at him with a single expression.

Relief, Cam realized, *relief that Devon wants me and not them.*

Bending over, Cam curled his fingers around Tara's wrist and pulled her up. Her skin felt cool from the ocean wind.

She bit her lip and put her hand on Cam's bicep, "What are you doing?"

"What does it look like I'm doing?" he answered. "I'm going to play a little game of Live or Die with the friendly mutants."

"This isn't just a race. You almost beat him, Cam, and

now he really wants to hurt you."

"Aren't you the one who told me that I'm fast enough, strong enough?" His eyes felt hot as they searched Tara's face.

Her grip tightened. "I meant fast enough to get away, not beat him. Did you see what he just did to Austin?"

"That's all I have to do, Tara, get away. Stay away. He can't hurt me if he can't catch me," Cam pulled his arm out of her grip.

Tara glanced at Jake, then backed toward the railing to watch, her brows tight with fear. "Be careful, Cam."

Cam pinched his lips, refusing to look behind him at Jake with his pale face and bandaged arm. *It's not like Devon and I are straight out fighting each other. I wouldn't be stupid enough to do that.*

Players and onlookers settled into their positions on the deck or along the railing. A new team captain, replacing Austin, waved Cam behind him to join the back half of his players, which were the smaller, faster kids. Even though he stood behind the defensive pack, Cam didn't expect them to go out of their way to keep Devon from plowing him into one of the hooks.

Squinting, Cam leaned onto the balls of his feet and tightened his gut. The sun that the ship had chased out of the river was high above them now, light bouncing off the deck boards and the water that went on forever in all directions. His heartbeat fluttered, *fast, skip, fast, slow, skip, fast* and his throat felt dry and his hands damp. *You just have to be fast enough that he can't catch you. Stay out of his way long enough for Smith to make it back on the deck. That's all. Just be fast enough.*

Devon made a noise and the front lines pushed against each other, the ball making it out toward Cam. He skipped to the side and looked at the kid next to him, recognizing the big nose from the night he watched them play in the paved yard of the train depot. The kid looked back at Cam and yelled at him to get the ball.

Keeping Devon in sight, Cam shook his head and danced around the ball until another of their team players finally picked it up and ran. She only made it a few feet before she threw the ball behind her and it landed in Cam's gut. Grunting, he curled his arms around it and ran, jumping over another player who had knocked a defender aside and slipped on the deck. Devon saw Cam with the ball, but too late. Cam made it past the rest of the opponents to the railing.

Two kids moved over so that Cam could touch the ball to the metal bar that stretched around the deck. He turned and smiled at Tara, and then Jake. He knew nobody in the game had followed him to the railing, but he hadn't realized they would just be standing there, staring.

An *immune* had scored.

Now his team was winning. Cam hadn't expected that to matter to him much, but it gave him a rush and he felt *alive*.

Tara's glare could have seared the ship in half, but Cam's teammates slowly shared a smile. As he walked back to reset for a new start, the girl who had passed him the ball patted his shoulder, and the big nosed kid folded his arms across his chest and nodded at the other team, "Take that, suckers."

Prepared for Devon's anger, Cam's stomach sank when the blond boy smiled. *That's what he wants. He wants me to take the ball, to be the target.*

The teams set up and this time one of Devon's players got the ball. A few tackles later, they scored against the wall where Devon had driven Austin into the hook. Devon, however, had waited, mirroring Cam across the invisible centerline, staying out of the play to trace his steps.

The next start gave the big nosed boy the ball. He gained

a few feet before passing it back to the girl. She found another player for a pass when the other team's defense plowed over the deck at her. That player got tackled, but not before sending the ball back to Cam.

He ran.

Devon grinned.

Keeping his eyes on the blond head, Cam cut an angle toward the metal railing, positioning the players down from the tackle between them so that Devon would have to go around them, or wait for Cam to clear them. A few steps forward, with Devon in the corner of his eye, strong arms wrapped around Cam's waist and pulled him down hard. His face smashed onto the deck and the ball popped out of his arms.

Warm fluid trickled past his right eye and he blinked it away. A hand hovered above him. Cam took it and watched as the world righted itself, looking at the girl who had tackled him.

"You're fast," she offered. Her hair was a damp brown, left wild and ragged, like somebody had given her a haircut with a pair of sheep shears. Otherwise she was cleaner than most of the orphans and less bloody than most of the players, her eyes a deep brown in a face already red from the sun.

"Thanks," was all Cam could think to say.

She nodded and headed back behind Devon as the ball was reset. Her team had stolen the ball and scored.

As Cam settled himself between the boy with the big nose and the girl on his team, he watched Devon shift his weight from side to side and flex his hands in and out of fists, hazel eyes on Cam.

He knows as well as I that Smith could be back any moment. He knows he's running out of time. Leaning onto the balls of his feet, Cam tensed and widened the scope of his vision so that he could see most of Devon's team. The tackle caught him because he had been singularly worried about the blond mutant. He only needed that lesson once.

Play started and this time Cam picked up the ball, realizing that Devon purposefully lost the opening scuffle so that Cam's team would be on the offense. It wasn't about winning or losing, it was about getting to Cam. The opposing defense broke through, close to catching him but also opening up the deck behind them for a clear run to the railing.

Except for Devon.

Jumping and twisting, Cam cut across the deck sideways, heading for an opening as far away from Devon as possible. Knowing the mutant would take the straightest line to where Cam cut through, Cam wanted as much time as he could get to reach the railing and then get back to his team.

It worked. Devon angled across at full speed, aiming to hit Cam about three feet from his goal. Just before impact, Cam slowed and fell back a step, and Devon flew by into the railing.

As he touched the ball to the metal, Cam smiled to himself but hurried back to his side, settling next to the boy with the big nose, who patted Cam on the shoulder, "Nice score, kid."

"Name's Cam."

"Joel," the boy held out his hand.

Cam took it, keeping Devon at the edge of his vision. The blond boy scowled now, clenching his jaw and pressing his fist into his palm. The sight crawled along Cam's nerves.

As the teams lined up again, Devon set himself to start on the opposite end from Cam, shaking his legs and arms to keep his blood pumping as the rest of the players settled into place. Just before the center group of defenders locked shoulders over the ball, Devon crouched to the deck floor like a mountain lion. Instinctively, Cam's chest tightened with a wave of fear and he backed away, glancing behind him for an escape. He could run to the upper deck, or he could squeeze past Alex to find where Smith and Myla had taken Austin.

Or he could stay in the middle of the game and evade Devon by speed and luck.

He didn't have time to decide. The ball thudded into his gut, passed back by Joel, and the defenders worked to disentangle themselves. The pass had cut an angle back to Cam, where he had a straight line to the railing, again, with only a few of the other team's offensive players scattered in his way.

Sprinting, Cam spun through two players, their hands sliding over his tee shirt as they tried and failed to find enough grip to bring him down. Once they fell behind, Devon had a straight shot at him.

It was like a repeat of the last play, giving Devon a second chance to catch him. The blond boy ducked his head and leaned in, pushing his full speed toward Cam and the ball. Cam did the same, but spinning through those players had cost him a few precious seconds of time.

A body length from the railing, Devon's fingers brushed his shoulder. Cam angled over, four steps away...

"Cam!"

He faltered, Myla's voice breaking through his focus. It only cost him a heartbeat, but it was enough. Devon's arms circled his waist and pinched in like a vise, squeezing the air out of him and popping the ball out of his arms. The contours of Devon's face pressed into Cam's back beneath his shoulder blade, the mutant's forehead, cheekbone, and jaw denting the muscle along his spine. Cam went down, his shoulder and head slamming onto the deck boards as he slid toward the edge of the ship.

He didn't see the support bar for the railing until it cut along his neck and bit into his shoulder. His legs swung wide and wrapped on another support post, Devon clutching at him to keep from flying off the edge himself and into the blades that churned the water below.

Pain shot down Cam's spine, and his arms went numb as sticky warm liquid ran into his eyes and down his neck. He blinked and watched blood crawl down the ball links of his chain and pool around the tags that had settled on the deck floor as Devon grabbed the railing and pulled himself off of Cam.

A rush of faces blotted out the sky and rough hands gripped Cam's arm and stretched him to a standing position. The motion made him sick and he swallowed bile. Squinting through the crowd, Cam caught Tara's golden head and focused on her. Her hazel eyes sad, she seemed to be saying something, but Cam couldn't make it out through the darkness that closed over him.

Chapter 16

Antiseptic

Sucking in his breath, Cam swiped at the sting. "Ah!"

"So you are awake. I didn't think it would take you long to come around."

Opening one eye, Cam caught a blur of gray hair and blue eyes. "Smith," his own voice sounded like the old man's.

"Easy there, this will sting."

Something cold and wet dabbed at his forehead, then the sting set in and Cam flinched when he saw white gauze floating above his head. He closed his eye and took a deep breath as Smith cleaned the side of his face.

"Not so bad here," the gauze went away and the smell of antiseptic burned Cam's nose.

Cam opened his eyes and looked down at the gauze that Smith had just tossed in a trash pile on the floor. The piece of white fabric waved on top of a small heap of blood-soaked squares, red streaking the floor.

Smith dabbed antiseptic onto another piece. "I thought you learned your lesson yesterday when Devon dumped you in the water, son, but your stupidity has increased overnight."

Bracing himself, Cam sat up. His shirt and tags were gone and he sat on a cot in a small room with pipes and peeling white paint. The room swam, swaying with the motion of the ship and the pressure that shifted in Cam's head. His stomach complained the most, settling a little after he closed his eyes and waited for the nausea to pass.

Cam swallowed and peeked through one eye.

Smith steadied the right side of Cam's face with a calloused hand and took a deep breath. "This is going to hurt a little more. Got a lot of blood to clean up. You shredded part of your neck on that deck railing where the screws went in. 'Bout near went off the back of the ship and into the propellers."

Squinting his eye shut again, Cam gripped the edge of the cot and waited for the sting.

Smith started under Cam's ear. It felt cold until he swiped about halfway down, then Cam felt the gauze catch on a piece of ragged skin, the full sting setting in. He tightened his grip and gritted his teeth. "I thought I could just stay out of his reach until you came back up to the deck."

"Looked like it worked until that dark girl called your name," he huffed and wiped more gently. "She was sure a pain in the ass when she came down here to watch me doctor *him* up." The Regulator's blue eyes glanced toward another cot in the room, then dropped the gauze in his discard pile and dabbed the antiseptic onto another square.

Glancing over, Cam saw Austin stretched out, the boy's eyes closed and a bandage wrapped around the back half of his head. The thick shoulders didn't look very intimidating now. "You mean Myla?"

"Is that the dark girl's name? She and that blond one both tried to follow me down here with you, but I told them that if they wanted to help you, they should keep you from being stupid in the first place." Smith's face stayed steady as he dabbed at the open wound along Cam's neck.

Resisting the urge to reach up and touch it, Cam forced his eyes to focus on the opposite wall. The room was about the size of the stall he had shared with Peter. His cot and the one with Austin met in the corner, leaving just enough space for the Regulator to move around his pile of gauze. A bleak lantern-style light hung from a painted pipe that crossed the low ceiling and snaked down the wall behind Smith.

Cam frowned. "Like you said, I was fine until Myla called my name. If she hadn't done that, I would have been in one piece long enough for you to stop the game."

"You're mostly in one piece. I wouldn't say that any part of you has exactly become detached, except maybe some skin you left in that railing post." Smith soaked more gauze pads with antiseptic.

Cam kept his head still, "The girls tried to come down here with me?" He was getting used to the sting, and he no longer felt tempted to flinch.

Smith snorted, "Both of them, giving each other pouty looks. At least the blond one isn't like her brother, or she'd be after the dark one for that mean cut she gave her. Don't think those two will be friends."

When Myla had run Tara into the brick post at the depot, Smith had cleaned up the cut and told Tara to be strong. He used Dom's words, and Tara never thought he was a Regulator. *Who is he?*

Studying the far wall while Smith dabbed at another section of his neck, Cam chewed on his lip. "You were alive during the First Wave."

Smith frowned and sat back with a deep breath. "Ten. Twelve when the Scouts came. Fourteen when they started training me for the arena."

"Did your family get sick?" Cam asked.

Nodding, Smith tossed the gauze on the floor, then leaned against the wall and folded his arms. "Two days after my birthday, my parents and my sister all showed those sores on their necks, pus oozing out on everything in the house. I felt sick, too, but not like them. I didn't know what to do. I was a city kid. I played baseball in the street and spit loogies and rounded up change to get a hot dog from the cart on the sidewalk. They died quickly, less than a week, I think. I had no idea why I didn't get sick, just went on surviving. A few of us kids with marks formed a little gang, scrounged for food, fought off the dogs. It was crazy how fast those dogs went wild, like the one that chewed up your friend."

Jake is up on deck with Devon. . .but I need answers.

Smith continued. "You'd think, with the population disappearing overnight, there would be plenty of food for the rest of us. It didn't work like that. People stole it, hid it, whoever was faster and stronger got everything that mattered. A few of the more self-sacrificing types stayed around to burn the dead. The more people lived in a place, the more of them died.

"The stench hung over the city for weeks, and then they started sending us over to Salvation. We were kids nobody wanted to clothe or feed or burn. Why not ship us off to somebody who wanted us? We were killing each other, anyway." He swung his legs up onto the cot next to Cam, nearly dumping the bottle of antiseptic on the floor. The stool squeaked as he shifted his weight and locked his fingers behind his head, pinning Cam with a clear, steady look. "Enough bedtime stories. Why don't you ask me what you really want to know?"

Cam studied the older man, the scar that ran along his cheek and twisted his face beneath the eye and chevron brand, the gray hair, the serious eyes. Mama Lucy's warning tracked through his mind. *He works for the other side. Can't trust him. Can't trust anybody.* But so far, Smith seemed to be the only one who knew he was a no-code and still wanted him alive. *Be strong.* He took a deep breath. "You're not a Regulator, are you?"

Smith shook his head, "Not really."

"Then what are you?"

"I'm a soldier," Smith answered.

"I thought you were a gladiator, a mutant. Soldiers are for war."

"Salvation is at war, son. At war with the Nests, fighting over the cure. Once you set foot on that shore, you will be on one side or the other."

"I thought you said they had promised a cure, that we were payment."

"I did say that, and it's true. It doesn't mean they'll give it to us, but there is a cure." Smith kept his eyes locked on Cam.

A *cure*. He swallowed, "What is a no-code?"

Smith smiled, "Now that's a question that matters." He pulled his feet off the cot and sat up on the stool. "A no-code is a live carrier of the plague virus."

Cam didn't move. "Do you mean I'm killing people? Making them sick?" He thought of Dom, the sores on his body leaking pus, the strain in his voice when he asked Cam to bring him water. Guilt burned at the back of Cam's throat.

Smith gave him a tense smile. "We don't know exactly how no-codes work. It's all been guesses and theory, but just look at you, Cam. All of those nasty gashes from the dog are gone, not just healed, but gone."

Cam ran a hand over his belly. Smith was right. The skin had healed perfectly. Then Cam's fingers found the burn on his chest, a round knotted scar directly above his heart.

He met Smith's eyes. "Why do I have this?"

Smith straightened on the stool. "Still a lot we don't

know, Cam. All of the other no-codes have been killed."

"Killed?" Cam's heart pounded against his ribs and his arms felt numb. *You're not anything, an accident. You're not even supposed to be alive.*

"Rounded up and killed. I knew a few after the First Wave, kids from my city. They were put on the ship with the rest of us, then shot and thrown in the sea. Think about it, Cam. Why do we need the tags? You can see who the mutants are because the virus marks them. The only reason for the tags is to find the ones who won't code, who still carry the virus. We need that live virus to make the cure." Smith's eyes became intense, heated.

"Then who wants me dead?" Cam swallowed.

"Jayden Winters."

The coin in Cam's pocket seemed like it weighed a hundred pounds. "Mama Lucy warned me not to trust anybody."

"As much as I think Lucy Malin is a sniveling, self-serving leach, she gave you some damn good advice. Think hard about it, son. You wouldn't have gotten this far without me. As far as you can tell, I'm the only one who wants you alive."

"That's why the Scout shot the Regulators at the outpost. They knew." Cam remembered the way Carrigan had pointed the gun at his face, the Scout's hand shaking so hard he had almost pulled the trigger from fear.

Cam jumped off the cot and picked Smith up by his shoulders, pinning him against the wall. He felt his own breath, hot off the older man's burned and scarred face. "What's going to happen to the others who know? Tara and Jake?" He shook him, "What about them?"

Smith swallowed. "Stay by me and I can make sure you all

get to the Nests. Then nothing will need to happen. They'll be with us, soldiers."

You better learn when to kill. Cam thought first, but as he searched Smith's eyes, he understood what Mama Lucy had been looking for in his when she held the knife to his throat in the kitchen of the Stalls. She had been looking for a promise, not just what she could make him say to her, but a promise that dug all the way into the soul, and what Cam saw in Smith's eyes surprised him.

He saw *hope.*

Dropping Smith's shoulders, Cam backed up to the cot. "Okay."

Austin moaned. Smith shot a look at the mutant, then gave Cam a nod. "Let's get that bandage on."

They sat in silence as Smith layered gauze and tape over the curve of Cam's neck. When he was done, he handed Cam his tags to put back on over the bandage, his blood still smeared over part of the chain. The gray tee shirt Carrigan had given him after the dog attack lay on the floor among the gauze, stained and stiff. He left it there.

Before he left the small room, Cam paused and looked at The Bull. The boy's thick shoulders stretched the width of the cot, forehead drawn in pain. "Will he be okay?"

"Yeah," Smith nodded, "he's breathing. Bad deal. Puts your blond mutant friend in isolation for the next two days, and we'll only let him out if he promises to be a good boy."

Cam knew the hunger in Devon's eyes had only been a warning. "He's not my friend."

They came out on the deck through a narrow stairwell, their steps echoing in the shaft. Smith continued to the upper deck to find Jake for new bandages, and Cam looked for a place to go, a place away from Tara's moods and Myla's flirting, away from Alex's constant sniffing. A place to be alone.

Shouts and cheers from the game floated on the wind from the back deck. Cam headed toward the front of the ship, passing a handful of acquisitions who were scattered along the railing before he came to the small foredeck. The late afternoon sun hung behind him, throwing his shadow in front of his bare feet. The wind pricked at his bare chest and ran fingers along his scars. He pulled the coin out of his pocket and leaned on the railing, clutching the cool metal in his hand and watching the prow slice through the deepening waves. The ocean seemed endless, bottomless, like he could jump into the water and sink forever in the silence.

You promised.

He looked at the coin. *So many promises.* Cam spit on it and wiped it on his pants. The edges caught the late afternoon rays, taking on a red tone in the full light. Blood. The Death's Head smiled at him, the stained edges adding an ominous dimension to the image. *Ash and blood.*

Cam flipped it over and studied the snowflake on the back. *Winters*, he had overheard the Scout telling Smith. *Salvation is at war, son. Once you set foot on that shore, you'll be on one side or the other.*

Or I'll be dead. Cam tucked the coin in his pocket and pulled out Dom's tags. The sight of them caused him physical pain, a pressure in his chest that tightened around his lungs and made it hard to breath. I'm sorry, Dom. *I'll keep my promises.*

I'll be strong.

CHAPTER 17

Distractions

Sun bleached everything. Cam had never seen so much pure light, bright and unbroken and endless. He stretched his legs in front of him and leaned back on his hands, staring at the water.

"How long are we going to be on this boat?" Alex had shed his coat, the tee shirt underneath it considerably cleaner, though he smelled like a year's worth of body odor. Cam had to wake him up from where he had slept through the night by the bench and drag him up to the deck with the other immunes.

Folding his legs under him, Jake settled upwind of the smaller kid, his movements unbalanced with his bandaged arm pinned to his chest by a sling. He still wore his coat, one arm through the sleeve and the other side hanging from his shoulder. "Two rules for five days, kids," Jake mimicked Smith's gruff voice. "No killing anybody, and no doing something stupid enough to get yourself killed."

Myla rolled her eyes and smiled, her legs hanging off the edge of the deck, a rail post between her legs.

Alex's face fell and he groaned. "Five days?"

Jake pointed at Alex with his biscuit. "Yeah, but at least you're not puking anymore."

Cam cradled his breakfast ration of two biscuits on his outstretched legs. He squinted past the bright sun at Jake and frowned. Jake was the one who looked like he was going to puke.

"So we have four days left, right?" Alex held up his fingers, counting to himself.

"Yes, genius," Myla huffed, almost close enough to Cam to brush elbows.

Jake sniffed at his biscuit, then put it on the deck floor. "You know, Alex, for a kid who knows everything, you don't know much."

"I do, too. I know a lot of things," Alex pushed his glasses up on his nose.

"A lot of useless things, like how they used to make ice cream and what pirate ships looked like," Jake cradled his bandaged arm in his good one.

"Those aren't useless things," Alex blinked.

Myla tightened her ponytail, "We have four days left. Four days on a ship with nothing to do. I'm going to go crazy if I have to spend it listening to you two."

Four days, Cam closed his eyes and felt the sway of the ocean through his belly. With their destinies looming in Salvation, this quiet morning on the ship seemed like a strange suspension of time. He needed a distraction—a distraction from secrets and promises, from Jake's pale, drawn face. A distraction from living.

Alex huffed and Cam opened his eyes to see Alex squinting at him through his dirty glasses. "Why is she here, anyway? She's a mutant."

"She's a friend," Cam answered.

Alex looked at him with his lopsided eyes. "We can't be friends with mutants."

Bobbing her head side to side, Myla turned to Alex and mocked him with a whiny pitch. "We can't be friends with mutants." Her face fell, "Did it occur to you that I'm the one hanging out with you?"

"Nobody asked you to," Alex shot back.

Jake cleared his throat. "I could referee if you need me to. Cam could keep score. Alex the Immune versus Myla the Mutant. Kind of has a ring to it. We could charge the other kids each a biscuit to come and watch."

Myla ignored him, leaning back so that she had a straight line of sight to Alex. "Nobody has to ask. It's a free ship. If you don't want to hang out with me, go somewhere else."

"It's the immunes' deck," Alex sniffed.

Jake caught Cam's eye and gave him a weak smile.

He knows I'm a no-code, but would he still be my friend if he knew what that meant? Cam returned an uneasy smile, then lifted his face to the sun and closed his eyes again. He wanted to smell Crix and Sparta, lie down in the hay, smell the spring rain, and listen to the river break its edges of ice. He wanted to go home. But all he had was the endless ocean and dangerous promises. *Be strong.*

He scratched at the bandage on his neck and opened his eyes. Myla and Alex glared at each other, like they were having a staring contest.

"Hey, Cam," Jake poked his shoulder and pointed. "Tara." She stood at the top of the stairs from the mutant deck, scanning the spread of immunes.

"Maybe she's coming to thank you," Jake raised an eyebrow. "You did stop Devon from hurting her."

Cam shook his head. "Devon was only hurting her because of me." He glanced from Tara to Jake's arm. *Too many people have been hurt because of me.*

Myla scoffed. "Well, I think in the end you paid for it. I tell you, you can sure bleed."

Cam shrugged. His neck already itched more than it hurt, and under the sun he was starting to sweat off the tape. He sat up and picked at a biscuit.

"I didn't know you got into the game because of a mutant girl," Alex blinked.

"It's not that she's a mutant girl," Myla's eyes narrowed slightly, "it's that she's covered in thorns and follows that crazy brother of hers around."

"She's nicer than you think," Cam said. Done trying to force his biscuit down, he offered it to Alex, who took it tentatively, his face still slightly green.

"Yes," Myla rubbed her arm, "I'm sure she's all soft and gooey inside, full of rainbows and butterflies."

Jake pointed at Tara again, "I think she's looking for us." Myla shook her hair out of her face when the wind whipped it onto her lips. "I don't think she likes me."

"You did cut her face open," Alex offered through a mouthful of biscuit.

"Not on purpose," Myla hung her head.

Swallowing, Alex set his hand over his stomach. "I don't think it matters if it was on purpose or not. She has a scar forever now."

Tara saw them and frowned, but she walked toward them, stepping around abandoned shoes and jackets.

"Well, here's a little secret for you, immune boy," Myla leaned over Cam.

"My name is Alex." The glasses slipped down the boy's nose and he sniffed.

I wonder if Myla thinks Alex is ordinary.

The girl half-crawled over Cam to get closer to Alex, her nose inches away from the boy's dirty lenses. She smelled like sea and wind and spice and made him think of a lake at night, her shoulders bare above the water and her mark a soft shadow on her skin. Some of it peaked out from the edge of her tank top as she stretched.

"Well, Alex, we are going to Salvation, where us mutants will be trained and thrown into an arena to give each other scars for the sake of fun and entertainment. By the time we're done or dead, we'll all look a lot worse than that. And you immunes," she dragged out the last word, "get to stay your pretty selves and serve tea." She sat back on the deck and hung her legs over the edge, hugging a railing post and looking at the water instead of the blond girl who sat down next to Jake.

Tara scowled at the back of Myla's head as she folded her legs under her, then turned to Jake. "Smith wants to check your bandages."

Jake looked down at his arm and tucked it more tightly into his belly. "Not now."

Myla twisted around and pulled her feet onto the deck. "Running errands for the Regulators? Making friends?"

Tara narrowed her eyes at the other girl. "Not as much as you're making friends with my brother."

"I'm not making friends with your brother. He just won't get the hint," Myla shot back.

Tara bit her lip, then lowered her voice. "Is Cam getting your hints?"

Oh, no. Cam sat up.

Myla glared.

Jake interrupted. "You could both give me hints. I'll get them, I promise."

Myla opened her mouth to say something else, but a pair of dirty feet settled on the deck floor and they all looked up at black skinny jeans, a faded green tank top, and a head of freckles and messy brown hair.

Hannah smiled at Cam when he reached her eyes. "Hey, we got a ball. Do you want to play?"

A boy stood behind her, barefoot and dirty, holding the Live or Die ball in his skinny arms.

A wicked smile peeked on Myla's face as she threw a glance at Tara, then disappeared when she turned enough to face Hannah and the immunes who were collecting behind the skinny girl. "I'll play."

Hannah looked at Myla. "No. I was asking Cam."

Oh great, more mutants versus immunes, Cam swallowed. He had felt relief when Hannah interrupted the argument brewing between the girls, but the tension hadn't left, just shifted.

Alex's hand shot in the air. "I'll play."

Screwing up her face, Hannah shook her head. "We'll see if there's room left on either of the teams for you, Puddles."

One of the other kids piped up, "Yeah, we don't want to break your glasses."

Laughter rippled through the immunes standing behind Hannah. The girl's freckles danced as she chuckled.

Hanging his head, Alex turned his attention to the biscuit in his hand.

Hannah folded her arms, "What do you say, Cam?"

Everyone looked at him, including the small crowd behind her. He flushed and stumbled on his words. "I don't think I can play yet."

After another glance at Tara and Cam, Myla caught Hannah's eyes. "I promise to be a good girl."

"Okay," Hannah shifted her weight. "I guess you can play. But I'm in charge."

Shrugging, Myla grabbed the railing and pulled herself up. "That's fine. I'm never in charge, anyway." She pushed past

Hannah and put her arm around the boy's shoulders, sliding the ball out from his arms.

Jake looked at Tara through the side of his eye. "You aren't down playing with the mutants?"

Tara's fingers went to her cheek. "I don't really like the game. Besides, I came to find you."

Myla said she's covered in thorns, but she really is kind of soft on the inside.

"Thanks," Jake gave her a weak smile.

Alex quietly chewed on his biscuit and picked at a thread on his pants.

Myla led the pack of immunes to a clear space on the upper deck. Larger than the lower deck the mutants had claimed as their territory, this level of the ship also had an empty pool near the back, and gaping rusty holes that marked where some large objects had been torn out.

Biscuit sprayed onto Cam's arm as Alex coughed. "Sorry," he said, his mouth full. "Got some in my throat."

The spots of half-chewed dough flaked off when Cam ran his hand over them. His skin had already turned a dark golden color, and the burn scar gleamed white in contrast. He scratched at his neck and watched Myla organize the immunes into two teams and go over the rules of the game, her face patient. She even smiled a few times as the kids caught on, her dark eyes bright in the stark sunlight.

Hannah stood against the railing, her arms folded and a scowl darkening her freckles.

The immunes organized into offensive and defensive groups and set up for a game to start. Myla pulled Hannah into the middle of it, placing the girl with the offense of the team facing Cam. A smile replaced Hannah's scowl as she settled her weight forward on her bare feet and picked up the ball once it came out of the starting huddle.

It was a short play. Myla stopped them and collected the ball, explaining some rule or other, then helped them set up again, a lot like Austin did with the twins the night they played at the depot. As Cam watched them, he found himself comparing the immunes to the mutants. The way they moved, the way they played together. The immunes had a harder time staying balanced on the moving floor of the ship, one boy tripping and almost losing the ball over the edge. Myla snatched it just in time and helped the boy to his feet, then handed the ball to Hannah to set up.

"She's good at this." Tara bit her lip and nodded toward Myla.

"Who would have guessed that she would have so much patience?" Cam asked without thinking.

Tara frowned and touched her fingers to her cheek again. Cam wanted her to smile, to shine in the sun like she had while they moved the rocks. He wanted to say something, do something that would pull her out of her thoughts. *We all need a distraction, a real distraction.*

Next to him, Alex swallowed and leaned his face on his hands.

"You really want to play this?" Cam nodded his head toward the mob of kids concentrating on the ball, and on Myla.

"Um," Alex shrugged, "I don't know. They didn't want me to play, anyway."

"I'm kind of bummed they didn't ask me," Jake said.

Alex smiled at him.

Cam squinted into the sun. "I can tell you, it's not that great. A lot of running and bruises." Waving his arm, he swept it the length of the deck, "Look at how many other kids aren't playing."

A couple dozen immunes dotted the edges of the deck like scattered leaves, some of them hugging the railing and looking out, others sleeping in the sun.

"I guess."

"What's with you and Hannah, anyway?" Cam asked.

Alex picked at a thread on his pants. "I told her once that I think she's pretty. That's when she started making fun of me, calling me 'Puddles' and punching me and stuff."

The crowd of immunes playing the game rippled open as Austin and two other mutants stomped through them. He stopped nose to nose with Myla, the mutant girl half his girth. Straightening her spine, she looked him dead in the eye and smiled.

The wind carried away their words as Austin's face twisted and he snatched the ball from Hannah, who had tried to hide it behind her back.

"Come on," Cam hopped up and pulled Tara to her feet. They pushed their way past some of the immunes, getting close enough to hear what the mutants were saying.

Myla had her hand on Austin's chest, her smile replaced by an angry scowl. "I can do what I want. I told you, those are your rules and not mine."

"When will you get it, Myla? We are *different*. Immunes and mutants don't mix." Austin's eyebrows pinched together and he swatted Myla's hand away.

"We're not that different, Austin. We're all still people. Maybe you need to get *that* through your thick skull." Myla leaned away and folded her arms. "Now give me the ball and get out of here."

The immunes watched in silence, some of them even holding their breath. His heart pumping, Cam edged through the crowd, stopping just behind Myla's elbow.

Austin's eyes shifted to Tara, who stood on the other side of Cam. He gave her a tense smile, "Hey, Tara, I was looking for you."

"Well, I wasn't looking for you," she put her hand on Cam's arm.

Chewing the inside of his cheek, Austin studied her for a moment, then held the ball in front of Myla's nose. "Fine, I'll leave you alone," Austin slapped his palm on the ball, "but you don't get this."

Austin and the two mutant boys who had come with him turned and pushed back through the crowd, disappearing down the stairs to the lower deck.

"Fine! We'll find something else to do, something that's better than your old game!" Myla shouted after them, stretching over the other kids on her tiptoes. When she came back down, she met Hannah's frown.

The skinny girl held out her hand. "Thanks for teaching us how to play."

Myla took it. "You're welcome."

Hannah smiled.

The crowd dissolved, everybody looking for something else to do. Several of them went to the back end of the deck, skirting the pool to find a place to watch the mutants who would be playing again below.

Austin had taken their ball, but at least he offered some entertainment.

Tara walked back over to the railing where Jake waited and Alex chewed on a biscuit and mumbled to himself. Cam caught a few syllables as he and Myla walked back over.

Dragging her feet, Myla flopped down onto the deck by Jake. "Ugh, Austin is so stupid, and I'm so bored."

Tara watched the ocean go by in little white capped waves, her back to them while the others sat where they had been before.

Cam caught the word 'engine' in Alex's mumbling and sat up. "I know what we're going to do."

They all looked at him.

"What are you talking about?" Myla asked.

"I'm talking about the ship. Smith said we could go down there, right?" Cam breathed more easily now, the thoughts of being a no-code retreating behind the possibility of an adventure.

"It better not be a game, or involve mutants and a ball in any combination," Myla looked at him sideways.

"No ball, but Smith did mention rats," Cam said.

Myla's eyebrow shot up. "Rats?"

Tara turned around and huffed. "So the tough Live or Die girl is scared of a few rodents?"

Myla looked at Tara and frowned. "They creep me out."

Tara's voice dropped. "There are worse things than rats."

CHAPTER 18

Rats

"Are we really going in there?" Alex backed away, his hand on his stomach.

Sighing, Cam stepped back and ran his fingers through his hair. "That's the only way to see the engine, Alex. We have to go inside the ship."

At their feet was a set of metal stairs, utilitarian, that twisted down through the ship in a square spiral. The railing and the steps looked like they were made of rust, with occasional smears of metal peeking through the dusty orange. Cam stood on the top landing while the others waited behind Alex on the deck galley that ran along the side of the ship. Alex clutched the doorway. Parts of the hinges still clung to the casing, but the door was missing.

Wrinkling his nose, Cam looked down at the metal stairs that turned back on themselves until he couldn't see them anymore. It smelled wet and slightly like urine.

He squeezed Alex's bony shoulder. "I think they're some kind of service stairs, you know, for the ship workers. Smith brought me up this way after he bandaged my neck."

"But you said there would be rats," Alex frowned at the metal and darkness.

"That's why I borrowed a flashlight," Cam pointed at Myla, who swung the flashlight from a short piece of rope.

She raised an eyebrow at Cam. "Where did you say you

got this?"

He shrugged. "I borrowed it."

"From who?" Myla asked.

"One of the Regulators. He wasn't using it."

"He handed it to you and said, 'Have a good time, kid.'?"

"Not exactly," Cam looked at Tara, who hovered next to Jake.

She blushed and smiled. *Nothing.*

Jake cleared his throat. "Cam is very good at borrowing things without the owner knowing about it."

Myla gave Cam a half smile. "I knew you stole it."

Cam returned the smile. *Unleveraged trade.* "I'll put it back and he won't ever know it was missing."

Tara peered at him over Myla's shoulder. "Like Mama Lucy's scissors?"

"You knew about that?" Cam was surprised.

"You're not the only one who knows how to steal," Tara huffed.

Alex sniffed. "I don't think I can go down there. Let's find something else to do."

"But you're fascinated with ships," Cam's shoulders tensed. *He's the one who won't shut up about the engine, and he doesn't want to go?* A thin tendril of anger curled in his gut, and he held on to it, using it to burn away the want—need—for a distraction from his secrets.

Alex nervously twisted his shirt around his finger, stirring up his smell and making Myla wrinkle her nose. For a moment, Cam couldn't tell if the urine smell came from the ship, or from Puddles.

Pushing his glasses up on his nose, Alex squinted at Cam. "Those were pictures," he held his hand to his stomach, "not something moving that has rats."

The tendril of anger singed along the back of Cam's neck.

"I'm with him on the rats," Myla put her hand on Alex's shoulder and leveled her eyes at Cam.

Tara chuckled.

Myla shot a glare over her shoulder at the blond girl. "I'm sure you're afraid of something. Happiness? Daisies?" She lowered her voice, "Your brother?"

Tara narrowed her eyes. "Like I said, there are worse things than rats."

Myla turned to Cam. "See, what did I tell you? Rainbows and butterflies."

"What is that supposed to mean?" Tara frowned.

Cam opened his mouth to interrupt when Alex sniffed and said. "Okay."

They all looked at the boy with the lopsided eyes.

"Okay, what?" Myla asked.

"Okay, I'm ready to go down there," he pointed down the staircase.

Cam snatched the flashlight. "C'mon," he half-hopped down the stairs and half-slid with his arms on the railing. Alex followed him, his bare feet testing out the first couple of steps before he met Cam at the next landing. Myla hopped over the railing and landed next to them, a grin on her face when she startled Alex and he almost fell down the next stretch of stairs. Tara and Jake were last. Jake was the only acquisition who had kept his boots and coat, the shoes echoing loudly on the metal treads.

Signs bolted into the wall at the small landing had lists and maps on them, grooved into plastic plates and painted. The decks were laid out in red and green lines, each section neatly labeled in tiny words. Other than some rust on the screws, the signs had held up well.

Cam moved over the list to the right of the maps. "Grand Ballroom, Golden Seahorse Buffet, Gilded Casino, Mermaid Theater, Black Pearl Spa, and Captain's Library." Cam looked over the railing and down the spiral of steps. "The engine room must be down there."

"We could start with something else, like the Gilded Casino," Myla tapped her finger on the tiny letters.

Cam turned to meet their eyes. "But I promised Alex the engine, and it's down there," he waved his hand at the abyss that sunk forty feet below.

"I agree with Myla, but I'd rather see the library," Tara said.

Myla gave her a surprised look, then asked Cam, "We have all day, right?"

Alex pushed his glasses up and sniffed. "Actually, we have four days left on the ship if you include today."

"Fine," Myla folded her arms, "we can start with the library."

Cam smiled. *At least they agree about something.* He waved them down another flight of steps. "Level 5 it is, boys and girls. Are you all sure you can handle the library?"

Myla elbowed Cam as she went by. "You're not supposed to be the funny one. That's my job."

Cam looked at Jake, expecting him to say something to top Myla's comment, but Jake just watched his boots thump down the stairs.

The door to Level 5 had only a few letters left before the number and read ' ev l 5.' The lock was completely broken off, and Cam had to pinch his fingers around the edge of the thick metal slab to pull it open. They walked into a short hallway with a windowed door at the other end that swung a little as the boat swayed. Myla stepped in behind Tara and Jake and the metal door behind them banged shut. The hallway went dark.

Alex gasped, and Cam switched on the flashlight. The beam streaked the white walls and hedged the door inside its bright white circle. Cam padded down the hallway and pushed the second door open.

It smelled like dusty, salty fish. They spread out in what appeared to be a lobby of some kind, couches in the shapes of shells circling scalloped posts that held a ceiling at bay, lounging chairs stretched in the shape of fish tails waiting by carved tables. The fabric on the couches and chairs was ripped, holes gaping where the stuffing had been pulled out. There was even a piano, the keys gleaming in the light. Everything was made of curves and scrolls and waves.

Cam paused as the flashlight passed over a tiny black nose with whiskers sniffing at them from a hole in one of the couches, then turned around and shined the light on the wall surrounding the door. A metal sign scrolled out *Black Pearl Spa* in gold letters.

"Was that a rat?" Myla hugged herself and stepped closer to Cam.

"Yes," Cam kept his eyes on the beam, "but I'm sure he's just as scared of you."

She scowled. "Maybe."

"Where do you think the library is?" Tara asked in a whisper.

"I don't know," Cam scanned more of the room with the flashlight. Toward the prow of the boat, small round windows dotted the tops of the walls, letting light leak in. "Let's see what we can find up there."

Tara nodded, hanging back by Jake, and they all followed

Cam as they crept further into the great expanse of the lobby.

The dark and the shadows suited Cam's mood. Even the rats that scurried along the edges and under the furniture reflected what he was hiding. *Maybe I'll end up in the dark, too, where nobody can find me. Maybe this is where I belong, buried alive in the middle of the ocean where nobody will be killed or die because of me.*

"Ugh," Myla said, "it really smells down here."

"Sorry," Alex groaned. "That's me."

"No," Cam felt sorry for the kid, who had been sick since they stood on the deck and listened to Smith give them the two rules. "It actually smells down here."

As they made their way toward the front of the ship, Cam switched off the flashlight and paused while his eyes adjusted. Something scuffled on the marble floor and squeaked. One of the girls sucked in her breath and whimpered.

Tara stifled a chuckle. "Just remember you're bigger than they are."

Myla's voice came out in a squeak. "This was supposed to be fun, right?"

"I'm having fun," Tara answered. Cam turned to smile at her, but she looked at Jake and wove her arm through his.

Jealousy twinged as Cam shoved the flashlight in his pocket and scratched at the bandage on his neck. He continued toward the prow, impatient now to find the library and get to the next floor.

Dim light streaked in through the thick, dirty glass of the windows and caught the edges of posts and counters and ornate pieces of furniture that Cam couldn't name. He walked behind a stretch of counter, bolted to the floor like everything else in the vast space, and caught the glint of metal out of the corner of his eye. Hesitating for a moment, he looked more closely. It was a knife, the blade about the length of his finger, wedged into one of the wood cabinets that formed a small bar. Cam reached behind him and ran his fingers over the scar at the base of his neck.

"There it is," Tara pointed to a set of thick doors, their wood gleaming in the subtle light. The other library walls were made of glass and the outer wall of the ship, three of the round windows arcing along the curve of the bow.

Captain's Library. It was in the same scrolled lettering as the sign for the spa.

"Ahhh!" Myla squealed as three black lumps snaked across the floor in front of her toes. She knocked Alex to the floor as she stepped back, cringing.

Jake leaned against another wall and offered a weak smile. "You know, Myla, they can smell fear."

"I can smell them, too," Myla pulled Alex off of the floor and looked at Cam. "Can I have the flashlight since you're not using it? I appreciate that you can see all of these creepy things in this dirty light, but I would like to see them before they see me."

The flashlight pulled the inside of Cam's pocket out with it, the coin and Dom's tags clinking onto the marble floor. Cam snatched the coin up before anybody else could, but Tara picked up the tags.

She ran her finger over the fire-smudged metal. "Dominic Landry," she looked up at Cam. "You have your brother's tags?"

Cam swallowed and stretched out his hand. The nightmare flickered at the edges of his vision and pressure filled his chest.

She held his eyes, her scarred mark hidden on the shadowed side of her face, like it had been when she stood in Mama Lucy's basement stealing fruit and canned goods. The others waited, hushed.

Slowly, Tara pooled the chain and the tags in Cam's palm. "That's where you went, isn't it? When you ran away from the Stalls?"

Nodding, Cam slid the tags and the coin back into his pocket and handed Myla the flashlight. The nightmare retreated, for now.

Biting her lip, Tara slid past all of them and pushed her way through the doors. The library was a single room, cozy compared to the vast lounge, with bookcases lining the walls and arranged back to back to create private nooks with cushioned chairs. A bench curved against the wall under a window, the cushion on it dusty but otherwise undisturbed except for a few of the books that had fallen off the shelves and landed there.

"This is what we came down here for?" Myla cleared the books from the nearest chair and propped Alex in it. Jake cleared another chair and sat down, his face withdrawn and strained.

Cam frowned and looked away.

"At least there doesn't seem to be many rats in here," Tara shrugged. Her face glowed as she ran her fingers along the spines, then she pulled one off the shelf. "Spartacus." She looked at Cam, "Wasn't one of your horses named Sparta?"

He cleared his throat. "Yeah. The other one was Crix."

"Did you name them?" she asked.

"No," Cam coughed and swallowed. "My mother did. That was her favorite book." He blinked back tears, grateful for the shadows.

"Her favorite book," Tara repeated as if to herself. She stretched the binding open, the ancient pages crackling in the gloom. "My mother used to read to us when we were little.

Devon and I would fight over her lap until she made us both squeeze between her arms and we would have to hold the book for her." Tara ran her fingers over the letters. "I loved turning the pages."

Myla left Alex groaning in the chair and stepped next to Tara. "My mother never read to me."

Tara glanced up from the book and met Myla's dark eyes. *Sunshine and shadow,* Cam swallowed.

Myla rubbed her arm and took a deep breath. "I didn't mean to do that to your face. Where we played before, there wasn't anything like that to run into. I wasn't watching." She held out her hand, "I'm sorry."

Tara closed the book and reached her hand up to her face, looking at Myla's outstretched fingers. Her hazel eyes glanced at Cam before she clasped Myla's hand. "I know."

CHAPTER 19

Fingers

Two levels below the library, the engine room door wouldn't budge. Cam tried to open it anyway, pulling against the lock and bracing his foot against the wall.

"Well, I guess our little adventure is done," Myla shrugged. "Or we could go for the casino."

Cam stared at the painted white metal and balled his hands into fists. Heat washed through his body and he broke into a sweat.

"What are you doing, Cam?" Tara asked in a low, careful voice.

"I'm going to take Alex to see the engine, Tara. I promised," Cam looked at her. "I promised him."

"It's locked," Tara argued.

Cam waved her away and faced the door. He grabbed the lock and tried to pull it off, grunting. When that didn't work, he kicked at the heavy metal with his bare foot, the impact vibrating through his leg. He tried with his fists, angry now like he had been when Smith shot the puppy in the head, and managed to dent the metal but the door still didn't budge.

He turned to the others, breathless and sweaty.

They all stared at him. Alex hid behind Myla, hugging the flashlight. The dark girl frowned and held on to the stair railing, her foot on the bottom step of the flight they had just come down, and Tara had bit her lip hard enough to make it bleed.

Jake sat down on the stairs and leaned his head against a metal post.

Reaching around Myla, Cam grabbed the flashlight from Alex and pushed past Tara to descend the final flight of stairs. A shallow layer of water covered the landing.

"What are you doing?" Tara called after him.

"Looking for another way in," he stopped in front of the door to Level 2, the light from the top of the stairs dim this far down.

It was unlocked. He pulled at it just to make sure, and it let out a loud creak.

"Hey, come down!" He could see their feet through the space between the stair treads, not moving. "Hey!"

Myla's head peeked over. "I don't think Alex wants to go any more."

"I found a way back in, only one level down from the engine room. I'm sure we can find a way in there."

She shrugged.

Cam raced back up the stairs. "Hey, Alex," he put his hand on the other boy's shoulder, then pulled it back. His knuckles were raw, blood smeared across the backs of his hands. He looked at the door.

Thin streaks of blood marked the dents in the metal.

He turned back and looked at the face with the lopsided eyes. "Hey, Alex, we can get in on the level below the engine room. I'm sure we can find a way up to Level 3."

Alex looked at him a moment, then stepped back by Myla. She put her hand on the boy's shoulder. "It'll be okay. I'm sure there's nothing down there worse than the rats."

Squinting, Alex twisted his head around to meet her eyes. "Are you talking to me or to yourself? I'm afraid of the rats, but not even like you."

Myla rubbed her arm and shrugged.

Alex turned back to Cam. "Okay, I'll go, but just to see the engine. I'm done after that."

Cam nodded and smiled. His knuckles started to sting as he gripped the railing on his way down to Level 2, this time with the others following. Myla and Alex kept up right behind him, but Jake and Tara were only a couple steps down.

Hovering near Jake, Tara caught his good arm when he stumbled.

Cam swallowed, "Jake, are you up for this? Maybe you should find Smith first, get that arm cleaned up."

Jake's face looked pale and yellow in the shadows of the stairwell, dark circles clinging to his eyes.

Tara opened her mouth to answer Cam, but Jake cut her off. "I'm just tired."

Tara shot Jake a look, then bit her lip and nodded.

Cam ran his fingers through his hair. *Something's wrong.* Jake, who never let anybody speak more than two sentences without cracking a joke, had only said one thing since they had found the entrance to the stairwell. "Maybe you should stay out on the deck in the sunlight."

"I'll stay up there with you," Tara gently squeezed Jake's arm, her fingers pulling on the fabric of his coat sleeve. "We should find Smith."

Tugging his arm out of her grip, Jake wrapped it over his bandaged one, wavering before he settled his balance. "I'm not staying up there while he gets to go," he pointed his chin at Alex, then gave Tara a pleading look.

She frowned and met Cam's eyes. "He's just tired."

The door to Level 2 opened into a hallway like on Level 5, but instead of another door at the end, this hallway stretched farther than the flashlight would shine. It was lined with doors, rust leaking onto the white walls from hinges and knobs. It looked like the hallway Smith had walked him through after bandaging his neck, only that one had higher ceilings and most of the lights worked.

This one looked more like a nightmare.

The water on the landing continued inside, parting around Cam's ankles as he waded into the hallway far enough for the others to follow. The door creaked loudly as it swung shut, leaving them in the fringes of the glow from the flashlight.

"This is what we left the library for?" Tara's voice echoed eerily off of the metal doors and the water that covered the floor.

"Better than a bunch of books," Myla kicked at the water and it splashed onto Cam's leg.

"Hey!" he jumped back, his toes landing in a strange slime.

"Well," Myla said, "is it just me, or isn't the water supposed to be on the *outside* of the boat?"

"I don't think this is right," Alex looked down. "What are we standing on?"

Cam dug his big toe into the muck. "Carpet, I think. Old, mushy carpet. Must have been under this water for a few years." Something slid past his ankle and he shuddered. "There are things in here, in the water."

"I felt one, too," Tara said.

"Rats?" Alex's voice shook.

Cam shined the flashlight on Alex's glasses, the light reflecting in the dirty lenses. "Yes, I'm sure it's just rats, Alex."

"Better be just rats," Myla mumbled.

A sign on the wall pointed left to the engine room. "This way." His neck was hot and itchy, and he reached up to scratch it, forgetting about the bandage until the gauze caught on his fingernails.

They sloshed down the hall, this time Alex behind Cam, then the girls and Jake. Some of the doors were closed, their room numbers peeling from decorative seashell-shaped doorplates, while others swung open on rusted hinges with broken knobs and blackness beyond. Except for the beam from the flashlight, there was not even enough light for shadows to live.

Keeping the beam high, Cam pointed it into the empty rooms as they passed. He saw beds, television sets mounted on the walls, toilets—each one was like a separate, small house. *People could have just run away on boats when the plague came, just lived out at sea. They could have done something other than die.* A drip echoed from somewhere in front of them, the sound hollow and vibrating. He sucked in his breath as something bumped against his leg, floating up and down as the water waved with the sway of the ship. He stepped back against the wall, his elbow catching on an open door that hung unevenly from a single hinge.

The impact jarred his arm and he dropped the flashlight. It fell in the water, the beam shining like a strange beacon on the debris caught in the ankle deep water. A bloated rat brushed against Alex's leg and he screamed, leaping onto Tara as Cam snatched up the flashlight. Myla whimpered and hugged against Tara, who now looked like a deformed monster made of extra limbs and round eyes. Jake leaned against the wall behind them.

Cam shook the water off the flashlight and aimed it at their knees so he wouldn't blind them. "Sorry, I won't do that again." The saltwater stung on his raw knuckles.

The monster unwound into three separate people, Alex

fixing his glasses but staying right by Tara, and Myla kicking
at the rat to send it into a room they had just passed.

Tara scowled at Cam. "Why do we want to see the engine
room?"

"Alex likes to see how things work," he answered.

She didn't say anything, just waved at him to keep going
and pushed Alex along, who took a deep breath and kept his
hand on the wall.

They came to another hallway that branched to the right,
and another string of doors and room numbers. Cam shined
the light on the walls, searching for the sign that would tell
him which way to go.

There wasn't one.

He swallowed. "There aren't any directions here."

The other three stopped behind him, and Cam pointed
out where the sign had been broken off. "Which way do you
think it is?"

"I say we go back," Myla was quick to answer.

Tara gave Myla a smirk, "Scared of a little water?"

In the small hallway, Myla didn't even have to move to be
inches away from Tara's face, the dark girl's narrow eyes mere
slits. "Did you see that rat? What if we get lost down here?
We'll be dead, or worse, we'll have to eat Alex to survive."

"Huh?" Alex sniffed, "Eat me?"

Cam put his hand on Myla's shoulder. "We're not going
to get lost. I know exactly where the stairs are."

She nodded and screwed up her nose. "It smells worse
down here."

"I know," Cam waved them down the hall to the right,
keeping the flashlight beam too high for Myla to see anything
floating in the water.

They passed three doors that were closed, then Cam

shined the light into a room that had no door at all, not even part of one hanging from the hinges. He saw the toilet and the TV, like all the other rooms, but when he scanned the flashlight over the bed, rats scattered at the light, screeching as they hid themselves in the crevices of the room.

There was a body on the bed.

He wouldn't have seen it, leaned up against the wall at the head of the bed with its legs sunk into the rotting blankets, but a hand hung over the side, the fingers curled like claws. It had been the fingers that caught Cam's eye as the flashlight passed over the room.

"Hey, guys?" he lowered the beam, whispering. The dripping sound seemed to echo more loudly as he waited for them to say something.

"Cam?" Tara stood beside him by the doorway and looked into the room.

He lifted the light. She gasped and stepped back into Myla, who was waiting for them to move on.

"Hey!" the dark girl whispered hoarsely. "What are you doing?" She tried to peer over Tara's shoulder. "Is it more rats?"

Tara shook her head. Then Myla saw it, too, and swore.

Alex didn't even look, and Jake was still leaning against the wall in the hallway.

Creeping into the room, Cam swept the light over the bed to flush away any more rats. Tara followed him, but Myla stayed in the doorway.

It was a boy, probably their age, with no shirt, his tags hanging against a hollow chest. The rats had eaten through most of his face and the tops of his shoulders, but the rest of his skin was a pale, almost translucent white and the exposed flesh bloodless. Past the end of his pants, the rats had also eaten the soft skin from between his toes.

"Was he an acquisition?" Tara whispered.

"I don't know. He looks too, um, eaten to be one of our shipment." As Cam reached for the tags, he heard a retching sound and stopped.

"I think Alex is ready to move on now," Myla held Alex's shoulders, the boy bent over and heaving.

"We should tell Smith about this," Tara pulled on his arm.

Cam took one last look at the face that was nearly a skull, the eyes black and hollow even in the direct beam of the flashlight.

Death's Head.

Then the flashlight sputtered and went out.

CHAPTER 20

Nothing

Cam heard a splash and a strange gurgle as he shook the flashlight back on. Alex had fallen face first into the shallow water, his arms flailing as he struggled to get back to his feet. Myla pulled him up by his pants and half carried, half dragged him down the hallway. Cam followed, keeping up with the flashlight.

Out in the stairwell, Alex heaved in the corner. Cam wrinkled his nose at the sight, but the air was a lot fresher than inside Level 2. Myla waited a couple of steps up and Tara leaned against the wall next to the door.

"Where's Jake?" Cam looked at them.

Tara bit her lip and looked through the door that squealed on its hinges.

"Jake," Cam bolted back inside, the flashlight flickering as he splashed down the hall, trying to remember the turns to the room with the dead boy. He found Jake sitting in the water, slumped against the wall with his bandaged arm cradled against his belly.

"Hey, Jake," Cam tucked the flashlight by Jake's bandaged hand, wrapped Jake's good arm over his shoulders, and scooped his friend up in his arms. Jake moaned and his head flopped against Cam's cheek. *He's burning up,* Cam's heart raced at how little his friend weighed. *As easy to break as a chicken's neck.*

Cam kicked the door open with his foot and stepped out

into the shallow water of the landing.

Myla still waited on the steps, and tears brimmed in Tara's eyes.

The tendril of anger that had been simmering all day burst into flame.

"You knew!" Cam yelled at Tara. "You knew he was sick, didn't you?"

"It's an infection, Cam, in his arm. Smith saw it before we got on the train, and he still let him come. Smith was hoping he'd make it to Salvation. He said they have medicine there."

Cam clenched his teeth, trying to think through his rage. "Smith?"

Alex wiped his face on his sleeve, silently watching next to Myla.

Tara blinked away her tears. "He might be in the infirmary."

"Take me there."

Leaping up the stairs, Tara led Cam up two flights and in through the Level 4 door. Cam remembered it from the day before when Smith bandaged his neck. The 'infirmary' was a service room near the front of the ship on Level 4, an internal room with no windows and the hanging bleak light that washed out the already white walls.

No Smith.

The cot where Austin had been sleeping was stained where the mutant's head had been. The pile of gauze had grown, shoved under the other cot, and smelled of blood and antiseptic.

Tara held the door open, avoiding Cam's eyes. He laid Jake on the cot and felt his friend's cheek. The fever painted streaks of red on his pale face, and he fought for quick, shallow breaths.

"Find Smith," Cam heard the click of the door as he tugged Jake's coat off and looked at the bandage. Blood spotted through where the arm had been pressed to Jake's stomach, the red tinged with yellow and green.

"Hey, Jake," Cam spoke softly as he picked at the bandage. Jake looked at him through glossy, fevered eyes. Cam continued, "Smith is coming. He'll know what to do."

Pus and blood crusted the gauze, the smell running down Cam's nostrils and sending bile up his throat. Fear squeezed at his temples.

Jake's breathing paused as the boy shook, then the panting resumed, faster than before.

"Move over, son," Smith's hand was heavy on Cam's shoulder.

The sound of Tara returning with the Regulator—or soldier, or gladiator, or whatever he was—had been drowned out by Jake's panting. Cam backed up so that Smith could squeeze by, and he bumped into Tara.

"You knew," Cam fought to keep his voice steady. "You both knew."

Smith kept his back to Cam. He fished a syringe and a bottle out of the med box and bent over the fevered boy.

Behind him, Tara's voice was soft. "He asked us not to tell you."

"Why?" Cam asked.

"He said you had enough nightmares."

Images of Dom flashed through his mind, no longer held at bay by panic. The pus and blood, the smell of rotting flesh, the pain in his chest every time he thought of his brother.

And now Jake was dying.

Cam slid his hand in his pocket and ran his fingers over Dom's tags. "Why didn't you stop him?" he spoke softly at first, then turned to Smith and let anger fuel his voice. "Why didn't you make him stay?"

Smith set the box down and faced Cam. "His blood is poisoned. And he knows, Cam. If I had left him behind at the depot, I couldn't have waited for the infection to kill him."

Cam's fingers curled into fists, his raw knuckles stretching over his bones.

"You don't want to do that, son," Smith's hand settled on his knife. "We need you. We all need you, but we can't keep you if you are too much of a liability."

I don't care. You are Salvation's bastard, and Jake is my friend. He swung, but Smith saw it coming and had Cam pinned to the wall by his throat. The knife had just been a warning, meant to scare Cam into backing down, but the old man didn't need it. His hands were enough, iron claws that cut into Cam's windpipe and crushed his wrist. Cam grasped at the fingers pinned around his throat with his free hand.

Smith's eyes burned through him. "You don't get it, do you? You are the one we need, *alive.*" His eyes flitted toward Jake. "You could let this get easier, you could practice *watching* your friends die. One by one, killed by the plague or by each other in the arena. Or you could save them, save us all."

Cam tried to swallow, Smith's hand squeezing tears from his eyes.

The old man let go and took a step back. "I have done everything to get you this far, but if you don't decide that you want to live, not even the fires of hell can save you. You have to stop taking chances, son," Smith pressed his finger to Cam's chest, "because in Salvation, when someone threatens to kill you, they mean it, and then this," he pointed his finger at Jake, "will have been for nothing." He looked at Tara. "Take care of his neck, and his knuckles."

Tara nodded, and the old man left.

Fighting for a steady breath, Cam swiped at his tears.

"Here," Tara said gently, taking his arm and setting him down on the stool. Cam stared at Jake while she fussed with the medical supplies. Jake's chest rose and fell, his breathing shallow, but steadier. He had his eyes closed and his head lolled to the side. Whatever Smith had given him had at least eased the pain, though Cam could almost see the heat of his fever. A single layer of gauze still clung to the mangled arm, stained and stinking. Jake had always been gangly, but now he looked hollow, like a piece of fruit eaten through by a worm.

I promise I won't leave you to rot in the dark. I won't let the rats have you. He turned at the smell of antiseptic. Tara lifted his hand and dabbed his knuckles. Her fingers pressed into his palm, warm and distracting. She stood with her right side to Cam, and he studied the thin, jagged scar that cut her strawberry mark in half on an angle.

Like butterfly wings. Cam tilted his head to match the angle of her scar. He glanced over at Jake, relieved to see his chest rising and falling, then studied Tara's face as she concentrated on his hands. A lock of hair escaped her braid and hung by her eye, catching on her lashes. He tucked it behind her ear and a tear fell down her cheek.

She drew a deep breath and leaned close, the base of her throat at his nose, and ran her finger over the tape by his ear. The touch drew Cam's anger and hurt into a line of heat and sent it down his spine as he watched the pulse in her throat. *One, two, three...*

Then she pulled back her hand and her breathing shifted as she inhaled and held it. She worked her fingertips along the tape again as she exhaled, and Cam realized she was shaking.

He put his hands on her shoulders and stood up, holding

her steady.

"Hey," Cam said softly.

She looked at him, her hazel eyes swimming with fear and pain. "Jake...that boy, the water," she said with a fragmented breath.

Wrapping his arms around her, Cam's heart skipped, then raced. She trembled against him, her head tucked against his neck by his jaw. Her hair smelled like straw and salt air and sunshine and she was warm through the thin cotton of her shirt, pressing his tags into his chest.

He held her as her trembling slowed and her breathing settled, memorizing how her body fit against his. Then she pulled away and looked up at him, tears trailing heartache down her cheeks. *I always thought you were beautiful*, he had said to her out by the rocks.

He brushed a tear away, tracing the scar from her ear down to her chin. And he kissed her.

Warm and soft, she tasted sweet, like apples. Cam pulled her to him, his body tingling from a heat that simmered low in his belly, flaring out and rippling up his back and down his arms. He trembled then, dizzy, afraid he would crush her if he held her too tightly.

Then she pushed away and gasped, stumbling a little as the boat swayed, and fell against the wall.

"Tara," Cam choked out, not sure what to say. He reached to take her hand and she waved him away.

"Cam," her eyes were dark, pained. "We can't..." she didn't finish, just shook her head.

"Why?" The heat that had filled his body when he kissed her turned back into frustration. "Why? Because of Jake?"

"No, Jake wanted us to be friends."

"Because I'm a no-code?"

"It's not just that," she stood up, matching his frustration. "It's a lot of things."

"Like what? Things like Devon?" Cam hit his hand against the pipe on the ceiling and winced.

"That's not it."

"But it is," Cam put his hands on her shoulders and tried to make her look at him.

"No," she pushed him back onto the stool and grabbed the gauze.

Cam swallowed. "I thought you were… I know you stayed in here for Jake, but I thought you also stayed for me."

She picked at the roll of gauze. "I did stay for you, but it's more complicated than that, Cam. I can't just do what I want, like Myla."

Cam watched her fingers work angrily at the flimsy fabric, then she realized that she still had to take off the old bandage and dropped the gauze on the cot. She leaned over his neck again and picked at the tape, tearing a small section off before Cam grabbed her wrists and brought her hands together.

"Why can't you do what you want? Tell me," he said softly, controlling the heat in his body that was a mix of frustrated desire and his anger over the boy dying on the cot.

"I can't," her face fell and tears glossed her eyes.

"Why?"

She bit her trembling lip. "Because I don't know how."

"Just tell me."

She pulled her wrists from his hands and leaned over him, the heat gone from her as she worked at the tape surrounding Smith's neat bandage. "Just tell you? It's not like you and I have had a lot of conversations, you know, like two humans." She taunted him with his own words from Mama Lucy's cellar.

I'm the one who's not human. Cam's heart sped as he thought of Mama Lucy's words, *You're not even supposed to exist.* Heat still coursed through Cam's body, flaring as she leaned over him, and he gripped the edge of the cot to keep himself from touching her.

She finished picking the tape off halfway down his neck and slowly peeled off the rest of the bandage. Her hand froze, holding the gauze stained with blood and antiseptic inches from his neck.

Cam's heart skipped a beat. "What?"

"No-code," Tara exhaled.

Cam caught her eyes. "What's wrong with my neck?"

"Nothing," she said with surprise.

Like the scratches from the dog.

"Here," Tara took his hand and pulled it across his chest to his shoulder, "feel it."

His skin was clammy from the antiseptic and gauze and his fingers stuck a little as he ran them along where the railing had shredded his neck. But she was right, his skin was smooth, like he had never even hit the railing post.

She circled a fingertip around the edges of the burn from Devon. "All you have left is this. Why?" She took a step back. "What are you?"

"I don't know," Cam answered softly.

She pointed at him. "Immunes don't heal like that."

He stood and ran his fingers through his hair, careful to avoid the ceiling pipe. "I'm not a mutant. I don't have a mark, Tara. You've seen me," he leaned toward her, "You've seen *all* of me and you know there's no mark."

She bit her lip. "I tried not to look..."

"But you did, didn't you? You watched the Scout search my entire body and find nothing."

She didn't respond.

"Please tell me you saw that, Tara." He put his hands on her shoulders, pleading. She still stood there, a pained look on her face. "You have to see, then. You have to know," Cam unbuttoned the top of his shorts.

Blushing, she stopped his hands with hers, the color almost making her left cheek match her right. "Okay, I looked."

Cam exhaled and fastened the button. "I don't know why it's like this, but I'm not a mutant, I swear. I can't be one of—" he cut himself off and looked at her.

"One of what?" The color quickly drained from her face.

"I meant to say," Cam sighed, "that I can't be like Devon."

"You mean a mutant," she folded her arms. "I don't know what you are, except that Smith says you're special, that you could be the cure. That I could be killed because I know." She searched his eyes. "But I'm a *mutant*, Cam, like Devon."

Cam was at a loss. Everything he had just said echoed in his head.

Tara swallowed. "He's my brother," her voice dropped, low and secretive. "I know he's cruel and careless, but he wasn't always like that. He changed, but it wasn't his fault," her voice broke on the last word.

"What happened, Tara?" Cam reached for her.

"Nothing," she answered. Tears filled her eyes and she stepped over by Jake, out of Cam's reach, and ran her fingers over the dying boy's cheek. "Goodbye," she whispered softly, and walked to the door.

Cam caught her and curled his fingers around her arm.

She glanced over her shoulder at his tags and his scars, the butterfly-shaped mark turned toward him as she waited for what he wanted to say.

"I want to be friends, Tara," his heart caught as she met his eyes. "I want you."

She blinked. "That's what you want?"

He nodded. "What do you want?"

"Forgiveness."

Cam would have asked who needed to forgive her, but he already knew. He was somewhere else on the ship, shut away as an uncontrollable beast, with a matching mark and blond hair.

What Cam didn't know was *why*. But whatever it was, it sat like a dark thing inside of her, sucking away her light.

I always thought you were beautiful.

She looked at him one last time, pain flashing through her hazel eyes.

I wasn't talking about the outside.

And she walked away.

Chapter 21

Friends

Cam blinked in the harsh light, his neck tight from leaning on his arm. Jake's hand was cold, his fingers stiffening within Cam's.

Sitting up, Cam watched Jake's chest for movement even though he already knew what he would see.

Death. He had seen it before, when he carried his mother out to the stack of wood that he and Dom had built to burn their parents. Death was silent. Death was cold. Death was endless.

I'm sorry, Jake, Cam fished Dom's tags out of his pocket, along with the coin from Mama Lucy. *I wasn't fast enough. Dom told me to be invisible, and I couldn't do that, either.* He looked at the coin, the skull watching him from the burned and bloody metal. *But I have one promise I can still keep.*

He put the tags and the coin back in his pocket and stood up. He wondered what time it was since the bleak light in the infirmary never changed, never even blinked at the stained gauze piled on the floor. Jake's tags sat on top of his shirt, gleaming silver. Cam gently slid the chain over his friend's head, remembering the way Tara had touched his cheek to say her goodbye.

Jacob Lee, Immune. He rubbed his thumb over the name etched in the metal, then slid the tags in his pocket. *I will remember.*

The body was even lighter than it had been only hours ago when Cam had carried Jake out of the blackness of Level 2. *Empty.* Cam hugged him close, ignoring the smell of his infected arm.

The gray twilight of morning hovered over the ship. Cam blinked, the memory of rot and wet and blood blown away by the ocean breeze. He headed toward the front of the ship, toward the foredeck where the sun teased the horizon. *Because the rats run from the light.*

White caps foamed along the prow as the ship cut through the ocean. Endless. Cam leaned the body against the railing and looked at the gray surface that stretched forever. He had thought about what it would be like to sink into the deep, dark blue. To be done seeing, hearing, *feeling.*

I think, in the end, you are the lucky one. Cam looked at Jake's face, the skin pale but no longer drawn in pain. *I will see the arena for you, I will see them fight, I promise. I'll be strong.*

He knew it was time, but he couldn't let go. Instead he held the body closer, feeling Jake's ribs shift under the pressure. The sun peaked up, lighting the edge of the world with a stripe of gold. *The others will be up soon.*

Cam leaned over the railing with the body, tears choking him. With a single sob, he flung Jake out into the water and watched as he floated on the waves, then slowly sunk beneath the surface, disappearing as the ship headed relentlessly east.

Not now. Cam took a deep breath to stop the tears. He pulled out the tags, holding Jake's in one hand and Dom's in the other, gripping them so tightly they cut into his palms. He took the pain and the tears and shoved them down in his gut where they would wait until he was ready.

I will remember. He put the tags away and closed his eyes. I will remember.

Bootsteps crossed the deck, the weight and rhythm familiar.

"Long night?" Smith kept his voice low, rough against the sunrise, and leaned on the railing next to him.

Cam nodded and kept his eyes on the ocean.

Smith stood next to him for a long moment, then cleared his throat. "Pretty damned sometimes to be one of the living."

"Seems like I'm pretty much damned either way."

A little higher now, the sun glowed like the eye on Smith's cheek, the reflection of the clouds rippling in the water like the four chevron marks, two on each end of the eye.

The old man shifted his weight, his voice underscored by the rush of the water against the prow. "I know something about goodbyes," he glanced at Cam, "and losing friends."

Cam kept his eyes on the water.

Smith took a deep breath. "She was dark, black as night, but her eyes shone like the glint of the sun on a polished piece of steel. Your girl Myla would look pale as the moon next to her. A mutant. Fought like a tiger, she did," he chuckled, "in the arena and out of it. We were both in the House of the Four Horsemen, trained under the same whipmaster, although we rarely fought in the arena together. We fell in love, I would say, but I was too young, like you, to know what that was."

But none of us are too young to know what death is. Cam swallowed and curled his fingers on the railing.

Smith's voice wavered for a heartbeat. "I lost her. We were no longer kids, but seasoned fighters, both of us with our House signs complete. It's discouraged for mutants to form attachments. They caught us together one night, behind the weapons room. The owner sold her to another House."

"Did you ever see her again?" Cam asked quietly. The

wind was calm, riffling through his hair and brushing along his bare chest.

"Once."

Behind them the acquisitions stirred.

"What do I have to do?" Cam's throat hurt from swallowing tears. He swallowed and looked at his hands on the railing. His knuckles were smooth, not even a hint that he had raged at the engine level door only hours earlier.

"Stay alive, son."

"Yes, stay alive no matter how many other people have to die, how many of them you have to kill, how many of them you have to dump into the ocean," he choked on the last word, pausing to breathe. "What if someone shoots you?" he looked at the Regulator. "What happens to me and Tara if someone shoots you? What happens if they find us?"

Smith toed the deck with his boot before he looked at Cam and answered, "Get to the House of the Three Kings."

"One of the gladiator Houses?"

Nodding, Smith looked back out at the water.

Cam stood straight and stared at Smith until the old man met his eyes. "If something happens to Tara, or to Myla or Alex, I'll make you pay." He put his hand in his pocket and curled his fingers around the tags and the coin. *Promises and secrets.*

"If something happens to you, we'll all pay," Smith's blue eyes were steady.

The Regulators called for rations. Cam followed Smith to the back of the ship where the acquisitions lined up in two rows as mutants and immunes. They looked even more ragged than they had the day before, and Cam raised an eyebrow when he saw Myla and Tara next to each other.

A Regulator with sandy blond hair and freckles walked

the lines and counted, his face sunburned from long days of pure sun and dry from the wind. Several of the immunes were also sunburned, including Hannah, who looked quite pink under her brown hair, but the mutants were merely shades darker than they had been when they boarded the *Princess Katherine*.

"One hundred seventeen," the Regulator finished counting.

Two missing. Jake and Devon. Even through his grief, Cam was relieved that Devon was in isolation for one more day.

Breakfast was more hard biscuits, two each, with mold coloring the edges. Cam scraped the bluish green fuzz off and found a place to sit by the railing, watching the water churn behind the ship. Alex followed him over and plopped to the deck.

"What kind of food do you think they will have in Salvation?" Alex picked at the mold on a biscuit and sniffed at it.

Cam kept his eyes on the water. *Numb,* he put a name to how he felt. He didn't even know if he *should* care about what Alex was saying. After talking to Smith, he had put the grief and the anger behind a wall. *A day until Devon gets out, then two days to Salvation. Always waiting.*

Alex looked at Cam with his lopsided eyes. "Are you going to eat that?"

Half of Cam's biscuit sat in a pile of crumbs on the deck, protected from the breeze by his legs. He handed the rest to Alex.

"So, do you think they'll have them?" Alex asked. From his tone, Cam guessed that Alex had asked him the question at least once already.

"Have what?"

"Tomatoes?" Alex blinked.

"Sure," Cam watched the other acquisitions mill about the deck, slowly organizing themselves into groups. The immunes gathered in pairs or groups of three, and the mutants gravitated toward the Houses that Austin had organized on the first day aboard the ship.

Alex chewed the biscuit, smacking his lips.

The sound grated on Cam's spine and he scowled at the other boy. Alex didn't seem to notice.

"Hey, Cam," Myla's voice sounded warm behind him before she and Tara circled around and sat down.

Tara offered him a shy smile and something in the numbness stirred but disappeared without breaking the surface.

Squinting, Alex looked at each of them. "Where's Jake?"

Myla snatched his arm and held him inches from her black eyes. "Jake's dead."

His face pinched in pain, Alex nodded and Myla let him go. He stared at his feet. "Sorry, I always say stupid stuff like that."

The scar on Tara's cheek twitched and tears filled her eyes, but she bit her lip and blinked them back. Something stirred in the numbness again.

Myla shrugged and rubbed her arm. "Just pay attention, Alex."

Alex took a bite of biscuit, still staring at his feet.

The mutants spread out into a circle, the crowd cutting off Cam's view of the center and all he could see were bruised legs and the edges of frayed shorts.

Laughter carried by on the breeze, and Cam looked up at Hannah and her friends skirting the mutant crowd as they headed to the stairs. The skinny boy who had held the Live or

Die ball the day before walked closely behind her.

Cam watched her dirty feet pad by until she stopped. She scowled at the two mutant girls, then pinned her eyes on Alex.

He glanced up and squirmed like a bug.

"Hey, Puddles, gonna puke up that biscuit when you're done?" Hannah stood with her hand on her hip. Her friend must have caught the look on Myla's face because he scurried away as fast as he could.

Myla jumped up and grabbed Hannah by the throat, suspending the girl above the deck. "What did you say to my friend?"

Hannah couldn't answer, only claw at Myla's hand as her face went red. Her freckles stood out on her cheeks, and Cam's heart thumped. *Peter.*

"Let her go, Myla," he stood.

She dropped Hannah onto the deck and frowned at Cam for a long moment, then glanced at Tara and Alex. "I'm going to see what the mutants are doing."

"I'll go with you," Tara hopped up, avoiding Cam's eyes, and followed the dark girl.

Cam rubbed at the scar on his chest and watched the two girls disappear in the crowd. The immunes were gone, scattered along the galley or on the upper deck where Hannah had hurried as soon as Myla let her go.

"They're gone," Cam told Alex. With the reminder of Peter, pain had broken through the numbness and Cam panicked as the tears threatened.

"I know," Alex kept his head down.
"Let's go," he tugged the boy to his feet. As much as Alex annoyed him, Cam had more fear of being alone with his memories.

"Where?" Alex struggled to keep up.

"I want to watch," Cam ran up the stairs to the upper deck.

Alex tripped halfway up and cut his shin on the stair, wincing.

They settled on the railing that looked out over the mutants' deck. Smith stood several feet over, frowning at the scene below.

The mutants crowded around an open circle, creating an arena with their bodies. Austin and the kid with the big nose faced each other in the middle.

One against one. Cam didn't think that the big nosed kid had a chance against Austin. He saw a couple of the other Regulators on the edges of the deck, glancing at the crowd, but not nearly as interested in the situation as Smith. *At least they're even out here. Smith is the only one I've really noticed around.* He studied the old man with the scar on his face, who had been a gladiator, a fighter, a slave. *What would he face if the others found out what I was and that he knew? Would they shoot him? What would happen to Tara?*

The two mutants in the arena locked arms, and it was only a breath before Austin had the other boy on his back crying for it to end. With a grin, Austin stood and raised his arms as the crowd cheered.

"I can't see," Alex squinted down at the mutants.

Cam ignored him as Myla pushed her way into the center, and Tara followed. He gripped the railing until he felt the metal threaten to give under the pressure. *Tara?* From what Cam had witnessed, Tara had reluctantly joined the House teams for games, but now she stepped willingly into the makeshift arena with the girl who had tackled her into a brick post and cut her face open.

As the two girls circled each other, new cheers and taunts

carried up from the crowd. Even a few of the immunes yelled and made bets on who would win. Cam fought the urge to jump onto the lower deck and stop them, then Tara looked up at him. She touched the scar on her cheek before turning to face Myla, her shoulders set and her weight on the balls of her feet.

What is Tara doing? Cam ran his hand through his hair and clenched his jaw. He trusted Myla in everything except this. In this she was ruthless.

Myla rushed at Tara, but Tara stepped aside, catching Myla's arm and spinning her into the crowd. Myla swept Tara to the ground and followed her down. They grappled, forcing the front row of onlookers back into the second and third rows, then moved back into the center. Finally, Tara held Myla down with a knee and pinned both of her arms to the deck. After a few moments, Tara stood and helped Myla to her feet. The crowd cheered. Tara looked around, dazed, as if she had forgotten they were watching. Myla took Tara's hand and held it up, and the cheers grew louder.

"Thank you," Alex said next to him.

Caught up in watching the girls, Cam had forgotten the other boy was there. "For what?"

Alex shrugged and ran his hand along the railing. "For being my friend."

CHAPTER 22

Expectations

A cloud blotted out the stars and Cam watched as the inky black space passed and the tiny shards of light winked on again. The moon arced high to his left, a growing crescent that shone like the silver of Cam's coin. He lay on the deck, turning the Death's Head Dollar over and over in his palm. Beside him Alex slept, rolled tightly in his coat and snoring.

Thank you for being my friend.

I never meant to be your friend, Cam confessed to the darkness. *I never meant to be here at all, but I made a promise.* Peter's small face floated in the stars. *I made a pinky promise.*

The Stalls and Peter seemed far away and with every breath Cam took, Salvation and the unknown grew closer. But right now there was the Death's Head Dollar, the tags collecting in his pocket, and the endless water.

Cam thought about the mutants on the lower deck, mangling each other in fun. The new game was wrestling, like he and Dom had done as brothers, but with a layer of deadly tension. He had watched Smith as much as he had watched the pairs of mutants grab at each other, trying to pin their opponent and earn the win. The grizzled Regulator had just watched.

Is that what it's like in the arena? Cam had asked him after the head count that night. The old man had leveled him with his eyes and said No, then left to bandage a few who were bleeding too much, even for mutants. Myla seemed to relish it all, cheering when she wasn't fighting. The initial excitement became serious as the competition went on, ending with a match between Austin and a boy who was taller and almost as thick whom Cam had not really noticed before. Austin pinned the other boy as the Regulators walked the deck to call for the head count, the crowd of mutants dispersing reluctantly to form a bruised and bloody line.

As the matches had gone on, Tara had slowly worked her way back into the crowd, her golden hair moving away from the center and out of the sea of mutants who pushed and pulled for their turn.

But thoughts of the fighting were only a distraction from what kept Cam awake, stretched out on his back, watching the clouds pass over the stars. He was awake because he didn't want to dream, didn't want to remember. Visions of Jake and the dead boy in the cabin below mingled with his final memory of Dom, and when he closed his eyes, he saw pus oozing from the dead boy's neck and the hollow eyes called his name, *Cam...*

Even across the ocean, the chains of memory bound him.

The silver dollar had become a familiar weight in his palm, and Cam ran his thumb over the skull and crossbones etched over the face.

Footsteps padded by, almost silent on the smooth deck. Cam craned his neck and caught a shadow creeping through the sleeping acquisitions toward the front of the boat, a shadow with long black hair.

Myla.

The deck felt clammy under his hands as he pushed himself to his feet. The shadow slipped past the stairs and hugged the railing toward the small deck at the front of the ship. As he followed, Cam noticed the curves and nooks the immunes had found to sleep in out of the wind, their clothing and hair not so ragged and torn in the thin moonlight.

"Cam," a hoarse whisper breathed. It came from behind an arched section of wall, something that might have once offered privacy to a couple sitting in lounge chairs and sipping drinks like in the cruise ads Cam had seen. He peered at a thin girl leaning back into the corner, a boy curled up on the deck beside her.

"Hannah," Cam answered.

"Where are you going?" she started to get up.

"No, wait," he stopped her, "I wanted to be alone."

Her eyes narrowed, "Myla just went that way."

"Did she?" Cam ran his fingers through his hair, "I'll have to watch out for her, then. Goodnight, Hannah."

He left the girl glaring after him and found Myla on the foredeck, wrapped around a post with her legs dangling over the edge of the ship. She didn't turn around as he sat beside her, but she smiled, her full lips pushing against some new cuts on her face.

"Couldn't sleep, either, huh?" her voice was warm in the cool night. "Nothing else to do on this forsaken hunk of rust, and we still can't sleep. Seems unfair, doesn't it?" Her legs swung with the motion of the ship, the wind gusting and pulling at her ponytail. "At least sleeping lets you forget."

Cam shuddered as the images of death fluttered through his mind. "You don't seem to sleep anywhere."

She shrugged, "No, not really. Haven't slept much since I was dropped off at the daycare."

"You went to a daycare?" Cam asked. He thought of Peter and the other kids who had come to the Stalls from a daycare.

Nodding, Myla scratched at a cut on her arm. "Yeah, when I was three." She tilted her head back to look at the stars, and grew quiet. Usually Myla did most of the talking, sometimes even too much, but tonight she seemed more thoughtful, lost inside somehow.

Cam had been thirteen when the Second Wave passed over the world, and Myla was about his age. "Did your parents die of a rogue strain?"

She shook her head and the wind picked up for a moment, flipping her ponytail across the back of her shoulders. "They didn't die, at least that I know of. I assume they died in the Second Wave like almost everybody else's parents, but I don't know."

The railing was cool against his cheek, and Cam watched the water billow out like wings as the prow of the ship sliced through the ocean.

Myla continued, her story punctuated by the wind. "I wasn't taken to the daycare because my parents died. I know that's how most of us get there, picked up by the Regulators, but my parents took me there. My mother, actually. All I remember is the woman who ran the daycare, Mrs. Jansen, giving me some bread, and I remember that the walk to the daycare with my mother was the longest walk of my life," she frowned at the water. "I don't remember her, not much, anyway, but I already had the mark on my shoulder. Mrs. Jansen told me that my mother brought me to the daycare because she couldn't feed me anymore."

Three years old. Cam thought of Peter, who had been taken to his daycare by the Regulators in the manner that most orphans were collected. Like Myla, he had been only three. Peter was seven by the time he was sent to the Stalls, and he still whimpered in the straw at night. Cam sat quietly and closed his eyes, feeling the night air against his bare legs as they dangled next to hers.

"The daycare was okay, and I think Mrs. Jansen actually cared about us. We slept on mats on the floor, six or seven of us in a room, and there was a window. It came down low enough that I could see outside," she rubbed her hands on her legs, "but she never came back."

He opened his eyes and looked up at the stars. Now he understood why Myla wandered in the dark, restless. *She's still waiting for her mother.* Goosebumps prickled Myla's arms, and Cam shivered against a gust of wind. Even though he didn't feel cold, the gusts teased him, and he could tell that Myla was worn, bruised from a day of fighting.

"Do you know what it's like to be a mutant your whole life?" She looked at Cam with a sad smile, "To be different like that?" She sniffed, fighting tears, and looked off at the distance, at the water that was deeper and darker than the night sky. "Once the other kids were old enough to understand what I was, that I was different than they were, they wouldn't play with me anymore. Mrs. Jansen hid my mark by making me wear shirts with sleeves, careful that they didn't have any holes in the wrong place, but somehow they always knew." She shivered against a gust of wind, "I knew."

Cam had thought mutants were like Mama Lucy and Devon, cruel and somehow missing a piece of their humanity. Then he had gotten to know Tara, met Myla, and started believing that maybe they weren't like that, that maybe mutants and immunes were the same.

Rubbing her arms, Myla looked at him with her black eyes. Moonlight streaked her hair, her caramel skin pale in the silvery light. "You're lucky to be an immune."

"Lucky?" Cam nearly choked on the word. Mama Lucy

had called him an accident. *You're not even supposed to be alive.* What would Myla think if she knew?

Her face fell. "You're lucky that you don't have... *expectations.* Everybody thinks they already know what a mutant is, what we're good for. How we'll live, how we'll die," she sighed. "When I was small, young enough that I still had friends, I wanted to be a daycare lady, like Mrs. Jansen." She smirked at herself, "I thought I could choose."

"Why can't you?" Cam had never looked at it that way. *What would it be like to know your whole life that you'd be sent away to fight? Probably die like that?* Myla was gritty and fought hard, but she also had a kindness in her, and a patience that Cam had seen in few people.

"Do you really not understand?" Myla's eyebrows went up. "Do you really think that we all *like* being mutants?"

Cam shrugged. "Well, yeah."

She looked at him stone-faced, then burst out laughing.

"Shhh!" Cam swept his eyes over the deck to see if anybody was awakened by the sound. "How can you find that funny?" Even though he tried to keep a straight face, Cam could feel himself frown.

"Listen to us!" she whispered between giggles. "Do you hear what we're arguing about?"

"No, I don't," Cam could feel the heat crawl up his neck.

She took a few breaths and smiled at him. "We're both on this ship bound for Salvation to be whatever they tell us to be. We didn't decide any of this, Cam. We didn't decide if our DNA would bond or if we would be immune."

I didn't decide to be. . . whatever it is I am.

Her eyes looked out at the darkness, and she rubbed her arms. Her voice was soft, "We should be fighting together, against them."

Once you set foot on that shore, you will be on one side or the other, Smith had told him. He looked at the girl in the moonlight, her black eyes and caramel skin. *We will be fighting, Myla.*

"What would you fight for?" Cam asked out loud. Images of burned houses with weeds growing through the windows, broken toys and bike wheels, and streets littered with rusting poles and smashed glass was most of what Cam had seen of the world. But there had been people, too, families in front of their homes, with children *playing.*

"I don't know," Myla said, "but there's got to be something."

An end to the dying. Cam cleared his throat. "Yeah, something."

Myla's voice took on a playful edge, "What has you up tonight?"

Dead things, Cam thought, but said, "Thinking of that game the mutants played today. It's just wrestling, right?"

"Yeah, but Smith talked about what it was like in the arena, what the fights are really like," Myla became animated, her hands talking with her.

"When did you talk to Smith?" Cam narrowed his eyes.

Myla looked down at her swinging feet. "When you were down in the ship with—" she paused and looked at Cam.

"Jake," he finished for her. "When I was down in the ship with Jake."

She took a deep breath and shifted her eyes to the ocean. "Jake."

They listened to the water and the wind and watched the clouds carve blackness out of the stars.

Myla finally broke the silence. "Did you watch us?"

Cam nodded, his eyes still on the stars.

"The game that Austin obsesses over is only part of it.

They also pit us against each other one on one," she sighed. "Austin's game is getting boring, anyway. It's hard to play it for real, on a ship, with the Regulators watching."

His blood pumped at the memory of the mutants fighting. "I saw you and Tara."

"Exciting, huh?" Her eyes sparkled as she waited for an answer, a mischievous smile playing on her lips.

"You let her win." It was a statement.

She shrugged. "Maybe."

"You did."

"She needed something, Cam," Myla leaned her cheek against the railing post. "She doesn't believe she can do it."

Cam nodded. "Do you believe *you* can?"

She held his eyes for a moment. "I have to."

"Expectations?" Cam raised an eyebrow.

"Exactly," she smiled. "I could see you as a fighter. Some of the other kids told me you played like a champ against Devon, even scored a couple times."

"I was just trying to stay out of his reach until you and Smith came back up, that's all." Cam shrugged and looked up at what stars he could see. The clouds grew thicker and the wind settled as the deep night sky started to fade.

"Still," she shifted against the railing post and brought her legs up onto the deck, "if you can do that, I bet you could do pretty well in a fight."

"Yeah," he avoided her eyes, "but going against Devon in the game had nothing to do with strength, just being smarter."

She pulled herself up and held out a hand, the smile still on her face. "Are you kidding me? I watched you dent a metal door. Let's see what you got."

Hesitating, Cam leaned back, glancing at the sleeping ship.

"C'mon," Myla waved her fingers. "I promise I won't hurt you."

Her hand was cool and dry and slim in his as she tugged him to a standing position and led him to the middle of the small foredeck. Backing up, Myla spaced a body length between them and made him look into her black eyes.

"You're faster if you keep your weight on the balls of your feet and your stomach tight. Almost all of the kids start out with their hands up like this," she followed her own instructions, setting her body into a semi-crouch, her fingers curled like claws. She looked like an upright mountain lion, one with long legs and caramel skin.

Cam copied her, the deck slightly gritty under the balls of his feet. "Like this?"

Her ponytail twitched when she nodded. "And keep your eyes on me, but not on one spot. Make sure you can see all of me, especially my arms and legs."

Cam nodded and smiled at her. "You know all of this just from the fights on the ship?"

"It works for the game, too, same principles of balance and speed, but you only have to watch one opponent instead of a whole field." She started to circle, her bare feet silent.

Matching her, Cam became aware of the way the pressure on his feet traveled through the rest of his legs and through his torso, small muscles twitching and tensing as he moved. "You sure you don't mind being a mutant? You seem pretty excited about the fighting."

She chuckled and lunged After a flash of black eyes and white teeth, Cam lay on his back with Myla's hands pinning his shoulders and her knee on his chest.

"I do like the fighting, but I like winning even more," she looked at him, the light of a gray dawn cutting across her narrow eyes, and Cam could see her heart beating at the base of her throat. She pulled her knee off his chest and slid down next to him.

"And I like you," she whispered, and kissed him.

Cam's heart pounded and heat spread from his chest. Her lips were full and warm and her body stretched against his. She tasted sweet and bold, like honey and spice and adrenaline, and she *wanted* him. Cam ran his hand up her arm to her face, and she kissed him harder, her fingers tracing his collarbone, his shoulder, and down his chest. His other hand on her hip, he rolled her on top of him and her fingertips dug into his skin.

A Regulator shouted for the acquisitions to line up for the head count.

Myla pushed herself up and gasped, her breathing ragged. Trembling, she stood up and offered Cam her hand. "I guess we're done," she smiled.

The sun hid behind the clouds, the air heavy and tense. The foredeck sat empty except for him and Myla, but Cam could hear the Regulators pacing the ship and waking the others. Her hand was warm this time and her caramel skin flushed. As soon as Cam was on his feet, she skipped toward the back of the ship, her black hair swishing behind her.

Cam followed, running his hand along the railing as the acquisitions who slept in the nooks and crannies stirred. He passed the arc of wall where Hannah had stopped him, and she stepped out and poked her finger into his chest.

"Is that what you mean by 'be alone'?" her brown eyes accused him, "Making out on the deck with a *mutant?*"

He frowned. "It's none of your business."

Hannah planted her feet, blocking his path. "Can't be around the immunes anymore, huh? We're not good enough for you now that they let you play their little game?"

"Why do you care, Hannah? It has nothing to do with you," Cam said.

She dropped her arms. "They get everything."

"Well, they'll get our breakfast if we don't get in line," he pushed past her, shaking his head. *Nothing's fair, she should know that.*

As he rounded the wall that hid the service stairs, he froze. It had been two days.

Devon.

CHAPTER 23

Before

Devon saw him as soon as Cam stepped onto the deck.

Cam swallowed and got in line next to Alex, on the other side of the ship from where Devon stood next to Tara. Her hazel eyes were sad when she looked at Cam, and her mouth formed a warning, *Run.* Then her twin grabbed her face and turned it away.

Devon rubbed his palms together and shifted his feet, agitated as he waited for a Regulator to count heads. *One hundred eighteen.* No one in the infirmary. No one in isolation. The only one missing had been given to the sea.

Clouds hung overhead, dampening the early morning light and casting shadows over the ship.

Tracking the other players on his imaginary game board, Cam saw Myla waiting with her hip cocked and a smirk on her face as she sized up the other mutants, probably thinking about the new game, and Smith stood at the head of the lines, scowling at Devon.

At least Smith's watching, though Cam doubted the old mutant could get down in time to stop Devon if he came straight for him. The other Regulators seemed to be paying more attention than they had been the past two days, but Cam didn't trust them to *do* anything. The line dissolved into a scramble for the last few biscuits, and Cam backed away through the crowd, his eyes scanning for Devon's blond head.

He caught sight of a golden braid and hesitated.

Tara pushed through the acquisitions and handed Cam a stale biscuit, her eyes frightened. "Go," she pushed him toward the front of the ship, then disappeared into the crowd. Searching for Devon, Cam saw the blond mutant looking over the railing of the upper deck. Although still tan, Devon was pale next to the other acquisitions, having been deprived of the sun for two days wherever they had been holding him, and Cam knew there were dark places on the ship.

"Hey, Cam!" Alex yelled at him. "Where are you going?"

Devon's head snapped over and he grinned. Cam met the hazel eyes for a flash and his belly tightened. *Run*, Tara had warned him with her sad eyes. But on the ship, Cam couldn't run, he had to hide.

Cam edged toward the section of metal wall that hid the service stairs, trying to get out of Devon's sight before the mutant saw where he was going. He made it past the bottom of the deck stairs just as Devon got to the top, the other boy's steps a soft slapping on the treads as he came down. Ducking into the service stair entry, Cam heard Devon behind him.

"Piggy boy, come here, piggy boy. I got something for you."

Looking down the stairwell, Cam realized he wouldn't make it to the darkness at the bottom in time to hide, and Devon would have him trapped on the stairs.

"Piggy boy," the voice that had haunted him for seven months echoed like a snare down the narrow shaft.

Cam gripped the railing and swung himself over the side, hanging from his hands, and shifted his fingers to the support beam below the stair treads.

"Piggy boy," Devon whispered from the doorway into the stairwell.

His heart pounding, Cam willed himself not to shake as he swung one arm to the beam on the other side of the treads. Hanging from his fingertips below the top landing, he tucked his legs up and gripped the back edge of a tread with his toes, praying that Devon would look down the stairs instead of at them.

The blond boy stepped onto the platform, sending vibrations through the metal. Cam's muscles twitched with strain, sweat beading on his skin in the heavy morning air as he held his breath.

"Where are you, Pig Boy?" Devon leaned over the railing and chuckled. "You dropped your breakfast." His voice fell on the last word, deep and ominous, as crumbs of biscuit sprinkled like dry rain from the landing above.

Blood pounded in Cam's ears and he adjusted his grip. The edge of the beam cut into his fingers and the tips started to throb as he looked down and swallowed. *He knows I'm here.*

Another voice echoed off the metal and emptiness, "What are you doing here?"

Smith, Cam nearly lost his grip as his heart skipped with relief.

Metal creaked as Devon turned around and leaned his back on the railing. "Just eating my breakfast alone, sir."

"I know where you can go to be alone. Otherwise, stay on the deck," the Regulator growled.

"Yes, sir," Devon answered, and the metal groaned as the boy left.

Cam dropped to the landing below, cringing as the hollow 'boom' echoed through the stair shaft. He sucked in his breath and listened, crouched and ready. After several heartbeats, Cam exhaled and fell back against the wall.

Blood still pumped through his body, but it was easing,

and his fingertips stopped throbbing.

He chases you because you're the hardest to catch, Tara had told him. And Cam had swallowed the bait—the race by the docks, the game that sent Devon into isolation, and now this.

Will he ever stop chasing me? But Cam knew the answer. *When he catches me. For good.*

The morning light that managed to filter down through the stairs was dim, casting a gray shadow over the already dark stairwell. *If he won't go below, then I will.* He listened, but the sounds of the acquisitions on the ship were distant, small fragments of shouts and cheers that floated on the still, heavy air.

They're playing the game. I hope Devon is with them, and that someone pushes him into the rudders.

The door to Level 5 was one flight below him as he stood up, the paint peeling off and the lock missing. *The library.*

Cam paused and played with the tags in his pocket. That wasn't where he needed to go. There was something else he needed to do, something he needed to know.

Level 4 was lit, as it had been the other two times Cam had been down to the infirmary. *It's the same as Level 2, only this level is the dream and Level 2 is the nightmare.*

The bleak light still washed over the white walls, and the bloody gauze on the floor smelled rank. Cam only looked at the cot where Jake had died long enough to find the flashlight on the floor below it.

Back out in the stairwell, Cam hurried down two flights of stairs to the landing on Level 2. He stared at the door and weighed the flashlight, cold water sloshing over his feet. It wasn't fear of what he thought he might find in there that had him frozen, it was what he knew he would find.

Hinges squeaked as the door swung with the sway of the

ship, and Cam looked up at the sky. Clouds choked out most of the blue, a mix of white and gray that drifted over the hole at the top of the shaft.

A storm is coming. He switched the flashlight on and pushed the door, the water licking at his ankles as he stepped into the long, black hallway. The smell of rot and decay hit his hollow stomach and Cam gagged. Holding his breath, he swallowed, then crept past the rooms that waited like empty coffins in the dark.

He came to an intersection he recognized and stopped, shining the flashlight down the shorter hallway to the left. *A few more steps. . .*

The flashlight went out, and Cam braced his hand on the wall. His heart raced in the pitch black of the ship's belly as he shook the flashlight and it sputtered on. The beam was dim, like the light in a fog, and Cam waited for his breathing to settle before he sloshed through the water to the room with no door.

The boy's hand hung off the bed, the fingers clutching at some invisible thing. Cam watched the rats scurry into the shadows as he stepped into the room and stood next to the bed. The boy would have been smaller than Cam, built more like Jake. His tags nearly sunk into the concave depression of his half-eaten chest.

Now that Cam stood more closely, he saw a patch of discolored skin on the upper part of the arm that sat between the boy and the wall.

He's marked. Cam ran his hand through his hair. *How did a mutant die here?*

The boy answered him with hollow eyes.

A rat climbed out of a hole that had been eaten through the boy's chest, its long whiskers twitching on its nose, and took a bite off the edge of the flesh that stretched over the corpse's shoulder. Shuddering, Cam took a step back and turned to leave, then stopped.

He shined the flashlight through the hole in the boy's chest, scaring the rat back into the dark as he leaned in to take a closer look. The rib bone had been split, the ends shattered and splintered.

He was shot.

The memory of the outpost Regulators' dead eyes flashed at Cam and he stumbled back, sick. He wretched over the end of the bed, his empty stomach twisting in on itself until he closed his eyes and forced it to stop.

Why? He grabbed the tags and pulled, the boy's head bobbing onto his shoulder as the chain slid out from behind it. Cam's stomach turned as he shoved the tags into his pocket with Dom's and the coin, then he hurried to escape the room, and the rats, and the dark.

As he hugged the wall down the hallway, he stepped on something hard that sunk under his foot into the mushy carpet. *Alex's glasses.* He stepped back and fished through the water, pulling the frames out and stuffing them into his other pocket.

Out in the stairwell, the air hung thick and gray. Switching off the flashlight, Cam looked through the treads and railings at the low, dark clouds. Shouts carried down from the deck, eager and aggressive. Cam set down the flashlight and sat on the steps, out of the water.

I can't hide down here forever. Anything left down here is just food for the rats. But he wasn't ready to go back and face Devon. Not yet.

He slid the boy's tags out of his pocket and pulled the chain up, feeling queasy when he saw a few tendrils of pale flesh clinging to the round links. The tags dangled in front of him as he looked at the name etched on the front, the name the boy's parents had given him, who he *was*.

But Cam forgot about the name as soon as he looked at the slices of metal. Where they should have said 'Mutant,' they were blank.

Cam dropped the tags in the water. *Why isn't there a code? He was marked. Why don't his tags have a code?* Cam fished the other two pairs of tags out of his pocket, then retrieved the dead boy's out of the water.

Both Dom's and Jake's tags had 'Immune' etched below their names in precise letters, but those of the dead boy had nothing. Cam curled them hard against his palm. *He had a mark but he was a no-code.*

And he was shot, left for the rats.

Cam stuffed the tags in his pocket and picked up the flashlight.

Level 5. The heavy metal slab swung in with a groan and Cam switched on the flashlight. The beam was dim but it was enough, and the lobby opened up behind the second door at the end of the short hallway.

Everything curved in elaborate exaggeration, couches and chairs spread out among fluted columns. *All this for the rats and the ghosts.*

As he neared the front of the ship, he came to the counter and bar that he had passed the first time he came through with the others. The knife was easy to dislodge from the wood, still sharp and small enough for a degree of precision.

It would be enough, better than the long hunting knife that hung from Smith's belt.

Light through the foggy round windows dispelled enough of the shadows that Cam could turn the flashlight off. His eyes scanned the ornate furniture, watching for the sleek, black bodies of rats. He saw one poke its head out of a hole in a velvet lounge chair, but otherwise they all seemed to be hiding. *Like me.*

The heavy wooden doors to the Captain's Library swung silently as Cam stepped into the room. Bookshelves, cushioned chairs, and the padded window seat waited in the dust.

He dropped into a chair, shaking. The small scar was a tiny ridge at the base of his neck, and he pressed on the tiny cylinder lodged to the left of the bone. His tracking chip.

He set the tip of the knife on the scar, but it slipped as his hand trembled and he brought it back down to his lap.

No-code. Shot. You're not even supposed to be alive. Salvation is at war, son. Cam pressed a hand to his face. *I promise.*

He stared at the blade, willing his hand to steady. He knew the cut would heal with no scar. In just the last few days he had changed. He had grown inches since leaving the Stalls, taller than Tara now. The gashes from the dog attack that had riddled his chest and belly were gone, along with the scrape on his neck, only the burn from Devon remained. He didn't think he could survive a bullet to the heart.

If they can find me, they can kill me.

The air smelled of molding velvet and musty paper as Cam sucked in a deep breath and raised the knife again. He found the cylinder with his fingertip and gritted his teeth. The blade sunk in half an inch before the pain followed, shooting down his spine and up into his skull. He grunted as he slid the blade out and fished the cylinder out of the cut. It was solid black under the blood, as long as his finger was wide, and smooth. He threw it on the floor with the knife and dropped his face into his hands.

Let the blood run, Cam shivered as it trailed down his spine. *I deserve the pain.*

He sat like that for several breaths, counting his heartbeats as they forced the blood down his back. He sat up when it slowed. *It's already healing.* The wound was wet and sticky with blood, but the skin around the knife cut had started to knit back together.

I can run away, but what about Tara? Cam had studied the scar on Peter's neck, looking for a way to cut out the small boy's tracking chip so that Cam could take him when he ran, but the muscle had grown around it, and the chip sat deep and too close to the spine. In Tara, it would be even deeper.

Tara. Ever since he had caught her stealing from Mama Lucy's basement, Cam had looked at her differently. He had always thought she was beautiful, like human gold, despite the mark on her face. But he had seen her as part of Devon, and everything Devon touched became tainted.

Now he knew that she was not like Devon, that she cared and grieved and liked to help things heal. *She's like sunshine, and just as hard to hold.* But he had held her, long enough to taste the heat inside, long enough to see the darkness in her that was drowning her soul.

What do you want?

Forgiveness.

He dropped his head and pressed his hands to his eyes. *What am I doing?* A short while ago he had been on the foredeck with Myla, her body pressed to his. She had kissed him with the same kind of determination she had when she played the games.

And he had kissed her back.

Black hair and black eyes, Myla was the night sky and the sea, her caramel skin warm and inviting. She was easy to talk to, easy to find, and she wanted him.

But in the end, they were both mutants and he was a no-code.

Cam sifted through a pile of books on the floor. He picked one up, a big, thick book about sea life with color photos, then another that had to do with politics and citizenship. Moving to the shelves, Cam found poetry and plays, and as he reached for a volume of short stories, he saw a blue spine with the title in gold.

Spartacus. His mother's favorite story. Tara must have put it here when they left the library, tucked between illustrated myths and an encyclopedia of Roman gods. He pulled it out and sat down on the window seat, the light gray and even through the round window, and ran his fingers through the pages. They were yellowed with age, crisp and brittle but still flat, the words arranged in neat lines as they spelled out a story of blood and freedom.

His mother had been a kind person who laughed easily and loved pretty things like flowers and lace. But she had also been practical and their survival had come first, giving her a firm hand when it came to dealing with nonsense from her sons.

Cam had loved her more than anything. His father had been a good man, too, but more reserved, and he had always spent more time with Dom than with him.

The fire that consumed his parents' bodies had lit the predawn sky, the smoke heavy. Dom and Cam had built the pyre together, finding branches and damp straw in the cold frost of early spring. But Dom had been the one to set the blaze, nursing a pile of tinder until it caught and flamed. He had been calm that day, his face flat and thoughtful as he held a sobbing Cam. It wasn't until three days later that Dom gave in to his grief, smashing all of the windows and punching the brick, his hands shredded and bloody. Cam hid that day in his parents' closet and cried himself to sleep.

And now he had watched Jake die. He had buried his friend in the nameless, endless ocean, all because he had failed to save him from a dog. He missed Jake's jokes and the way he smiled, even after Devon gave him a bruise for saying something too loudly. He missed knowing that there was at least one person who would care when he woke from the nightmare.

What does it matter now? He's dead. They're all dead.

That wasn't the part that was hard, the part that hurt when he dreamed and remembered. What hurt, what suffocated him and stopped his heart, was that he had *survived*.

Closing the book, Cam hugged it to his chest and curled up on the thin, dusty cushion of the window seat.

And he cried.

Chapter 24

Burial

A boy's scream jolted Cam's spine as he stepped out of the Level 5 door and onto the landing, peering through the growing shadows for someone on the stairs. More shouts and cheering echoed from above, and Cam shoved the flashlight into his pocket with Alex's glasses and ran to the top of the stairwell.

Whatever's going on, I hope it has Devon distracted. The air outside of the stairwell was oppressive, and Cam felt like he was breathing water as he craned his neck around the wall that hid the stairs from the mutants' deck. No one, not even a straggling immune.

A cheer went up, followed by more shouting. Praying for his luck to hold, Cam shot out from behind the wall and took the stairs to the upper deck in twos, looking for Smith.

The old man was there, gripping the railing so hard his hands were white as he watched the deck below. It was surrounded by immunes shoveling and tussling around the empty pool, all of them trying to get closer to the edge to watch.

Watch what? Cam's heart raced. He spotted Hannah and hurried over, working his way through a small crowd of girls who cringed at the scene below.

"What's going on?" he asked as he secured a place along the railing.

She glanced at him, her freckles stark against her pale face, and pointed.

He looked down and his heart stopped. On the deck below, the mutants surrounded a small arena, shouting and shoving, those closest to the center holding the others back. Austin was one of them near the center, his thick arms stretched in front of a handful of yelling mutants. Myla was on the other side of the ring, her arms held in the unyielding grip of two boys as she fought to get free.

Two boys circled each other in a crouch, their bodies streaked with blood. One of them Cam didn't recognize, but the other...

Devon. Blood rushed to his ears as he scanned the roiling crowd for Tara. He found her a few rows back, fighting to break through the kids in front of her, screaming as the fighters locked arms and Devon took the other boy down to the deck.

The clouds churned overhead and the air moved, softly at first and then frenzied. Cam glanced at Smith. *Where are the Regulators?* Then he saw them at the edges of the crowd, battling to get inside, but they were held back by mutants.

More blood ran on the deck. Devon leaned over the other boy, his arm pumping as he punched him over and over again. Excited and sickened at the same time, Cam looked over at Smith again.

The Regulator held his gun, aiming carefully at the center of the arena. Cam watched the finger on the trigger as it slowly pulled back.

He's going to shoot Devon. The thought held both fear and hope. Cam held his breath, waiting.

Smith raised his arm in the air and shot the sky. Thunder rumbled and the clouds shook, unleashing a flood of rain.

Acquisitions scrambled to get down from the decks as the ship lurched sharply, but Cam's hands stayed locked to the railing as the Regulators shouted for everybody to go below to Level 4. He heard screaming and chaos behind him, and turned to watch one boy slip and skitter toward the stairs, then he saw Hannah fighting against Smith as the Regulator dragged her by the arm. Other immunes crawled or slid as the ocean twisted and stretched below them.

Get up, Cam urged silently as mutants scattered and the boy Devon had been fighting lay still in a puddle of rain and blood. *Get up.* But the boy did not move. One other figure still stood on the deck, her blond braid like a rope down her back and her white tee shirt becoming translucent in the rain.

The ship rocked as Cam let go of the railing and he slipped, going down on one knee, but he pushed himself to his feet and rushed down the stairs. Tara had fallen to her knees, braced on the deck by her hands, her eyes riveted to the mangled body.

"Tara!" Cam shouted, his cry muted by the rain as he ran to her and pulled her up. She stood like a rag doll, dead weight in Cam's grip, staring at the dead boy. His face and throat were smashed in on one side, his nose bent over to his cheek, and the blood that had been smeared on his body revealed gashes as the rain washed it away.

Cam shook her, "Tara!"

Slowly she turned her head, her eyes glazed over and distant. The ship heaved and she fell into him.

Cam wrapped his arms around her and hugged her close, bracing them both against the anger of the sea. "Come with me."

She grabbed onto him as the deck dropped, and they scrambled toward the stairs. The ship swelled and tilted as they reached the doorway, pitching Tara into the railing.

She screamed as her hand slipped off his arm and she slid toward the ocean.

Cam gripped the edge of the doorway as his body swung out, and Tara disappeared over the edge of the ship. Scrambling along the deck, Cam caught her wrist as her fingers slipped from the railing post.

"Cam!" Tara's fingers bit into his wrist and she swung her other hand up and grabbed his arm. He steadied his foot against the post and pulled her up, then kept a firm grip on her wrist as he led her into the service stairs and down to Level 4. The metal shaft was strangely quiet after the violence of the storm outside. Rain came in through the top, making the treads slick under their bare feet, and Cam listened to it slosh in the bottom as he reached for the door.

"No," Tara curled a hand over his shoulder, "Devon will be in there."

Cam turned and searched her eyes.

She took Cam's hand when he let go of her wrist and led him back up the stairs to Level 5. She pushed the door open, then hesitated at the pitch black inside.

"Here," Cam let go of her hand and pulled the flashlight out of his pocket and switched it on. The light flickered, then went out. He shook it but it didn't come back on, and Cam dropped it back into his pocket. Curling his fingers in Tara's, he tugged her inside. "Stay close."

She nodded and squeezed his hand.

The floor shook and moved, but it was calmer inside than out on the deck where the swells had nearly thrown Tara from the ship. In the hallway, they steadied themselves along the wall, but out in the open lobby they had to fight to stay on their feet, feeling their way through the dark past the chairs and columns. Meager light shone through the library's glass walls, and Cam tugged the heavy wooden doors open.

Books skidded along the floor and fell off the shelves. Cam shut them in the room and began clearing the shelves of one of the nooks. Tara came over to help, and Cam could see her shaking as she pulled volumes off and tossed them on the other side of the room. Snatching the cushion from a chair, he set it on the floor where the shelves met in the corner and pulled Tara down into his arms. She clung to him, her body shuddering from more than just the cold.

"Here," he sat up, shivering, and tugged at her shirt, "we have to get you warm."

Her hazel eyes questioned him, "I don't..." her teeth chattered and she couldn't finish.

"I promise. Just let me hold you." *I know you don't want me,* Cam thought about how she had pushed away from his kiss in the infirmary. "I promise nothing will happen."

She gave him a weak smile and managed a word, "Nothing."

He pulled her shirt off over her head, and she fumbled with her pants until Cam stood her up and helped her with those, too. Her legs were long and muscled, her hips curving out from a tight waist. Her arms and face were golden tan, but her skin was paler where her clothes had kept her hidden from the sun. Her tags fell inside the thick white fabric of her bra, and she wrapped her arms around her middle as she watched Cam drop his shorts. The heavy, wet cargo fabric had sagged down below the top of his underwear He emptied his pockets and spread the clothes on the shelves to dry.

"Here," his voice caught, and he settled her gently beside him on the floor. Her body curled against his, shaking, and he tucked her to his chest with his arms. Her hair dripped onto his arm, filling him with the smell of the ocean rain, and the ship, and of *her*—sunshine and darkness. Cam unwound the tie at the end of her braid and grazed his fingers through the golden length until it pooled in wet cords on the floor.

They lay in silence until Tara's shaking subsided to trembles. Cam watched the steam rise from their bodies as their heat dried the rain, and thought of the boy left dead on the deck, his face smashed in and the way Tara had been frozen by the sight.

"He killed him, Cam," Tara's voice broke the sound of the waves crashing into the hull. As she spoke, her trembling grew to sobs. "I watched, I w-watched that boy die, and I was so s-scared because Devon wanted it to be you. He couldn't find you, so he *killed* him." She buried her face in Cam's chest, pressing his tags under her cheek and clinging to him as she cried.

He wants to kill me. Cam's heart leapt in his chest and he tightened his grip on the girl in his arms. He had known it, somehow, known that for Devon it was more than just hunting.

That there would be an end.

But it was different hearing Tara say it out loud, hearing the fear in her voice, and realizing she was as afraid for herself as she was for him. He looked down at her, wracked with sobs as she let some of the darkness inside of her go. She was as tall as Myla, but wider in the shoulders and more curved at the hips. One of her long legs was wrapped over his.

"I'm sorry, Cam," Tara said. "I'm sorry he's like this. It wasn't his fault, it was mine."

"He's your brother, Tara, but he's not anything like you," Cam ran his fingers over her cheek.

"He was like me," she trembled, "until Brian drowned."

Brian? Then Cam remembered. *We had a brother.*

"I wasn't watching, and he fell into the river," she choked on a sob. "Devon pulled him out when we found him, but it was too late. He died because of me. And now that boy out on the deck." She pressed her face against his chest, "Devon's a monster because of me."

She bit her lip and let the tears go, but her sobs were all spent. Cam's heart slowed and he watched her breathing settle as the raging sea rocked her to sleep.

That's the forgiveness she wants, but she won't get it from him. Cam thought of Dom and the way he had screamed as flames licked at the house. *Dom can't forgive me, either,* Cam swallowed, *or Jake. At least I can still do something about Peter.*

Cam gently traced the scar that cut through the middle of Tara's pink mutant mark. *Like butterfly wings,* Cam remembered thinking in the infirmary. Her eyelids fluttered but did not open.

Like beautiful, torn butterfly wings.

He reached for his collection of tags and the coin with the death's head etched onto its face. *What are we?* He held them up to catch what they could of the sparse light coming in through the round window, shadows settling in the grooves of the metal. *What will happen to us once we reach Salvation?* As the final dregs of light faded, Cam curled his fingers around the mess of metal, and with the darkness came the pressing feeling that he was running out of time.

CHAPTER 25

Land

Something had changed. Blinking his eyes open, Cam squinted into the shafts of light that fought their way through the dirty window.

The storm's over, he realized. The ship's sway was gentle and Tara slept, her shoulder resting in the hollow of his and her head still tucked against his chin. She was dry and warm, her hair falling over his arm in soft waves. He breathed her in before waking her, and reluctantly let her go as he stood and gathered their clothes off of the shelves.

"Not quite dry," he handed her pants and shirt down to where she still sat on the floor. His shorts were still wet around the pockets as he slid them on and dropped the coin and tags inside, then he paused. Tara stood and slid her shirt over her head, her hair hanging nearly to her waist like golden wings as it caught the morning light, and he sucked in his breath.

"You are beautiful, Tara, even if you don't think so." He hadn't quite meant to say the words out loud, and his heart stopped as she met his eyes. She held his gaze for a moment, then finished getting dressed without saying a word and stepped over to him.

Her eyes looked like glass as she searched his, a sadness clouding the bright hazel. She ran her finger over the burn scar on his chest and picked up his tags. "Thank you," she whispered, "for being kind." She leaned in and kissed him, and Cam could taste the sadness on her lips.

Her touch still burned him from inside, creeping up to his lungs, and when she stepped back, he fought to calm his breathing.

She brushed her hair off her shoulder and gave him a crooked smile, then her face fell. "Maybe you should stay down here," she swallowed, "until we reach the shore. Devon would never find you in here."

Cam put his hands on her shoulders. "Tara, I'm not staying down here while you're up there, and if you're missing, he *will* come down here. He'll go everywhere on this ship until he finds you."

Her brows creased and she dropped her eyes. "What is this?" she crouched down by the chair and picked up the small knife that Cam had tossed on the floor with his tracking chip. She looked at the chair, blood staining the back cushion, then her eyes returned to Cam's. "This is where you were yesterday, isn't it?"

Cam nodded.

"What did you do?" She searched his body.

Cam turned around and pressed his fingertips to the tender flesh at the base of his neck. "Here."

Tara's fingertips replaced his as she traced where the knife had gone in. "You cut out your tracking chip." She stepped back and Cam faced her again. She had her fingers behind her, testing the space at the base of her neck. "Do you think...?"

"No, Tara," Cam grabbed her wrists and pulled her close. "No, yours is too deep. It would do too much damage."

"How do you know?"

Cam let her go and stood up. "I thought about running away. I was going to take Peter, but his chip was too deep. I didn't try."

"That's why you were in the cellar," she bit her lip and pressed the knife in his hand. "You better keep this."

"Devon should be locked up in isolation again, right? I'm sure Smith will keep him somewhere where he can't hurt anybody." Cam wanted to convince himself as much as he wanted to sooth her, but he kept the knife. Not sure what else to do with it, he put it in the pocket with the flashlight and the glasses.

She bit her lip. "Okay." Pulling his hands off of her shoulders, she wound her fingers in his.

Cam nodded and led her out of the library and through the dead lobby, listening to the rats scuffle in the shadows. The light that fell through the stairwell blinded him as he pulled the door open and stepped onto the landing. He blinked and paused.

The ship was eerily silent, like the moments before dawn at the Stalls when the other orphans still slept and Cam had shared the world with his memories and the frost.

Tara squeezed his hand and started up the stairs. Cam caught Smith's voice echoing down the stairwell and followed the blond girl up to the deck.

The acquisitions stood in their lines, somber and ragged. Smith held Devon at the head of the lines, the mutant's hands behind his back. They both turned as Cam and Tara cleared the corner, Smith's eyebrows going up as he saw them drop their hands. Based on the scowl that twisted Devon's face, Cam guessed that Tara's twin brother had noticed, too.

"One hundred fifteen," Smith announced as Cam squeezed into the line next to Alex. He pulled the glasses out of his pocket and nudged his friend. Alex squinted at him, then took the glasses and smiled.

Four missing? One had been killed by Devon, and Jake was dead. That meant that two others were missing. Cam studied the group as Tara found a place in the mutants' line, wondering who was no longer there. Hannah cried silently, tears carving streaks on her freckled cheeks, and Cam realized the skinny boy who had held the Live or Die ball was gone.

Avoiding Devon's glare, Cam searched the deck for signs of the boy who had been left dead as the rain washed away his blood. All he saw was the sun bleached deck littered with the dirty feet of orphans and the heavy boots of Regulators. *He's in the ocean with Jake.*

He caught Myla looking at him as he lifted his eyes, but she turned away and stared at the sky. *She saw me with Tara. I'll have to explain,* Cam decided to find her as soon as he had a chance. *She'll understand, right?* But by the clenching in his chest, he knew that his heart didn't agree.

Tara's eyes flitted to her brother, then to Cam, then to the other acquisitions. Fear, Cam recognized it in the way she chewed on her lip and rubbed her arm. She settled her eyes on Devon, her body tense and agitated. Her brother ignored her, his eyes pinned on Cam with a deadly promise. *I'm coming for you.*

The other Regulators edged the deck, surrounding the acquisitions with guns in their hands. *They're afraid of the mutants now. And Devon.*

He wished Smith had shot the blond boy while he had the chance.

The Regulators announced breakfast rations and the lines broke into an irreverent mass of shoving and insults, the immunes inevitably pushed to the back of the line. Hannah stared off into the distance, her tears gone, but she was letting herself be knocked around by the other acquisitions like a sack of grain. Alex followed Cam as he worked his way over to the thin girl and gently pulled her out of the crowd.

"Hannah," Cam shook her, keeping Devon at the edge of his vision. "Look at me, Hannah."

She blinked and looked at him, but her eyes still saw something far away.

"Maybe she's sick," Alex offered.

"No," Cam took her face in his hands. "Hannah, what's wrong?"

"The storm," she whispered, "I told him to hold on, but he didn't. Just flew off the ship like a leaf. He's gone, over there." She pointed toward the north, toward the water, and kept her eyes there.

"Sorry, Hannah," Cam didn't know what else to say.

"Land," Hannah said.

"What are you talking about?" Alex twitched his hands, frustrated.

"Look," she met the boy's squinted eyes and waved her finger, "land!" Hannah shouted the last word, and the crowed waiting for rations rushed to the north side of the deck. She followed them, her friend forgotten.

Cam's heart hammered. *Is this the beginning or the end?* For him, he hoped, it would be the end of running from Devon, the end of thinking of Dom every time he closed his eyes, and the beginning of being a *survivor*.

"C'mon," he grabbed Alex's sleeve and tugged him toward the upper deck. A few other acquisitions had already left the crowded railing and headed for the stairs, but Cam wasn't as interested in gaping at land as he was in having a clear view of Devon, and the top deck would let him see what he wanted.

The ship had slowed to navigate past the shoreline. The air was breezy but gentle, and the smell of salt mixed with something new. Land, Cam thought of what that meant for him. *Do they know I'm coming?*

He settled in Smith's favorite spot, leaning against the railing that overlooked the lower deck, Alex squinting next to him.

"Why is everybody over there?" Alex pointed at the acquisitions jostling for position on the north railing.

"Because they're looking at land," Cam answered.

"Well, what are we looking at?" Alex asked.

Cam glanced at him. "Devon."

"Oh," the smaller boy said.

Cam held his breath as he looked back down toward the deck. *Devon's gone.* Smith was missing, too. In a heartbeat, they had vanished. Gripping the railing, Cam scanned the acquisitions for the blond head, but all he saw were Regulators watching the kids smashed up against the north side of the boat.

Then he heard a familiar chuckle. "Hey, Pig Boy, looking for me?"

His heart pounding, Cam slowly turned around. Devon stood on the other side of the pool that sloshed with storm water, his hands stretching and clenching, broken handcuffs dangling from his wrists. A grin split his marked face, the strawberry half twisted in anticipation.

"Devon? Alex sniffed. "You should be with Smith for breaking the rules."

Frozen, Cam stared at the mutant. His body went numb and he felt like the ship dropped out from under him.

"Whatcha gonna do, Pig Boy?" Devon danced sided to side, "Gonna go tell Smith to lock me up because I've been a bad boy?" His voice dropped into a chuckle. "I helped Smith take a little nap."

Cam thought of the people he had watched Devon taunt and hurt. Little Peter with his coat choking him purple, Jake with the bruises on his back, the boy left dead in the rain… *Tara.*

You're strong enough…

Something burst in the back of Cam's mind and Tara's words pulsed behind his eyes. You're strong enough, fast enough. The world spun and then halted in startling clarity. Everything looked new, almost painfully stark. Sunbeams cut through the blue sky and onto the ship like blades of light and sparked against Devon's pupils. Cam watched the mutant's eyes dilate as the blond boy swallowed and tensed his arms.

Fast enough.

Pushing Alex back into the railing, Cam ran past him along the edge of the pool. Devon grinned and sprinted to cut him off at the stairs, but Cam kept his course straight and flipped over the railing, landing halfway down the staircase as Devon rounded the top and hurried to catch him. Cam did it again over the outer stair railing, this time landing on the south galley of the lower deck and gaining the service stairs before Devon caught on and landed behind him.

The library, Cam hurried for Level 5. He dropped to the second landing and winced, a sharp pain stabbing through his foot. Twisting it up against his knee, Cam gritted his teeth as he pulled out a shard of metal. From the storm? Blood welled up and dripped onto the landing.

"I'm coming, Pig Boy. I know where you like to hide." Devon's voice was deep, and his breath shook as he laughed silently.

Glancing at the door to Level 5, Cam wiped the blood off his foot and hurried down a flight to Level 4. The door swung in quietly as Devon's steps echoed in the stairwell. Cam pushed the heavy metal slab shut and looked for a lock on the inside, but it was broken off.

Cursing, he limped down the hallway, trying to keep his blood from leaving a trail, but it slowed him too much and he cut down a hallway that crossed to the other side of the ship. *Just stay ahead of him, like in the game.*

The floor vibrated and Cam heard the door slam open.

"Oh, Pig Boy," Devon called as Cam took another turn toward the front of the ship. The carpet muffled the sound of Devon's footsteps, but not his voice. "Here, piggy, piggy, piggy."

Cam made it to a set of stairs and ran up a couple of steps, letting the blood from his foot soak into the treads, then backtracked and popped the door open on a room and slipped inside, the lock shutting him into complete darkness.

"Naughty, naughty, Pig Boy. You're bleeding. You make it too easy to find you. I thought I'd actually have to try," Devon's voice echoed dimly through the door.

He likes. . . hunting. Tara had told him, and Cam had thought that was all Devon wanted, a good hunt and a few punches, until the mutant left a bloody body on the deck.

He wanted it to be you.

Cam felt his way back to the bed, the subtle sway of the ship playing with his tense muscles.

"Eenie, meenie, minie, mo."

Cam held his breath as a metallic shriek shook the wall next to him. *He's tearing off the doors,* Cam swallowed and stumbled up on the bed. The tip of the knife stabbed into his thigh, caught in his pocket under the flashlight. He pulled both objects out and hugged himself into the corner, gripping the handles.

Laughter and a loud clang. "Catch a piggy," another door shrieked, this one farther away, "by the toe." Devon was close.

Nails scratched at the edges of the door to Cam's room, then the hinges groaned and shrieked as light flooded in around Devon's silhouette.

"If he hollers," Devon threw the door down the hall and paused, squinting into the shadows.

"Make him pay," Cam flew at the other boy, smashing the flashlight against his face and pitching them both across the hall through a jagged doorway and into a light-filled room. Devon grunted as Cam's knee dug into his thigh, and Cam swung the flashlight again. The boy's skull caved in above his eye, and blood splattered on Cam's face, but Devon only grinned.

Voices called Cam's name, distant but getting closer. *Smith?*

The mutant tucked his foot into Cam's gut and launched him onto the bed. The headboard cut into Cam's spine and his head bashed the wall, blurring the lines of the room.

Devon stood at the foot of the bed, blood running down his face. He picked the knife up off the floor. "Looks like you dropped this."

At the edges of his vision, Cam noticed a set of glass doors that led out to a small balcony.

Wiping his hand through the blood on his face, Devon's shoulders heaved.

Cam smiled.

"You think dying is funny, Pig Boy?" Devon spit.

Cam chuckled, then winced. "I think killing you would be funny."

"Killing me?" Devon smiled at that, blood running into his teeth. "You think a puny immune like you ever had a chance? You're only alive because I like chasing things. But you know what I like better?" He spun the knife, the blade streaked with red. "Catching things. And now," his tags clinked softly as he put a foot on the bed, "I've caught me a little piggy."

As he stepped onto the bed, Tara and Myla rushed in the room. Myla tackled Devon around the waist and pulled him over into a table. The wood splintered as the table split, the crack echoing in Cam's skull as Tara pulled him to his feet.

"Devon, stop!" Tara screamed at her brother. Devon ignored her, pushing himself up and dragging Myla with him, his fingers digging into the dark girl's arms. He swung her into Tara, knocking both girls into the far wall.

Alex stood in the doorway, stunned.

"It's Pig Boy's new rat," Devon stepped toward Alex.

Cam threw himself at Devon, unbalancing the bigger boy. Devon's arms wrapped around him as the mutant stumbled back, shattering the glass doors and sending shards out over the ocean like broken snowflakes. They skittered into the railing, Devon's back and head crashing into the metal with a dull *thud*.

Scrambling to pull himself up, Cam wheezed as the blond boy's hands wrapped around his throat. *Tara,* was all Cam thought when Devon flipped him around and pinned him against the railing. Her blond hair covered her face where she lay, still. The edges of his vision blurred and faded, dark and pulsing like the clouds of the storm. Cam razed his nails on Devon's fingers, fighting to loosen the boy's deadly grip.

Behind the blond head, Cam watched as someone stood and crept toward the balcony. Black eyes. *Myla.* She raised her hand.

The knife.

Devon taunted him through gritted teeth, "You're not smiling, now, are you," he leaned in and breathed into Cam's ear, "Cam."

Cam's eyes flitted to Myla, and Devon spun around, knocking her back with his arm. The knife clattered on the balcony floor and Myla fell back into the metal frame of the shattered glass doors. Cam pried Devon's fingers off of his throat and dove for the blade. Devon came down on top of him, and Cam brought the knife up into his neck. *Be strong.* The blade sunk in the soft flesh, and Cam sliced it around the front.

Devon opened his mouth, and blood gurgled out. The mutant clawed at Cam's face and then convulsed and collapsed.

Shoving the bigger boy's body to the side, Cam rushed past Myla to where Tara lay. He turned her over, a cut on her forehead trickling blood, and held his breath until he saw her chest rise and fall.

A shadow disturbed the sunlight and Cam looked behind him at Myla. The dark girl stared at Devon's limp form on the balcony, then turned her wide black eyes to Cam.

"Myla," he stood and reached for her. She backed quickly away from him, out through the empty glass doors. Her heel caught on Devon's arm and she fell back against the railing, her momentum flipping her over the top.

"No!" Cam caught her wrist, and the motion pulled him off with her.

CHAPTER 26

Gifts

Salt water burned out of his lungs as he coughed, clutching at a boat deck made of weathered wood. The smell of fish and rot swam on the ocean breeze.

Myla. Cam squinted at her. She lay curled in a pool of water, hugging her arms to her chest.

"Well, well," a woman's deep voice said from above them. Cam looked up and saw a black shadow shaped by the sun. "Gifts from da sea." Her speech had a heavy rhythm, like the beating of the waves against the hull. The boat swayed and Cam's head spun.

The shadow disappeared and Cam raised his hand against the blinding light.

"Tie d'em up!"

He reached for Myla's hand, but she shrunk from him, her eyes wide. The expression on her face was different from the shock he had seen before they fell off the balcony.

She's afraid of me. Cam swallowed and winced as rough hands shoved his face onto the deck and wrapped thick rope around his wrists and ankles.

He didn't resist at first, then he panicked. *The coin.* He twisted away from the hands and wriggled his wrists out of a half-tied knot. His pocket was wet and stuck to his leg as he shoved his hand in his pocket and ran his fingers over the smooth metal of the tags and the ridges of the coin edge. *Peter.*

The rough hands dug into his shoulders and hauled him to his feet, then grabbed his wrists behind his back. His fingers caught on a chain and pulled tags out of his pocket. They landed on the weathered deck with a soft metallic ring. Fingers almost as dark as Myla's hair curled around the tags, the chain swinging in the sun.

Rich brown eyes met his then shifted to the man behind his shoulder. "Kill him."

Blood thundered in Cam's ears. His own tags were gone, paid for with blood just to be lost to the ocean. A waste like the grand buildings in the city and the velvet covered furniture on the ship.

"No," Myla pleaded.

The brown eyes flitted to where Myla lay twisted and bound, and returned to his, the woman's face turned down in a scowl. The frown pulled at the brand on her cheek, the same blank eye and chevrons that Smith had. Ropes of black hair swung past her shoulders, the sun casting a shadow in the hollow of her marked throat. She crouched down and lifted Myla's chin. "Do you know what he is?"

You're not anything, an accident. Mama Lucy's warning echoed in the woman's rhythmic words. *I'm a no-code, Myla.* I'm not supposed to exist. He thought of the body in the ship, the boy whose tags the woman dangled in front of Myla's black eyes.

"He's an immune."

"Look at da tags, child. See there? Nothing. A no-code."

Myla looked where the dark woman pointed.

"Those aren't mine," Cam croaked out past the blood throbbing in his head. "I have others."

The woman stood and shook the tags in his face. "Show me."

The hands holding Cam's wrists let go and Cam dug into

his pocket, careful not to pull the coin out with the other tags.

"Where did you get all these?" the woman took them. "Did you kill dem?"

"No, I didn't kill them," Cam watched the metal catch the sun. *But they died because of me.*

"So you collect them, from the dead," she rubbed her fingers over the names. "Careful, child, or you may join them." She nodded at the man behind Cam and the rope coiled back on his wrists, chafing against his skin. "It's good for you that you are worth more to me alive." She hung all three chains around Cam's neck, then turned and barked orders to the other men on the boat deck.

"She's a mutant," Cam thought out loud, glancing at Myla, who lay still with her eyes closed.

"Aye," the man shoved him down onto the deck and tied Cam's ankles. "Captain Styx."

She wore little clothing, her muscles rippling in the sun that bounced off the water. The ropes of her hair hung halfway down her back, and when she turned her head, Cam saw the eye with four chevrons burned at the base of her neck, the black ink that shaped the rest of the horse's head barely darker than her skin.

She came from the same House as Smith. A gladiator.

The wind shifted. Cam caught another strong whiff of fish and he wretched up more ocean water.

The man tying his ankles stifled a laugh, his smile deepening the weathered wrinkles around his eyes. "Smell of a fishin' boat," he took a deep breath. "Don't bother to get used to it. You'll have other things to smell where you're going."

"Where am I going?" Cam met the man's gray eyes.

His head was nearly bare, only a few wisps of silver thread floating from his scalp, and his arms and legs were the shade of old leather. He waved his hand toward the prow of the boat.

A shoreline wavered in the distance, hovels scattered on the ragged beach. Cam thought the hillside above might once have been beautiful, when the houses were still white and their terra cotta roofs crested like foam on ocean waves. Now everything was burned, black fingers weathered to gray by the salt breeze, empty and soulless.

People moved about the shacks below, men and women scarcely covered like Captain Styx.

The weathered man's voice held amusement at the expression on Cam's face. "Welcome to Salvation."

Acknowledgements

Thanks to my alpha readers Lehua Parker, Paul Davis, and E.A. Younker for being straightforward and on time. Also thanks to Lisa L. for letting me use her condo as an 'office' away from my kids. And thanks, Mom, for combing through the details.

I also appreciate the support of my writers group and the foresight of my publisher, Fox Hollow, for getting this dream rolling. I also appreciate my editor, Danielle Kent, for all the big and little things.

About the Author

Christine Nielson Haggerty grew up in rural Utah with three brothers, a sister, several chickens, a goat, and an outhouse. She always loved the escape of fantasy and the art of writing, and her passion for life is to craft stories of strength and survival.

With that passion, Christine taught high school language arts for several years, encouraging her students' perfection of language. Now she appreciates her background in classic literature and history as she draws on the past to write about the present and the future. Her first series, The Plague Legacy, is about a boy battling his own past and future to save the human race.

Her other interests are karate, drawing, reading, and hosting killer barbecues.

Check her out at: christinehaggertyauthor.com.

The Plague Legacy: Assets

Cameron Landry is lost.

After his brother died from a rogue strain of a bio-engineered plague, Cam was dragged from his home and forced to live at the Stalls until a stranger smuggled him across the ocean. On a rusty ship with its own secrets, Cam survived a fight with a deadly enemy and learned that he is a no-code—a live carrier of the plague virus that destroyed the world.

And some think he is also the cure.

Now with blood on his hands, Cam is separated from the one person responsible to keep him alive. He is a slave in Salvation, where the nine gladiator Houses fight to rule the arena, and the laws of mutants and immunes divide his friends. Alone with his deadly secret, Cam has a promise to keep, but his only chance for redemption could cost him his life.

COMING FALL 2014!

•

Made in the USA
Charleston, SC
07 March 2014